MOONLIGHT
OBSESSION

What Reviewers Say About
Sheri Lewis Wohl's Work

Drawing Down the Mist

"Vampires loving humans. Vampires hating vampires. Vampires killing humans. Vampires killing vampires. Good vampires. Evil vampires. Internet-savvy vampires. Lovers turning enemies. Nurturing revenge for a century. Kindness. Cruelty. Love. Action. Fights. Insta-love. This one has everything for a true drama."
—*reviewer@large*

Cause of Death

"I really liked these characters, all of them, and wouldn't say no to a sequel, or more."—*Jude in the Stars*

"*CSI* meets *Ghost Whisperer.* ...The pace was brilliantly done, the suspense was just enough, and I'm not ashamed to admit that I had no idea who the serial killer was until almost the end."
—*Words and Worlds*

"*Cause of Death* by Sheri Lewis Wohl is one creepy and well-written murder mystery. It is one of the best psychological thrillers I've read in a while."—*Rainbow Reflections*

"[A] light paranormal romance with a psycho-killer and some great dogs."—*C-Spot Reviews*

"There's a ton of stuff in here that I enjoy very much, such as the light paranormal aspect of the book, and the relationship between our two leads is very nice if a bit of a slow burn. The case was engaging enough that I didn't really set this title down once I started it."—Colleen Corgel, Librarian, Queens Public Library

"Totally disturbing, and very, very awesome. ...The characters were amazing. The supernatural tint was never overdone, and even the stuff from the killer's point of view, while disturbing, was awesomely done as well. It was a great book and a fun (and intense) read."—Danielle Kimerer, Librarian (Nevins Memorial Library, Massachusetts)

"This thriller has spooky undertones that make it an intense page turner. You won't be able to put this book down."—*Istoria Lit*

The Talebearer

"As a crime story, it is a good read that had me turning pages quickly. ...The book is well written and the characters are well-developed."—*Reviews by Amos Lassen*

She Wolf

"I really enjoyed this book—I couldn't put it down once I started it. The author's style of writing was very good and engaging. All characters, including the supporting characters, were multi-layered and interesting."—Melina Bickard, Librarian, Waterloo Library (UK)

Twisted Screams

"[A] cast of well developed characters leads you through a maze of complex emotions."—*Lunar Rainbow Reviewz*

Twisted Echoes

"A very unusual blend of lesbian romance and horror. ...[W]oven throughout this modern romance is a neatly plotted horror story from the past, which bleeds ever increasingly into the present of

the two main characters. Lorna and Renee are well matched, and face ever-increasing danger from spirits from the past. An unusual story that gets tenser and more interesting as it progresses."
—Pippa Wischer, Manager at Berkelouw Books, Armadale

Vermilion Justice

"[T]he characters are so dynamic and well-written that this becomes more than just another vampire story. It's probably impossible to read this book and not come across a character who reminds you of someone you actually know. Wohl takes something as fictional as vampires and makes them feel real. Highly recommended."
—*GLBT Reviews: The ALA's GLBT Round Table*

Visit us at www.boldstrokesbooks.com

By the Author

Crimson Vengeance

Burgundy Betrayal

Scarlet Revenge

Vermillion Justice

Twisted Echoes

Twisted Whispers

Twisted Screams

Necromantia

She Wolf

Walking Through Shadows

Drawing Down the Mist

The Talebearer

Cause of Death

Avenging Avery

All that Remains

The Artist

Witch Finder

Buried Secrets

The Guardians

Moonlight Obsession

MOONLIGHT OBSESSION

by

Sheri Lewis Wohl

2025

MOONLIGHT OBSESSION

ISBN 13: 978-1-63679-831-8

THIS TRADE PAPERBACK ORIGINAL IS PUBLISHED BY
BOLD STROKES BOOKS, INC.
P.O. BOX 249
VALLEY FALLS, NY 12185

FIRST EDITION: SEPTEMBER 2025

CREDITS
EDITOR: SHELLEY THRASHER
PRODUCTION DESIGN: SUSAN RAMUNDO
COVER DESIGN BY TAMMY SEIDICK

Dedication

For Zoey. My SAR partner, my travel buddy, my heart dog.
In memory of all our exciting adventures in Montana.

Beware of false prophets,
which come to you in sheep's clothing,
but inwardly they are
ravening wolves.

—Matthew 7:15
The Holy Bible
King James Version

PROLOGUE

Great Slave Lake, Northwest Territories
Ten years ago

Wolves were fascinating, from a distance. He slung the rifle over his shoulder before he pulled his kayak high onto the shore, tying it securely to a tree. For a couple of minutes, he stood in the sand to watch and listen. Gentle waves lapped against the shore, his kayak bobbing up and down, and a light wind moved the branches of the trees. The massive wolf with a silver face had followed the shoreline for at least a mile as he'd paddled north. As he'd pulled the oars through the water, the muscles in his shoulders kept telling him to turn toward land. He couldn't. Interesting at first, the wolf became worrisome as civilization faded behind him. Regardless of how slow or fast he moved through the water, the wolf had kept pace. A powerful predator stalking his prey.

At least until he gave in to his screaming muscles and headed to the shore. When he finally navigated to the beach, the wolf had turned and run into the trees. Not as though afraid of him. More like bored. Worked for him. Happy enough to see it go its merry way, considering this trip had been a long time coming. A nosy wolf didn't need to ruin it for him.

Plenty of room for his small camp and the animals that called this remote area home without infringing on each other's personal space. If not, well, he could deal with that too. He patted the rifle he'd slung over his shoulder and stood taller. Overhead, the sun dropped toward the west. He had to set his camp up. Pain in the butt to do it in darkness, although at least a full moon would rise tonight, and that would help if he got behind.

Rather than trek into the woods, he found a nice spot on the edge of the forest. The trees provided a good wind break should the weather turn, while still allowing him a beautiful view of the lake. Now at the end of tourist season, he'd hoped to enjoy this stretch of beach along Great Slave Lake all by himself. Blessed peace and quiet and he intended to savor every minute of it.

Within an hour he had the tent up, his ground pad topped with his sleeping bag, and a fire built. Flames danced and sparks popped into the air. Beautiful and serene. Better yet, no sign of the wolf. Of course, it wouldn't be wise to underestimate it. Pack animals by nature, more wolves would likely be somewhere in the trees. He'd keep his rifle close and his ears open. Live and let live was a motto he tried to embrace. Then again, if threatened, he'd protect himself, and if that meant killing a majestic animal, so be it. Better than becoming dinner for the pack.

The sky grew deep and dark, stars glittering and the moon golden as he held a stick with a hot dog on the end over the fire. At home, he ate only the fresh foods he raised in his garden. Organic and pure, they kept his body healthy and his mind sharp. Out here, he indulged in his guilty pleasures. First up, fire-roasted hot dogs.

After wrapping the wiener in a slice of white bread, he took a big bite and closed his eyes. It tasted like childhood back home and the wonderful times out camping with his dad. Pops had taught him about the no-rules, no-girls, no guilt trips. Not that he believed for a moment his mother had been unaware of their hot dog, candy, and soda-filled adventures. She always just sent them on their way with a stay-safe-and-have-a-good-time blessing.

Slowly, he opened his eyes and looked around. Not because the mystery pork treat didn't make him super happy. No. It struck him as he sat and enjoyed his very unhealthy dinner that the night had grown silent. No sounds at all. Not the whoosh of lake water lapping the shoreline, not the hoot of an owl, not the rustle of a rabbit or squirrel running through the forest. Silence, deep and disturbing.

He set aside his food and stood. Eerily quiet, as if he remained the only living thing in the world. He leaned down and pulled a headlamp out of his pack. The strap was snug around his head, and he clicked the button to turn the light on. It cut through the darkness like a surgeon's scalpel. The rifle once more over his shoulder, he walked to the tree line.

"All right, show yourself." Now he moved the rifle stock to his shoulder and pointed the barrel toward the trees. "Come on. I know you're there." Only an apex predator could cause a forest to go silent.

The rustle of the underbrush made his finger move to the trigger. *That a boy. Come on out.* He slowed his breathing, narrowed his eyes, and kept the barrel pointed in the direction of the sounds. The wolf stepped out, his eyes glowing red in the beam of his headlamp. The same silver face he'd seen running along the riverbank earlier. "There you are. What do you want?" He smiled, imagining what the wolf might say if he could talk.

"I don't want to hurt you, so how about you go hunt a rabbit or something tasty besides me. You're not going to want my delicious hot dogs." The wolf listened, his ears up, his body tense. Almost as though he listened and understood.

It took a step closer, tension in its body, hair standing up at the scruff of its neck.

"Go find somewhere else to be. I'm here." He stood tall, his shoulders back, and the beam on his headlamp remained on the wolf's eyes. Made himself appear as large as possible. For a second, he thought it had worked. Only for a second. The wolf charged. He screamed.

Chapter One

Ravalli County, MT
Present Day

Wyatt Foreman stood back and studied her latest project. The raised beds came together as she'd envisioned. These were the perfect height and would give her a break from leaning over to tend the massive gardens that provided her with food throughout the year. Not that she'd eliminated the in-ground version. This season, she'd have a multi-level operation. A well-thought-out experiment that, depending on how it went, might be expanded upon next year.

"That looks nice." Her nearest neighbor, Royal Fremont, walked through the garden gate. "I may have to copy this setup." His long black hair streaked with silver was pulled back in a ponytail, and he wore blue jeans and a University of Montana T-shirt. To the best of her recollection, Royal never went there. Tall and confident, he smiled at her as if they were a couple of good friends hanging out on a lovely afternoon. Except they weren't.

She forced a return smile, and it almost hurt. Maybe more a grimace than a smile. Less than a year ago, he'd moved back to Hamilton and, in that time, had made a bit of a pest of himself. No, more than a bit. He'd made a big pest of himself. While true enough they'd both grown up here, they'd not really been friends, given he'd been two grades ahead of her in school. The only reason she remembered him at all had to do with his name. Royal was the kind of name a person remembered. Especially if one acted like they believed they were royal.

"We'll see how it goes. Nothing like working the land itself." She wasn't making idle conversation about her dedication to nature. Pleased as she might be with her newest experiment in growing food, her parents would pale if they could see the raised gardens. They were, or had been, purists in the most basic sense. When they said they worked the land, they meant it literally. On their knees and without gloves. Dirt under their fingernails that refused to be washed away. These days, people called her parents' style of living earthing, and while it was important, she took a broader view and taught her classes that way. No reason the old and the new ways couldn't co-exist.

"Knowing your green thumb, my money is on it all going super good." His smile lit up his face. She'd give him credit for growing into his looks. He wasn't the Royal she recalled from their teenage years, the skinny guy who led the debate team to more than one state championship.

Wyatt narrowed her eyes at his words. Flattery would get him nowhere, and besides, how would he know what she could do? Well, maybe that wasn't fair. Around here, her classes in self-sufficiency and women-specific survival classes were well-known and quite popular. Actually, that wasn't totally correct. Her reputation went well beyond the borders of Montana. Routinely tapped to teach classes all over the country, she'd traveled coast-to-coast and border-to-border. Wyatt loved sharing her lifetime of knowledge and equally loved the enthusiasm of her students.

"Is there something I can help you with?" Maybe if she nudged him, he would get to the point and then be on his way. Something about him rubbed her wrong these days, though she couldn't pinpoint why. Perhaps he'd always been that way, and that's why he'd never been on the inside of her friends circle during their formative years. Today, she didn't have time for him and whatever was on his hidden agenda, as she had a lot more work to do. A custom-recurve-bow commission was due to be delivered in a few days and still needed its finishing touches. No bow left her workshop if it wasn't perfect. She built hers with the same attention to detail that she employed in teaching her classes. Her grandmother's famous bit of wisdom: if something was worth doing, it was worth doing right.

"There is." His smile grew. Now why was it she had the feeling he believed it made him more handsome? It probably worked on other women. Might be wise to tell him he was barking up the wrong tree, and if she thought it would help, she would. Singularly undeterred by any of her previous rebuffs, he wouldn't listen. Everything he'd done to date made it clear Royal would turn out to be *that* neighbor. Not fair either. She'd lived in this same house her entire life, and that meant, in essence, he was the intruder here regardless of being born in the nearby town. There were plenty of other homes in the area he could have purchased. Didn't have to be the place closest to hers. Damn the Andersons for retiring and moving to Phoenix. Montana winters weren't *that* bad.

"And that would be?" She hoped her expression remained neutral. As much as he bugged her, he was her neighbor, and a feud wasn't a good plan.

"Wondering if you might have some monkshood plants I could talk you out of." He stuffed his hands in his jeans pockets and continued to smile as though he hadn't just asked her to give him a poisonous plant.

She narrowed her eyes as she studied his face. "That would be a no. Monkshood, or wolfsbane, is dangerous, even fatal, and I prefer to cultivate healing plants. I don't do death, and I don't recommend you planting any, even if the flowers they produce are beautiful. Sometimes deadly hides behind beautiful."

His smile didn't waver at her rebuff. "My idea is that they'll create a beautiful fence around my place without having to spoil the view with traditional fencings. Animals won't cross the barrier."

His explanation had some merit. True enough that wildlife would steer clear. Not enough justification for her to help him. Not that she had any of the requested plants on her property now, or ever.

She shook her head. "To be blunt, bad idea, and besides, I don't grow Monkshood plants anywhere on my property. My advice to you is to stick with a regular fence if you want to keep animals out."

Now he pressed his lips together and shook his head. A shadow crossed his face. "Naw. That doesn't work for me. I'll figure something out."

He didn't sound like he'd let it go, and neither would she. "Stay away from monkshood. The risk is too high." Animals typically steered clear of the plant, but not always. He'd feel bad if he unintentionally poisoned someone's pet. Wouldn't he? As she studied his face, she wondered.

He spun and walked away. "Maybe."

She gazed out at her goats, chickens, and horses. "Bastard," she muttered when he was gone. Her animals rarely got out of the fenced pastures and off her property, but it did happen to anyone who had livestock, and now she had to worry about whether they'd make it home alive. That plant could kill in an hour if they were to ingest it. She left the garden beds to walk her fence lines just to make sure.

Mari Walker pulled up to the modest house with the natural-cedar siding and full front porch. Knowing it was always iffy to buy a property sight-unseen, she'd sent out a whole lot of prayers that the pictures on the Internet did it justice. So far, so good. The five acres that came with the house gave it the privacy she'd been looking for. A new start in a big way. Suited her current mood and mindset.

A woman with short, curly, brown hair waved at her from the driveway as she stood next to a late-model blue Ford pickup. She recognized the realtor from the half-dozen video calls needed to make the home purchase happen long-distance. "Welcome, Mari. Welcome." She held out her hand, a set of keys dangling from her fingers. Blue jeans and cowboy boots suited her. Personality and looks combined with a people-savvy instinct made for a top-notch realtor.

"Hey." She smiled as she walked toward her new home. "Can't wait to see it." Truth too. The outside of the place worked for her, and she had a hunch the inside would too. Sometimes, things did pan out. Sometimes they didn't, which is why she stood here now.

An hour later, seemingly content that Mari would be fine, her oh-so-perky realtor backed her big truck out of the driveway and drove away. Mari sighed as she stood in the empty living room. Her furniture wouldn't arrive until tomorrow, and that was fine, given she was too tired from the drive to want to set anything up. At least ten times during the last hour she'd been invited to stay the night with the realtor she'd liked the first time they spoke, and she liked her even more now that they'd met in person. She'd still turned down the gracious invitation.

Mari's work took her to some very remote places, and she'd spent her fair share of nights sleeping under the stars on hard ground. She'd be fine here inside her nifty new home even without furniture. The hardwood floors wouldn't be soft beneath her sleeping bag. They also wouldn't have rocks poking into her back. She would be fine until her bed showed up tomorrow.

Didn't much surprise her when her cell phone rang. "Yes. I'm here." No need to say hello. Her family were a caring bunch that gave her space at the same time. She loved that about them. Just as she loved that Jasmine had been her ride-or-die since the fourth grade.

"I still don't like it." Jasmine's words contained the same tone of disapproval they'd carried since the moment Mari told her best friend that she was leaving Oregon. "You should have stayed here and fought it out. You let the bastards win."

"Nope on both counts." So far, it had been impossible to convince Jas that moving several states away was a solid plan.

"Oh, please. Leaving like this only validates that SOB's actions. You deserved that job. It should have been yours, not that manipulating blonde's. Be nice to think the days of getting ahead based on big boobs and fake eyelashes were over. They sure proved they weren't."

Mari closed her eyes and sighed. Jas wasn't wrong. Mari had been massively more qualified for the chief's position, yet she'd been passed over as though she'd been nothing more than a first-year ranger. Oh, the powers-that-be had all the right words for their actions and didn't like it when she'd called it BS. Hadn't changed anything, and she'd opted not to stick around, even when promised that he'd get her promoted *if she were just patient.* The chief ranger in charge of hiring said blonde had the nerve to tell her to just get over it. As her brother would have said, fuck that. Besides, with the current cuts across the entire agency, if she'd stayed, she'd have been more likely to get axed than eventually promoted.

"Water under the bridge, Jas. Besides, I actually got the chief job in this district, and cherry on top, it's pretty nice here. The house is as good as it looked online. Better, actually. I'm pleased so far. Tomorrow, I meet with the ranger I'll be replacing, and he's going to give me the grand tour. This move is a good thing." She hoped.

"It's running away." Jas wasn't one to pull punches. "You folded like a load of laundry, and that's not like you. Makes me want to slap you up alongside the head."

"Granted, but you know, sometimes running away can be the start of a grand new beginning, and we both know slapping me is the last thing you'd ever do." She could picture her anti-violence buddy sitting at her table with her feet up on a chair, sipping herbal tea. No caffeine in her body, wrong as Mari believed that to be. What was the point of either tea or coffee without the kick?

"I'm missing you already." Her voice had turned somber. "Who I am I going to whine to when another guy breaks my heart?"

"I'm not that far away. Whining over a video call is perfectly acceptable."

"Hours and hours away. Not the same. I need to whine in person."

She smiled. Jas did have a point. It was fun to commiserate in the same room. "It's driving distance. All you'll have to do is get in your sporty little car and drive your butt over to Montana. I'll have furniture set up by the time you get there. And, to be clear, if you'd stop picking dicks for boyfriends, you wouldn't keep getting your heart broken."

Jasmine laughed, the sound light and full of mirth. "All right. You win, but I'm going to wait until you have both furniture and food. I'll work on the quality-control part of my boyfriend selection."

"Perfect. I'll make sure your room is set up post haste, just in case." It would be wonderful to have her here for a few nights.

"Call me after your tour and let me know if you still think it's the right move."

"You got it."

"Mari?"

"Yeah?"

"I miss you already, and I love you, girlfriend. Please take care of yourself."

Tears stung her eyes and her smile slid away. "Will do and back atcha." The tears fell as she put her phone back into her pocket. Leaving her lifelong home hadn't been an easy or quick decision. She'd waited a full year after the snub to make certain she didn't react out of anger. As she stared out the window, the sun beginning to set, she told herself again, she'd made the right decision.

"I don't know why I'm not enough for you." Inez had her back to him, not pausing in her preparation of the top sirloin he'd brought home.

Royal closed his eyes and silently prayed for patience. At first, Inez had seemed perfect for the family he wanted to create. Lately, his opinion of her fitness had begun to change. Physically, she was perfect. Lean, athletic, and attractive. Her neediness is what got on his nerves. How did he miss that before? Perhaps her beauty and enthusiasm had blinded him. He didn't like to think himself that shallow, but it kind of stared him in the face.

"You are a lovely person." He didn't add that a lovely person didn't equate to an acceptable pack member. That last part remained to be seen. Whining didn't work for him. Never had, and plenty of students had tried it on him.

Inez slapped the knife against the steak as if trying to beat it into submission. "You're sniffing after her like she's in heat. It's not attractive."

"Inez." He drew her name out. Stay calm, he told himself. A good leader kept emotions under control.

She put the knife down and turned to look at him. Really pretty, and that's what had drawn him to her in the first place. Bright too, and he'd always been attracted to intelligence. Might have been a better idea if he'd spent more time getting to know her better before taking that irreversible step. Attractive and smart didn't equate to someone being easy to live with. He took a couple of slow breaths. Only himself to blame. He created the problem, and he'd solve it somehow.

A contrite expression crossed her face. "I'm sorry, but geez, Royal. It's hard to be stuck here all the time. I don't know anybody in this hick town, and yeah, the forests are sweet, but it doesn't make up for the dullness the rest of the time."

"It's important to be here." Vancouver had been his home for decades so it wasn't like he didn't understand her feelings of loneliness. Born and raised here in Montana, he'd nonetheless loved Canada, and Vancouver in particular, with all the beauty and the bounty it provided. Things change over time, and the plain reality of that truth couldn't be ignored. The draw here had been equally exciting, and, in any event, the decision had been his to make.

"I know, I know. You've told me a hundred times." Anger crept back into her voice.

"And I'll repeat it a hundred more." He stared into her eyes.

She blew out a long, noisy breath, something close to a child-stomping tantrum diminishing her beauty. "I miss Canada." Her eyes closed as she leaned back against the countertop, all emotion seeming to drain out of her.

His nerves still trilled. The peace of home he'd hoped for had taken wing. Might have to arrange for her return if she kept this up.

Problem for her was that it wouldn't be quite the return she hoped for. On the other side of the border only exile awaited her. "I do too but it's nice here, and we couldn't stay up North. You know why." Wanted to be here was the part he didn't add.

Royal had plain and simple missed Montana in the many years he'd been in Canada. He appreciated all that he'd done during the years away, the people he'd met from the world over, and the lives he'd changed, whether through an early law practice or his years of teaching. His life had changed too in that time, and there came a day when leaving what he'd built was no longer an option. It became a matter of survival.

Inez nodded, frowning. "I do know. It's just that some days it gets to me, and especially when I feel you moving away from me. You're everything to me, and I don't like her. She's not one of us." The petulant child had returned.

Not yet. He had plans on that front. Plans he hadn't shared with Inez. If he told her, he'd have to listen to even more whining. Not interested in her complaints. The decisions were in his hands and always had been. In the early years, she'd been great and pleasant to be around. Funny even. Since they'd come here, she'd changed, and it wasn't for the better.

"Can we at least go out tonight?" Hope rang clear in her voice, and he didn't blame her. Night runs were unlike anything else. The beauty of the forest and the clear air were intoxicating, the warmth of the moon as it called for the change, thrilling.

He couldn't give her what she wanted. "No. Not tonight." There'd been a close call a couple nights ago, and he didn't want to risk it again. Smarter to let the incident fade from anyone's thoughts before they went out again. The right thing meant staying close to home for the time being.

"I think it'll be okay. Nothing happened." Said incident had been orchestrated by Inez, and it would be a nice change if she took responsibility for her actions.

"Almost nothing happened." If he hadn't stopped her, she'd have torn apart a large hare right in front of a couple of night hikers.

"Almost nothing," she repeated and frowned. He wasn't sure if it was because she felt bad about what happened or was upset that she'd been denied the spoils of her hunt.

Either way, he didn't care. The conversation bored him. Inez bored him. "I know what I'm doing, so how about you concentrate on dinner and let me deal with everything else." This impromptu meeting had reached its end.

For maybe ten seconds she stared into his eyes, and then she sighed and turned back around to her meal preparations. "You're the alpha." She stabbed the knife into the sirloin.

"I am." He left her at the counter and walked outside. A light breeze blew. Nice this time of year. Not hot enough for fire season. The winter chill long gone. Yes, he missed Canada, as did Inez. He had loved it there. Appreciated the welcome the Canadians gave him. The respect he got from his students. The gift he'd never seen coming.

Now, as he gazed out at the Bitterroot Mountains, it hit him how much he'd missed the beauty here. Life began for him on this land and had shaped him in many ways. He hoped that when his time came, it would end for him on this land as well. If all went to plan, with his chosen mate at his side and not for a very long time.

It wasn't the same place he'd said good-bye to all those years go. Things had changed in the years since then. The town had grown. A lot more people, though still a drop in the bucket compared to Vancouver. The culture had changed a little too. Hamilton's great mix of urban and country hit just the right note and was part of what drew him back. Little did he realize when he first returned that he'd glimpse his soul mate on the first day. The only word for it: destiny.

He tilted his head to the sky. In a matter of days, the Harvest Moon would shine, and all would be right with his world. He glanced down at his watch, did a quick calculation in his head, and smiled. "Soon, my love. Soon, we will be together forever."

CHAPTER TWO

Really, Daisy? Really!" Wyatt stared down at the broken fence and frowned. She turned to point a finger at the five-year-old Angora goat, her black coat speckled with grass and twigs. Daisy always knew how to entertain herself. "This isn't what I wanted to do today." Seemingly unimpressed by Wyatt's scolding, Daisy wandered off into the field.

Mending a fence wasn't anywhere on her to-do list for the day. The commissioned bow finished, she still had to get it boxed and shipped to the Arkansas buyer. Instead of heading back to the house to finish that task, she stared at the fence, mentally making a note of the supplies she'd need to grab for the repair. It could have been worse. Daisy and the rest of the herd could have made a break for it. Instead, she'd found Daisy snacking away on the front lawn, while the remainder of the herd remained out in the pasture blissfully unaware of the avenue for escape. No Daisy-assisted walkabout for the goats. Small blessings and all that. With a sigh, she headed to the equipment shed. The bow would have to wait.

Her cell phone rang seconds after she'd completed the repair. "Hey," she said after glancing at the display.

"What's up out in nature land?" Tracy Harris owned the most popular café in town and made the best espresso for miles around. They'd been friends since kindergarten, the kind of friend who saw her at her best and her worst. The kind of friend who would help her bury a body and bring the wine.

"Daisy." Didn't need to elaborate.

"Oh, sister. Sounds like you could use a big old latte."

"I would love you forever." She smiled and put a hand to her chest.

"You already do." Tracy laughed. "I need some eggs, so how about I bring you that coffee and you hand over a dozen or three?"

"Deal. Feels like a fair trade, don't you think?"

"It sure does. See you in thirty."

While it wasn't that she didn't appreciate the hand delivery of her favorite coffee drink, she also knew Tracy well enough to realize it wasn't about eggs. The odds were on local gossip her friend couldn't wait to share. Kind of like with hairdressers, people loved to come into the café and talk to Tracy. And talk. And talk. If it happened within thirty miles of Ravalli County, Tracy would be one of the first to know. Wyatt fell on the other end of that spectrum. She stayed miles out of the gossip pool. Not to say she didn't find a lot of what Tracy shared with her through the years amusing, because, yeah, she did. It was only that she preferred to stay out here with her animals, building her bows and sustaining herself through her own efforts. Town and the people who lived there didn't hold a whole lot of appeal. At least some of them. High school and young adulthood had been tough, and those things had a way of sticking with a person. Her person, to be specific.

In some ways that wasn't being fair to her community. Times had changed, and most of the good folks had changed too. What happened in the past would likely never happen now. She had to learn to forgive, and maybe when she wasn't so busy, she'd get on that. Or maybe not. Wyatt liked to think she chose the high road, except sometimes it was harder than it sounded.

Enough. She didn't have the time or the effort to go down that tired old track. By the time Tracy arrived with her perfect latte, super-sized, she had the tools and extra fence hardware put away and ready for the next time Daisy got it in her head to orchestrate an escape. She glanced toward the pasture where Daisy grazed with the rest of her pals. If her coat didn't result in the most wonderful angora yarn possible, they might need to have a talk about an alternative living arrangement. Probably not, given that no matter how many times Daisy created a problem, Wyatt cleaned it up. Something about that goat's attitude made her smile. Well, smile after she fixed fences and troughs and gates. At least she was usually a solo act and didn't often entice the rest of the herd into joining her shenanigans. After her conversation with Royal yesterday about monkshood, she planned to keep an even closer eye on the ever-creative Daisy.

"Looks good as new," Tracy said as she leaned against the fence and gazed out into the pasture. "And the goats seem happy."

"Daisy is always happiest when she creates havoc. The girl is a little left of center." Wyatt sipped the latte and sighed.

Tracy's bright-blue eyes looked into hers. "True enough but you love her."

Now she laughed. "I do indeed. So," she said as she turned and walked toward the house. "What's new in the big city?" She wasn't referring to Missoula.

Tracy snickered as she followed Wyatt. "Oh yes. Hamilton is hopping these days. A new mercantile shop opened up, and you're going to want to swing in. They have some sweet items, and I'm betting they'd love to stock your yarn. Maybe even a bow or two if you have any that aren't already spoken for."

"Maybe." She already supplied yarn to a specialty shop in Missoula and another one in Bozeman. "I don't know if I'll have enough to do a third shop, and I've got orders for three more bows. It'll take me the rest of the year to fill all those." As much as she found spinning the yarn relaxing and almost meditative, her real love lay with teaching survival classes and crafting custom bows. Something very satisfying about both those endeavors.

"I get it. Just something to keep in mind."

In the kitchen, Wyatt picked up four egg cartons, holding eighteen eggs each, and set them on the island. "Here you go. This should keep you for a little while."

Tracy clapped. "Yay. I'm down to my last two eggs and was near to panic. Then I thought, wait. I know who to call. My buddy, the problem solver."

Wyatt leaned against the counter and looked at Tracy. It was no wonder her café remained profitable. Not only did she make the best coffee for a couple hundred miles and have an uncanny business savvy, but she was beautiful to boot. Long black hair that still didn't sport even a single gray hair and eyes so blue they were like the morning sky. Top that off with a genuinely sweet personality, and success came as it should.

Wyatt patted her own long, dark hair, which did sport more than a few well-earned grays. She wore them with pride. A life lived with both joy and sorrow. "Go ahead and tell me while I drink the nectar of the gods." She sipped the latte again. Just as good as the first sip.

Tracy's smile lit up her face, and she winked at Wyatt. "I knew you'd want to know."

"Do I have a choice?" When Tracy got on something, it became her single focus. She had something she wanted to tell Wyatt. Bad.

"Hell, no. I mean, if I can't share with you, who can I share with?"

"Maybe every single person who walks into the café."

Tracy made a poofing sound. "Now you're just being mean. I was going with the BFFs-since-kindergarten thing, but you took it somewhere dark."

"Okay, okay, you win. Tell me." Actually, her curiosity ramped up.

"Here's the thing. Your buddy, Royal…"

She held up a hand. "Not my buddy." Bad enough he was making a pest of himself at her house. Now other people were connecting them. Enough already, and he hadn't even been back here that long.

Tracy let out a tiny laugh. "He sure wants to be yours. Anywho, the thing is, the prodigal son didn't return to the fold alone."

Okay. Interest now piqued big-time. That she hadn't known. "He's been over here umpteen times through the years, at least while his parents were alive. Always alone, or that's what I heard anyway. I guess I assumed he'd come back now by himself, although I haven't quite figured out why he'd want to return to live here at all. The way I heard it, he's some big-shot law professor. Why come back? We don't have a law school, and is there really enough business to sustain a law practice?"

Tracy shrugged. "Maybe the big city got too big for him and his pals. As much as I like our neighbors to the north, I wouldn't want to live in Vancouver. Way too large and noisy for my liking."

Wyatt circled back around to one word in Tracy's spiel. "Pals?"

Tracy blew out a noisy breath. Or was it an exasperated breath? "That's what I've been trying to tell you. He's not over there at his little ranch alone." Tracy pointed to the window that looked in the direction of Royal's place.

Wyatt's eyes narrowed as she stared at the window, thinking about what was beyond her line of sight. Wasn't good old Royal just full of secrets? She brought her gaze back to Tracy's face. "Tell me the rest."

"I don't know if there is more. All I know so far is there's a woman and a man with him. The guy is super hot too. If I didn't already have my sights set elsewhere, I'd sure be interested in tall and handsome. Maybe a little something for you too." She winked.

Tracy wasn't referring to Royal or the other man. They'd been friends long enough to know pretty much everything about each other. "What about the woman?"

Excitement flowed back into Tracy's voice. "I saw her in the car. Looked pretty, but I only got a glimpse when Royal and his buddy came in for coffee. Found out when I was down at the feed store that the three of them are living at Royal's place. Nice and cozy, don't you think?"

"Did he say who they were?" Royal could have other family that she hadn't known about. To the best of her recollection, he'd been an only child. Didn't mean there wasn't extended family out there. Or perhaps good friends that wanted to make a change too. All sorts of possibilities.

One particular question kept running through her mind. Why, in all the visits he'd made to her house since returning or during those casual moments of crossing paths, Royal had never once mentioned he didn't return alone.

❖

Mari parked her black Chevy Trailblazer next to the line of forest-service pickups. The small SUV was the first car she'd ever purchased new, and she loved it. All the bells and whistles, along with all-wheel drive for the snowy winters. Next to the trucks, it looked like a toy. Remarks would be made. She didn't care.

The tall, silver-haired man who stepped out of the main door didn't require an introduction. Besides the name tag on his shirt, he'd been the deciding vote in her hire. She'd liked Oliver Allridge right from the start of the lengthy interview process. She came here as his replacement when his retirement went into effect the end of the week.

"About time you got here, Fremont." Hands on his hips, he looked like the office guard dog.

"I didn't get in until late yesterday afternoon." She'd emailed him that information, which made her wonder if he didn't read it, or he liked giving her grief. She suspected it to be the latter. What took the sting out of his words was the expression on his face and the twinkle in his eye. No malice, only warmth. A friendly guard dog.

"You're in Montana now, Ranger. Speed limit is 80."

She laughed. "Going to take some getting used to. Not that I'm saying I won't in time."

"My money says you'll be used to it inside of a week."

"Sucker's bet. I like it already."

Now he laughed, one of those deep laughs that made everyone else join in, and waved her inside. "Let's get the paperwork done and then get out there. You're going to love our corner of the world, and I'm betting you won't even miss all that rain you're used to."

"The sooner, the better." One of the reasons she loved her work? She didn't get stuck behind a desk. Not to say she didn't have tasks that required her to be inside, but the fact that the majority of Mari's work occurred in nature made those times bearable. She wasn't wired for four walls, a desk, and chair. Endless meetings and team-building exercises.

She smiled at Oliver when she walked by and into the office lobby, her eyes nearly level with his. Suspected her height might have been one of the reasons he'd liked her over other candidates. A plus in this scenario, a minus in a promotion that should have been hers. One saw it as a positive, one as a detriment.

"What?" She knew the question even though it hadn't passed his lips. No, she wasn't in uniform, as she'd dropped hers at the tailor's shop to get the patches changed for her new duty station. No uniform aside, she'd shown up for her first official day in field-appropriate clothing. She still had her forest-service cap so she was also fully identifiable. "My uniforms will be ready tomorrow with the new patches."

He shook his head. "Not that." His frown wasn't angry, more disapproving.

"Then what's wrong?" Mari wasn't following.

"We do things a little different here for good reasons."

"Meaning?"

"Meaning, we carry." He tapped the Glock 22 in a holster clipped to his belt. "All the time."

Her hand went to her gun-free waist. "Oh." It had become more and more common for rangers to carry because of the increasing danger they faced out in the state and national parks. She'd resisted, and in the areas she'd worked thus far in her career, it hadn't been an issue. "I didn't need to carry often at my old duty station, and I checked my gun back in when I left." Not that she had a problem with guns. Unless she needed to, or was required to, she'd rather not.

"You know how to use one?" His frown deepened as though he suddenly questioned his choice in her as his replacement.

The shadow of disappointment in his face made her heart sink. Her honest answer might help. "Of course." Just because she chose not to carry didn't mean she wasn't fully trained.

The frown lessened and an eyebrow went up. Maybe she'd imagined the disappointed look. "You any good?"

She could brag, decided to go subtle. Sometimes men didn't like to find out she could outshoot them eight days a week. "I'm very good." Not an exaggeration. Dad had been a champion, and she'd followed in his footsteps. She'd aced the range tests at the mandatory federal law-enforcement training back East. A couple of the hotshots in her class were probably still pissed about that.

His smile returned, and he gave her an approving nod. "Good to hear. We'll get a service weapon checked out to you. Most of our guns are Glock 22s. That work?"

"Yes." She knew the gun well and liked it. If she had to carry, it might as well be a Glock.

"I'll also introduce you to the boys over at Fire Ridge Guns. They have an excellent selection and will treat you right if you need anything for home. They can hook you up at the range too. Clear out the cobwebs, you know."

"Sounds good." While she'd maintained her firearms certification, she hadn't been on the range in a while. Probably were a few cobwebs.

Things here really were going to be different, and it wasn't only about the need to carry. The real question wasn't about those differences but rather if they would treat her as an equal. She hadn't stood for the crappy treatment in Oregon, and she sure as heck wouldn't stand for it here either.

Royal sat at the table drinking coffee as sunshine streamed through the kitchen window. The suit he wore might be a little much, but it also screamed competence, and that's what he needed to portray to ensure that the good residents of Hamilton viewed him as a successful lawyer, which they would. True enough, he hadn't practiced in over a decade. Also true enough that no one needed to know that. It would be like riding a bike and would all come back to him once he got in the saddle. He had been an excellent law school professor, and he'd been an equally excellent practicing attorney.

At the bang of the back door, he swung his gaze from the rays of sunshine to the kitchen doorway. Two seconds later, Inez walked through, a bit of grass in her hair, her shirt untucked from the waistband of her dirt-streaked jeans. The moment her eyes met his, she stopped. "I thought you'd be gone."

He shifted his gaze from her messy clothes to her face, blood on her lips, eyes almost glowing. "Clearly." His jaw tightened.

"Look…" She took a step back and put out her hands as though protecting herself.

He leaned over and slapped his hands on the table. "No! You look. I told you not to hunt."

Her face darkened, she dropped her hands and squared her shoulders. Trying to look as big and bold as possible. Failing. "I needed to."

Hard to keep from yelling. He managed a level, "You need to obey me."

"Or what?" She brought her chin up, and she might have appeared confident if her body didn't tremble, her hands plucking the hem of her shirt.

He stood up, knowing full well that his towering height intimidated, and that was even before. Combined now with his enhancement, he could be menacing when he took a mind to. He'd heard the rumors at the university that centered around not bothering him if he were in a dark mood. The other professors who looped him in called them rumors. He saw them more as truths. "Or things around here will change. Permanently."

Anger entered her voice, a go-to tactic for Inez. "You're threatening me? After all I've done for you? After leaving my home for you? That's messed up."

He kept his tone level. Sometimes the calm could convey something far more powerful and frightening than explosive displays of anger. "I'm not threatening. I'm promising. I will not have you screw things up."

Like a flash in a pan, her bravado faded. "It was just a stupid mountain goat."

"Where?" Wondering where she might have made a mess, his mind raced. One thing in their favor were the nearby wolf packs that could take the blame if the remains were discovered. Deflect whenever possible.

"Out there." She waved in the air as though swatting away a fly.

"WHERE?" He couldn't read her mind, and he sure as hell got nothing from her hand-waving. Thousands of acres encompassed the *out there*.

Inez dropped her head. "The wilderness area."

Great. The Bob Marshal Wilderness Complex. About as public as she could have gone. A remote area, it still had enough people visiting it that someone could come across the remains of the goat. "You clean it up?" *Please, for once just tell me you cleaned up your own damn mess.*

She didn't bring her head up, shifting from foot to foot, still plucking at her shirt. A bit of grass floated to the floor.

He looked down at his suit and sighed. "I take it that's a no."

Inez shrugged. "Wasn't in the right form."

The calm fled. "Jesus Christ, Inez. You can't do that." How in the world would he get that goat out of there before somebody reported it, and knowing how she did things, it would definitely be reported.

"Nobody will give a goat a second thought. Nature running its course and all that good crap."

"You hope. Now, get showered and promise me this is the last time you chase and kill an animal." She turned to go, sliding her feet rather than picking them up. "I said promise me," he said sharply.

Inez paused and looked over her shoulder at him, darkness in her eyes. For a few seconds, she stared at him. Then she shivered. "I promise."

Royal breathed in deeply, sorting through damage-control options. Beautiful, quick, and talented on one side, Inez was impulsive, hot-headed, and unreliable on the other. Hundreds of miles north of Ravalli County, those qualities had been entertaining. Here, they threatened them all, and that wasn't acceptable.

"What did she do now?" Claude strolled into the kitchen, opened the refrigerator, and pulled out a bottle of juice. He downed the whole thing in a single drink. His torso bare and glistening with sweat, his shirt was tucked into his cargo pants and hanging down over his backside.

"Hunting. Again."

Claude wiped his mouth with the back of his hand. "She's pretty feral, but, dude, you knew that from day uno." He tossed the empty bottle into the trash. The guy could put away more calories than three people and still look ready to walk a runway in Milan.

Thing about Claude, despite his model-good-looks and easy talk, a darkness rippled beneath. Not quite feral like Inez. Something different that he'd never been able to pin down. Energizing to anyone in his immediate orbit. "She's going to be all right. And besides, she's one of us."

Claude laughed. "Yeah, right, one of us. You have high hopes, don't you?"

"If I hadn't been full of high hopes for you, think you'd be holding either that diploma or passing bar results?" Royal raised an eyebrow as he stared at him.

"That's different." He sounded a bit like the spoiled child he'd undoubtedly been once upon a time.

"Different scenarios, same optimism and chances for redemption." He might have been thinking of sending Inez away, but Claude didn't need to know that.

"I still say she'd be a risk." Wasn't going to give it up. Claude wouldn't ever admit he was wrong about anything. He'd go down fighting. Actually, the trait wasn't a bad one for a litigator. Particularly one who leaned toward defense work.

Right at the moment, they had other things to concentrate on. "I'll deal with Inez, and trust me, she'll come around. "You." Royal pointed his index finger toward the middle of Claude's chest. "Just focus on what we came here to accomplish."

Claude pulled his shirt from the waistband of his pants and ran it over his face. He slung it over his shoulder and looked at Royal. Cool, calm, and unconcerned. "Sure, right. Destiny and all that shit."

Royal took a deep breath and then blew it out slowly. "Yes. Destiny."

CHAPTER THREE

Wyatt parked her truck at the Bob Marshall Wilderness Area and got out. Only a couple other vehicles today, including a forest service truck. Probably Ollie. His love for hiking the trails here rivaled Wyatt's, and it wasn't unusual to run into each other. She'd miss him after he relocated, and while he might not be on the job any longer, he'd remain a wilderness guy because that was who he was. Made her wonder if he'd settle in somewhere besides Montana. Time would tell if Arizona would remain his new home, with its brown mountains and scorching weather. Secretly, she hoped he decided it wasn't for him and came back. Losing friends didn't sit well with her.

She grabbed her small day pack from the backseat and slipped the straps over her shoulders. Soon enough, she'd make this trek with six women who'd signed up for her ladies survival basics series. The first class always started with an orientation to the local wilderness areas. Bob Marshall was her favorite and thus her initial stop. It never failed to wow her students, who came from all over the country. Even though she'd grown up here, it never failed to impress her too. Truly a gem for her corner of Montana. Actually, a gem for the country, period. Not that she was biased or anything. Unlike Ollie, if she ever did retire, she planned to stay put.

With a blue, cloudless sky above her head and a warm breeze blowing soft against her skin, Wyatt started out on a familiar trail, or perhaps more accurately, the most familiar. The destruction from a wildfire several years earlier could still be seen, though nature had done a fine job on its renewal. Blackened earth and trees were surrounded by rebounding wild grasses and conifer starts. Soon, all traces of the damage done would be wiped away. She'd seen the massive wildfire from her house that fateful Sunday. At the time she'd sent up her pleas to the universe to keep the fire fighters safe and to let them stop the path of the conflagration sending tendrils of fire so high into the sky they could be seen from many miles away.

She gazed back and forth across the landscape as she hiked, identifying native plants and tracks of animals. Every so often, she stopped and picked up debris left by those who refused to abide by the carry-in/carry-out rules. In her classes, if a student failed to follow the rules, they got one warning. Those who ignored the initial warning found themselves on their way back home. No second chances. No exceptions.

With her handheld global positioning system, or GPS as they were commonly referred to, Wyatt marked her location. Retracing her steps without tech wasn't a problem. She liked to do her class prep in the same way she'd teach her students. Her motto was simple: train like you teach; teach like you train. At this point, she'd have them mark this spot. Nothing in particular here, just good practice at establishing coordinates.

As she turned toward the west, the wind blew across her face and with it brought a scent she didn't expect. She frowned, closed her eyes, and inhaled deeply. Blood. A lot of blood for the scent to be picked up and carried through the air. So much for her class prep. The unexpected had her following the information on the wind rather than planning a route for her students.

Wyatt didn't get far. "That's not good." A blood trail darkened the earth and spotted the leaves of plants and wildflowers. She followed it off the path and into the thicker brush. Bits of fur littered the forest floor. She continued to follow the trail to a small clearing. The source of the fur revealed itself. At first, she assumed the remains of the mountain goat appeared to have been left behind by an unethical hunter. "Piece of shit," she said under her breath, and she wasn't referring to the deceased animal.

She got closer. "What the hell?" Her assumption proved false. No bow or rifle had killed this animal. Something brutal and far more primal had ended this goat's life. She stood up and looked around. Predators didn't usually leave their prey behind. She didn't want to be in the way if it came back to reclaim its kill. Nothing in the immediate area. No sounds that would let her know she wasn't alone.

Once more Wyatt pulled her out GPS unit. As soon as she had the coordinates marked, she took her phone from her pocket. No service. She traded her phone for the radio in her chest harness. After she adjusted the frequency channel, she pressed the button. "Wyatt calling Ollie. Are you reading me, Ollie?" She took her finger off the button and waited. A couple seconds later, a crackle came over the radio.

"Go head, Wyatt. What's up?"

"Ollie, I'm here in the Bob, and I think you might have a problem. Got a goat here that's been torn apart."

"Come again. Did you say a goat torn apart?"

"Copy that."

"Give me the coordinates."

Wyatt held her GPS in one hand and the radio in the other as she read the coordinates to Ollie. He read them back. "Confirm. You want me to wait until you get here?"

"Up to you. We're not far from you so should be there in under fifteen minutes."

"I'll wait." Two reasons. She was curious to get his thoughts on what animal did this to the goat and equally curious about the *we* part. Could be another ranger from one of the managing districts or it could be his replacement. Rumor had it, they'd hired someone from Oregon, and like pretty much everyone around here, Wyatt was curious about the new guy.

While she waited, she walked the perimeter of the clearing. Looked like wolf tracks to her. First time she'd seen evidence of one taking down a goat. The more she studied the tracks, the more unusual they seemed. A little on the large side for the endangered grays that called the Bob home. Ollie would be able to tell for certain. Might know if a nearby pack had some larger-than-normal members.

"Whatcha got, Wyatt?" Ollie stepped into the clearing, his hands on the straps of his pack and a smile on his face. Years out in the wilderness witnessing the good, the bad, and the ugly, and still he smiled ninety percent of the time. She wished she could bottle that kind of attitude. Her face had a bad habit of reflecting whatever she happened to be feeling, like those moments when one of her students did something downright stupid. She worked on not letting it show. She failed most of the time.

Right behind Ollie followed a woman in civilian clothing. A beige, long-sleeved tech shirt and green cargo pants. Expensive boots that would hold up to the rigors of wilderness work told Wyatt in a flash that she was the new ranger. She had a forest-service cap on her short, brown hair. "Say hi to Mari," Ollie said. "She's stepping into my shoes."

Curiosity piqued even more, along with a healthy dose of optimism for the future of the service here. No new *guy*, and things just got a whole lot more interesting.

Mari had been focused on the remains of the goat and only looked up when Oliver introduced her to the tall, attractive woman with long, dark hair pulled into a single braid that fell far down her back. An aura of competence radiated from her, and Mari didn't have to wonder why the senior ranger responded as quickly as he had to her call. This woman knew the forest and the creatures that made their home here. The things that were right. The things that were wrong.

"Hi." She reached out a hand. "I'm Mari Whitaker."

Wyatt took her offered greeting, her grip firm. "Nice to meet you, Ranger Whitaker. I'm Wyatt Foreman."

Mari smiled. "Please, it's just Mari. No need to go all formal."

"Same to you. It's Wyatt. We don't stand much on formality around here and sounds like you're going to fit in great."

"Thanks, Wyatt." She smiled. "What can you tell us about this?" She pointed to the remains

"Wolf," Oliver said before Wyatt could respond. He walked a full circle around the remains. "Definitely a wolf." His smile had been replaced by a frown and narrowed eyes.

Wyatt turned away from Mari and looked down at the ground. "A big one. Look at those prints." She pointed. "You see that?"

Oliver squatted and studied the tracks. "Yep, I sure do, and you're right. A big one." He glanced up and said, "Mari, come take a look. I know your previous post didn't get a lot in terms of wolf population, but have you seen anything like this?"

True statement. Familiar with the wildlife in her home state, here she'd expected things to be a bit different. Different terrain and climate made for different habitats. The kind of challenge she'd come here for. Not running away. Nope. Not at all.

She put a knee down on the ground without getting too close and studied the prints. "From my limited interactions with Canis lupus, I'd have to say it does look like the print of a bigger-than-normal wolf." It wasn't like she hadn't been in areas with wolf populations. A good ranger had a well-rounded background regardless of their duty station, and she'd done a bit of temporary duty in areas where wolves lived. A couple months up in Northeastern Washington state had exposed her to some growing packs. Now, she supposed she'd need to get up to speed on the local packs in this region of Montana.

A bit of excitement rushed through her. As much as she'd loved her hometown, a change in scenery wasn't unwelcome. In fact, she kind of wondered if the universe saw this for her and that's why things had played out the way they did. Made the snub a lot easier to swallow.

"Except…"

She squinted as she looked down. "Except, it's really big."

"Yeah. My take too." Oliver stood. "That's one huge wolf. Haven't seen one that size around here before."

"A good year maybe?" She thought of reasons why members of a pack might grow larger than the norm. Lots of food, secure dens, plenty of small game to hunt. The goat, however, didn't feel like small game and an unnecessary kill for survival. She also wondered, if the smaller game was plentiful, why it would go for a more difficult prey like a goat. It wouldn't have been an easy takedown.

"Could be. We had a mild winter, and the spring is turning into a beauty, which all equates to a bountiful year around here. Thing is, I've never heard of it before, and you know, I've been in these parts a real long time." He rubbed his chin, the five o'clock shadow a pale gray that matched the hair on his head.

Mari stood and put her hands on her hips. "I defer to your expertise. My last duty station wasn't exactly a hot spot for packs of wolves."

Oliver laughed. "And I'd say to you, keep an open mind. I know a lot, and I'll be the first one to tell you that. I'll also be the first one to tell you I don't know everything, and nature has a way of making fools out of all of us now and again. Never take anything at face value, and never deal in absolutes. The minute you say *never* or *always*, it will come back to bite you in the butt."

Mari thought she'd end up liking this guy a lot, and it made her a little sad their time together would be short. He'd already told her he and his wife had bought a place in Arizona and were packing up to leave. Getting away from the harsh winters, he'd said. Retiring to a hot climate didn't appeal to her at the moment. After she spent her first winter here, she might change her mind. Portland's winters were pretty mild most of the time. Snow loved eastern Montana, while people in Portland freaked out if there was even a dusting of it. She'd had enough time in the mountains to have some skills most of her fellow-Portlanders did not. She hoped they would be enough not to embarrass herself come the first snowfall.

She gave him a nod and said, "I still defer. Nature does some amazing things, and I'm guessing you've seen a lot of that." With over a million acres here, she had tons to learn. Much she hadn't experienced before. Rugged peaks, alpine lakes, waterfalls, and massive meadows, along with a towering forest, filled her with joyful anticipation. Made her glad Oliver had her jump right in. Even the sight of the poor goat that lost its life in a bloody encounter didn't dampen her enthusiasm for her new position.

"True enough except..." He shook his head as he waved his hand toward the sheep carcass and the extra-large wolf tracks. "I've never seen this."

❖

Royal sat at his home office desk and stared at the unfinished email on his laptop. They'd be waiting to hear from him, and so far, he'd been unable to finish it. When he'd come here, he'd had what he thought to be a solid plan with a perfect timeline. Turned out the plan needed some tweaks and his timeline might not be workable. His optimism was partly to blame. Inez and Claude partly to blame. He'd overestimated his powers of persuasion, and those two weren't as obedient as he'd anticipated. Free will and all that. Inez, in particular. Who knew she'd turn into such a needy bitch? She hadn't come across that way before. Flew her flag with abandon now. Almost as though she wanted to wear her version of a scarlet letter, but rather than an *A*, she'd be flaunting a *W*. Couldn't allow that to happen.

It worried him that she'd left a mess out in the wilderness area. Chances of someone discovering her indiscretion ranked pretty darned high. He could only hope it would be attributed to one of the predators that roamed the forest. Unless someone had better-than-average skills, they wouldn't be able to discern the difference between a wolf attack and a bear mauling. Unfortunately for him, this particular area boasted more than its share of excellent trackers. If one of those folks saw it, they'd know, and that wouldn't do. Better to dispose of the evidence.

He stared at the email a minute longer before deleting it. Might not be his best decision to keep Inez's escapades to himself. For the moment, he would. He wasn't quite ready to give up on her, even though that would be easier. Instead of asking for help, he'd send the regular monthly report. What the council didn't know wouldn't hurt them. Him, maybe, but not them. Responsibility for Inez rested on his shoulders, and he would handle her without their intervention. Right now anyway. He began typing.

Amy. Relocation of the pack is proceeding as anticipated. Home is fully established, and I'm well into the process of setting up my law practice. Once again, I appreciate the council's authorization to relocate to my hometown. My plan still stands unaltered and am looking forward to the upcoming Harvest Moon and mating ceremony. I will keep you and the council apprised of progress.

He sat back in his chair and reread what he'd written. Short, sweet, and to the point, though he suspected that Amy would read between the lines. The feeling of failure kept him staring at the words and not hitting *send*. His pride stood in the way. Every great adventure had its ups and downs. Did anything ever go exactly to plan? Probably not. His hands drifted away from the keyboard.

The difference between ultimate success or complete failure came with the ability to pivot. To accept the defeats and still maintain forward momentum. That's exactly what he planned to do. One step back and three or four forward. Now he had to pivot, and he could do that without advertising to the council. Some of the elders were very set in their ways, and their idea of solving problems like Inez were quick and final.

"She took off again." Claude stood in the doorway.

"What?" Royal spun and stared.

"With a bag."

Royal jumped up and headed out to the driveway. "She took my car." The audacity of Inez never ceased to astound him. Bold even for her. "I'm going to kick her ass."

Claude had followed him outside and stood next to him. "If you can find her."

Royal smiled. "Oh, I can find her." He pulled his phone out of his pocket and opened a locator app.

Chapter Four

So, Ranger Mari, what do you think?" Wyatt decided the way both of the rangers studied the scene said a lot. Not a typical day in the Bob Marshall Wilderness Area. Certainly not for Wyatt, and it wasn't just because of what she'd stumbled upon. Not very often a good-looking female ranger showed up. Might be a little superficial on her part, but hey. It was still nice for several reasons.

"Again, please, just Mari. I'll be honest. I'm not familiar with the workings of the area yet, but even so, it seems odd to me. Oliver, what do you think?"

"Yeah, *Oliver*, what do you think?" She smiled at Ollie. Sounded so funny to hear him called Oliver. She wasn't sure she'd ever heard anyone call him that, except maybe his wife, and even then, it was only when she was mad at him.

He rolled his eyes as he shook his head. "Wyatt, you can be such a smart-ass."

"Mama taught me well." She waved a hand in the air. The apple didn't fall far from the tree in her case, and it made her proud.

Now, he did laugh a little. "That she did. Wyatt's mother was a bit of a legend around here," he said to Mari. "She knew every inch of this place for miles around. Was a better shot than probably eighty percent of the men in these parts and could cook well enough to sweep the blue ribbons at any fair. Like I said, a legend."

"What would she say?" Mari looked directly into Wyatt's eyes. Mari's were brown, like hers, and they were filled with intelligence. No slouch had been selected to step into Ollie's shoes. Not much she wasn't liking about this hiring decision.

Wyatt looked down at the remains of the poor goat. "She'd probably tell me to go back home, grab a bow, and come back to investigate."

Mari's brow furrowed, locks of short brown hair poking out from beneath her cap. "Investigate? A bow?"

Wyatt did things a little different from lots of folks. It was how she'd been taught, and she liked it that way. "I hunt exclusively with bows."

Ollie patted her on the shoulder. "She's being modest. She's not only one of the most skilled bow hunters in the West, but she's also one of the best bow makers in the country. This woman doesn't need to carry a gun."

"Interesting." Mari drew out the single word.

At least she seemed mildly impressed. Too often that fact was met with disbelief, as though only a man could possibly create an impressive bow or be a skilled hunter with one. Took a fair amount of time to establish herself as a creator, and that was okay. In the end, she'd proved to the skeptics that she could compete with the most accomplished craftsman anywhere. As for using a bow, she had to shoot only once to shut up the disbelieving.

She shrugged. Proud as she was of her work and skills, she didn't like to brag. "My parents were old-school, with massive talent. I seemed to have inherited it."

"Don't let her fool you." Ollie jumped in. "The lady has some serious skills, and she knows these parts almost as well as her mother. And me," he added.

"I don't know about you, Ollie, but that's why I'm feeling like that is a problem." She pointed to the remains of the goat. Not that predators didn't attack other animals. It happened all the time. Just the way of the natural world. Something about it struck her wrong, although if pressed, she'd admit she didn't exactly know why. More a feeling than anything else.

Ollie chewed on his lower lip for a few seconds. "Yeah. I don't like it either, and the size of those prints is like a wolf on steroids. To my knowledge, no one has reported anything unusual like a gigantic wolf."

"Could there be something in the environment causing a mutation of some sort? A chemical released in the water? I've seen some issues near Portland. Unintentional and yet damaging to the environment at the same time." Mari stared down at the goat, her words soft as though she were talking to herself.

Mari's thought process wasn't out of line. Particularly if she came from an area closer to a large metropolitan city like Portland. "It's possible, though not likely out here. Nothing nearby with the potential to release a toxic substance. Unless..." A thought occurred to Wyatt.

"Unless what?" Mari studied her face.

"Unless someone is doing something under the radar, and the results are affecting our wildlife." Some folks looked at national parks as their own personal property to do with as they pleased, and they'd found things like marihuana grows and even once an unauthorized cabin. Guy was pretty put out when his abode was dismantled.

Ollie stood with his hands in his pocket, a dark expression on his face. "Great. That's just what we need around here. Interlopers destroying nature. Big-city pricks." He glanced at Mari. "Sorry."

Mari shook her head. "No need to apologize to me. I'd use something a little stronger to describe the mofos who do things like that."

Wyatt decided she liked their newest ranger. People who abused nature pissed her off, and it sounded like they did the same to Mari. She might come to them from a place very different from their little piece of Montana, but she had spunk and honesty. All signs so far indicated Mari would fit in with ease. "I'll do some investigating. Need to work on some lessons for my upcoming classes anyway."

"Classes?" Mari looked at her.

"I teach women's survival classes. Things like how to start a fire without matches or a lighter. How to build a temporary shelter. How to feed yourself. Those kinds of things."

"A lot of call for that?" Mari took her cap off, ran a hand through her short hair, and then put her cap back on.

"You'd be surprised. I get students from all over." It still amazed her how many women came to her to learn. She loved it and loved them. Most of them anyway.

Ollie jumped in. "She's the one everyone comes looking for, male or female. Let's just say she knows her stuff, and if you want to hone your nature skills, can't get better than Wyatt here."

She smiled and patted Ollie on the back. "I think I need to hire him as my PR guy. Sure you don't want to stay around and work for me?" It was an off-the-cuff comment, yet the more she thought about it, the more she liked it. Could be fun working with him. The administrative side of her work grew larger every year, and it was the part she didn't particularly enjoy.

"Not gonna happen, lady. This boy is gonna kick his feet up and do nothing except eat, drink, and be merry. Oh, and all of it by the water. Did I tell you our new house has a swimming pool?"

"You'll be bored." Wyatt really couldn't see Ollie being a man of leisure. Too much energy even as he stepped into his sixth decade.

"Maybe, but I'm gonna give it a go. That pool is calling my name." He smiled, and Wyatt thought he looked ten years younger.

"All right." She laughed lightly. "So, today, how about you do your thing here, and I'm going to buzz back home and grab a bow, just in case, before I continue on my original route. Still have to get all my notes in order and ready for my next group of ladies."

Ollie patted her on the back, his big hand warm. "You call if you find anything."

She crossed her index finger across her chest. "Promise."

❖

The interaction between Oliver and Wyatt impressed Mari. She hoped she could forge something similar with her. Fascinating lady. Her reservations about leaving her life in Oregon faded with each passing hour. The grand plan of the universe at work. She liked it. As bad as it had gotten when it all went south in Portland, things here were new, bright, and encouraging. Dead mountain goat excepted.

For a minute, she watched Wyatt hike away from them. She carried a small olive-green pack on her back, along with a chest harness that sported a high-end GPS unit and an FRS radio. The best equipment to ensure coverage wherever she might be in the deep forest. She figured Wyatt to be around her age and pretty close to the same height. She liked her long, thick hair. She touched her own, short and practical. Never had the patience to mess with her hair, much to her mother's dismay. Mom had always wanted a girlie-girl and instead got one who ditched dance lessons to run in the woods. She had liked those tap shoes though. They'd made some great noise.

"Let's bag this bad boy up and see what our local vet has to say." Oliver stared down at the remains of the goat.

Reading between the lines, she asked, "Let's as in me?" She smiled.

"You catch on quick, newbie." He looked up at her, his smile large as he stuffed his hands into his pockets.

Mari shrugged. "I guess you've done your time."

"Damn straight. Now that you've arrived, I'm cruising from here on out, and I don't feel bad one iota."

She laughed. His honesty was refreshing, particularly after all the lies and deception that had sent her running this way. "I got your back, Oliver."

"Of course you do. Who can resist me? And, for the love of God, can you please stop calling me Oliver. It's Ollie to everyone except my mother, and maybe my wife when she's on a tear."

"You got it, Ollie."

Mari ran all the way back to the truck to grab a bag, gloves, and a small shovel, just in case. Her affinity for navigation came naturally to her, and she'd been able to retrace their steps without having to use a GPS. Sometimes she wondered if she'd been switched at the hospital. Her mother's longed-for princess got exchanged for a forest fairy's daughter. Thank goodness, Mom adapted to the daughter she got and not only loved her as she was, but encouraged her in her chosen vocation. Not to say she wasn't sad when she made the move here, although given how Mom liked to travel, she suspected she'd be seeing her soon.

The woods were alive as she ran, the sounds of birds and rabbits and squirrels. Made her happy when the forest came alive. Told her one thing for certain: the predator that killed the goat wasn't around now. The air was warm, the scent of spring heavy on the air. A little less humidity than she'd grown up with. Figured she could get used to the dry air pretty darn quick. At times coastal Oregon's damp weather got on her nerves. It would be nice to experience more sun and less rain. Maybe she'd been destined to come here all along, and she only now just realized it.

Ollie waited for her back at the scene of the crime. Not quite the typical crime, yet she thought of it as one. It rang wrong to her. Nothing like a good mystery on the first day of the job. When she got back, Ollie was leaning against a tree making notes on a small lined pad. She went right to work.

"This is weird." Mari rocked back on her heels and studied the goat's remains before she bagged it.

Oliver stopped writing, put the notebook back into his pocket, and leaned in. "How so? Looks like a dead goat to me."

She pointed toward it. "It's the condition of it that bothers me. Look close, Ollie. The predator didn't kill this goat for food. Too much of the body is here. The organs are still intact. What predator doesn't go for the best parts first? It's like whatever killed the goat was playing a game that ended once it was dead. Then it ran away, all the fun done and over."

He squatted down next to her and stared. "Well, I'll be damned. Good point, Ranger, and you're right. This doesn't look like a normal kill."

An uneasy feeling washed over her. "This looks like pure sport. Animals don't do that."

"People do, and everyone around here hunts."

Shaking her head, she continued to study the remains, a dark feeling washing over her. "This isn't the work of a hunter." She used a gloved hand to touch one of the wounds on the goat. No bullet or arrow caused it. Looking up at Ollie, she pointed. "More like intentional harm for fun. Something tore this goat apart and then just left him here. Why?"

"Predators don't do that."

"That's my point. No, they don't. This reminds me of a dog playing with a stuffie. They pick it up and shake it hard, but they don't eat it. It's a big, fat game."

"That's messed up."

"It is." She went back to work bagging the remains. Once done, she stood and slipped off the gloves, stuffing them into a small biohazard bag. One thing for certain, day one orientation was turning out to be more than interesting.

❖

"You have got to be kidding me." Royal sat in his truck and stared at the spot where they'd found his Jaguar. Inez had parked it right in front of Beautiful Buds. A damn dope store. Good thing he wasn't wearing a blood-pressure cuff. "She knows better."

Claude laughed and slapped the dashboard. "Got to give her props for having some big balls. That shit's funny."

"I'm going to kick her in those big balls, and no, it's not funny." He held out a set of keys. "Drive my car home." Heartburn kicked up heat in his chest.

Claude started to open the door and then turned to look at Royal. "You going in for her?" No laughter now. Probably more hope that he could go inside with him.

A shot of fire flashed up his chest again. "Absolutely not. She can bloody well get her ass home on her own. There are consequences to actions."

Claude tilted his head and frowned. "Kind of harsh punishment. It's like twenty miles back to the farm in broad daylight. No SkyTrain out here. She'll have to walk."

He glanced at the long stretch of highway. "Don't care. I won't put up with this kind of crap from her." Royal turned and stared at Claude. "Or you."

Claude held up his hands. "Bro, I'm not stupid. Besides, I like it here, and once I pass the Montana bar, I'm pretty sure I'll like it even more. The lady clients will come to us in droves."

"Let's keep it that way. Now, would you please get my car home." He wanted Claude out of here so he could be ready to move the second Inez came out and noticed him. The realization that she had no car or ride back home might be enough to finally get her attention. Let her know he was serious about her knocking it off. He'd had enough. Every alpha had their limit.

What he did like was how Claude got out to do as he'd been directed without being an ass about it. A good soldier. Most of the time. He had his quirks too. Didn't they all? For Claude, it leaned more toward indifference than defiance. Inez was the poster child for the latter. How he didn't see that before, he'd never know. Reminded him to be a lot more selective about those allowed into the family.

Claude was long gone by the time Inez walked out the door with a paper sack the size of a lunch bag in her hands. She stared at the spot where she'd parked the Jag. Instead of expletives or anger, she started laughing. Looking up, she noticed him in the truck. She held up the bag and shook it. A little like a red cape being waved in front of a bull. As she started to walk his way, he pulled out of the parking lot. Still no screaming. In his rearview mirror, he saw her lift her middle finger at him.

"Back atcha, bitch." He hoped that by the time she made it home, she'd once more be obedient. More optimistic than reality called for.

His phone rang as he drove toward downtown. Didn't even bother to look at the display to see the identity of the caller. No need. Didn't hit ignore either. Let it go to voicemail. She could leave whatever message she wanted. He'd ignore that too.

As he drove, it occurred to him that he could use a good beverage, and the best place by far was the café on the town's main street. Tracy sure did know her coffee and baked goods. Rivaled anything he'd had in the big city. Surprised him a little that she'd stayed around, given her skill level. She'd have made a killing in Missoula or Salt Lake City or even Spokane.

"Hey, Tracy." He remembered her from way back when and made big points with her when he'd called out her name the first time he stepped in the café. She hadn't recognized him initially, and he hadn't been surprised. The Royal who grew up here had been unremarkable, a little chubby, and the star of the debate team. No popular girls hoping he'd ask them to the prom. No letterman's jacket for football or basketball in his closet. Only shelves crammed with debate trophies. The Royal who came back was tall, dark, and handsome, and he figured that was being modest.

She smiled, and, as always, her average face went to beautiful. This was a woman who should always smile. "Nice to see you. The usual?"

"Please. It's been quite the day so far, and I can sure use a pick-me-up."

She moved to the very expensive espresso machine and worked her magic. "I can fix you right up." The scent of fresh coffee filled the air. He loved it.

"Appreciate it."

She handed him a cup. Knowing Tracy, she'd seen him parking and had the drink halfway prepped before he even got out of the truck. "Saw your Jag go by a while ago. Your girlfriend?" The question sounded casual. It wasn't. Tracy knew everything about everyone. He glanced at her. Almost everything.

He nearly spit out the sip he'd just taken before the girlfriend comment. "Ah, that would be a big no. She's family."

"You have a sister? Didn't remember that. I guess I always thought you were an only child."

"I am. You're remembering correctly. Inez is my cousin from up North." Close enough without having to go into details he had no intention of sharing. He took another sip of the most excellent coffee.

Tracy used a rag to clean the espresso machine while she talked. "Pretty, or at least that's what I thought from the fleeting glimpse I got. She drove a little fast. Might want to warn her that she'll get a ticket if she keeps driving like that."

He raised an eyebrow. "You interested?" He hadn't known that about Tracy. In fact, he could have sworn she had a boyfriend. No ring or he'd say husband, although that wasn't always an accurate representation of marital status.

She laughed. "No, not me. I'm as straight as they come. Just ask my man. Although I do have a friend. You know, if..."

Now he smiled. "I'll let her know, though I wouldn't expect much. Not sure how long she'll be here, and I'll warn her about her speed. She doesn't need another ticket."

"Well, you know how it is. Always looking out for the happiness of our friends and family."

"You're a good friend." He smiled, knowing it made him even more handsome. He could work it like the most polished boy-toy when he wanted, or needed to.

She smiled back. "I try. Hope your day goes better."

He held up the cup as he opened the door. "This will help. See ya."

Back on the road, he sipped the coffee and thought about Inez. Bothered him that Tracy noticed her at that level of detail. One of their unbreakable rules—keep on the down-low. Don't draw unwanted attention, especially not from law enforcement. Inez was moving further off task as each day passed. A rabid dog running wild. Wouldn't do. Couldn't be allowed.

He finished his coffee and set the empty cup in the holder. He'd throw it in the recycle bin once he got back to the house. Not that they had recycling pickup here. Didn't change how he viewed the natural world. Had to keep it clean and safe, respected, and that meant never littering and sending as little as possible to landfills.

Instead of going directly home, he pulled off the highway and drove down Wyatt's driveway. The coffee made him feel better, and an important, friendly face would help even more. Her driveway was empty and the house silent. He'd hoped she'd be here working. He'd hoped she'd be glad to see him. Hope springs eternal. Disappointment, crushing.

Royal sat and stared at the house for a minute before he backed out of her driveway and pulled out on the highway again. By the time he turned into his own driveway, he had a solid plan on how to clean up the mess Inez seemed hell-bent on creating, without having to bring the council into it. She wouldn't like it.

CHAPTER FIVE

It took Wyatt an hour to drive home, grab her bow, and return to the woods. She hurried to have enough time for a good look around before it got so dark it would be difficult to see things with any clarity. Lack of daylight didn't diminish her skills. It did make it harder to spot markers in the wilderness that might shed light on the attack on the goat. Any hope of tracking would be gone. As it were, she pushed it. Maybe she'd make it through before nighttime, and maybe she wouldn't.

Her truck parked and locked, she headed out at a brisk pace. The scents carried on the breeze were no longer of blood and death. Instead, they were light and fresh and hopeful. One of the things she loved about nature was the way it rebounded. Tragedies, man-caused and natural, attempted to destroy the natural world again and again. But goodness and light prevailed. Even if things were changed, they were not destroyed.

A good philosophy to hold on to. Her own life had changed a number of times, and at moments she thought it to be the end. That she couldn't go on. Never be happy. Never be loved. Each time, she returned to nature and listened to the sounds of hope on the wind. Smelled the sweet scent of the wildflowers and the fragrant grasses, and listened to the hoot of an owl or the chatter of a crow. Without exception, the foray into the wilds lifted her soul, and she carried on. As nature renewed itself, so did she.

More than one woman had come to her classes in the throes of despair and life changes that challenged their will to go on. Like Wyatt, time in nature brought them a measure of peace and lifted them up. When they returned home, they did so with a new outlook. Nature healed, as easy as that.

But she sought answers now. The death of the goat wasn't odd in the way of the animal world. Nature in its normal cycle of predator and prey. The difference in this instance unsettled her. No matter how she came at it, the killing didn't look right. As though the predator played with its prey rather than taking it for sustenance. Combine that with the massive paw prints, and it just didn't pass the smell test for Wyatt. She recognized strange when she saw it.

The silence that surrounded her as she hiked also unsettled her. Like something big and dangerous had walked through ahead of her, and all the smaller creatures had scattered in fear, leaving the forest silent and empty. What in the hell was going on out here? She needed to know. Not just to help Ollie and his attractive new replacement, but for herself. Her next class was scheduled to begin in a couple of weeks, and she couldn't bring her students here if it exposed them to unnecessary danger. These were novices, and few, if any, would be equipped to face down an unpredictable predator. Bears. Cougars. Wolves.

She stopped to look down at her GPS, and at the same time, her phone rang. Made Wyatt smile as she pulled it out of her pocket. Her mother would have hated the cell-phone generation. She'd have said something along the lines of it polluting the natural world. Not that Wyatt didn't understand the sentiment. Out here, all wilderness and wondrous nature. In her pocket, the twenty-first century walking right along with her, most of the time anyway. The forest had its moments of denying technology, and there were dead spots here and there. For her, the marriage of the two worked. She could still enrich her soul with the beauty all around her while staying connected to civilization. The world today wasn't the same one her mother grew up in. Even out here, danger lurked. Particularly if one happened to be a woman.

The number of missing and murdered indigenous women in her state alone hurt her heart. One had to stay vigilant. Cell phones helped.

The name on the display made her day. "Tell me you're here." Her smile grew despite being alone.

"Of course, we're here. Where, may I ask, is our hostess? We're locked, loaded, and ready to partay, if only we weren't bolted out." Tuesday Johnson had been one of her best friends since the day they met almost ten years ago, when Tuesday and her young K9 partner, Tripper, had come to do some human-remains-detection training north of Missoula. Wyatt hadn't seen Tuesday, a former federal probation officer, since she'd been shot in the line of duty, discovered her brother was a serial killer, and uncovered the deception by her mother, who turned out not to be her mother at all. Events like that would have broken most people. Not Tuesday. They freed her.

"I'll be there in thirty minutes or less. Here's the code to the door." She rattled off the numbers. There had been a time when locking doors hadn't been necessary. These days, even here, times had changed, and locked doors were important. She loved the cipher locks. No need to carry keys.

"Sounds great. It's been a hell of a long drive. Tell me you have coffee around here somewhere, right?"

"Does a bear..."

Tuesday laughed. "Perfect. I'll hunt it down. See you soon."

She'd turned around as she talked to Tuesday and hustled back in the direction of her truck. She couldn't wait to see her friend, her dog Tripper, and the love she'd discovered in the midst of the chaos. Video calls meant Wyatt had met Addie Caine, the private investigator from Omaha who'd been with Tuesday when all the insanity came down on her, though she had yet to meet her in the flesh. Even from a distance, it wasn't hard to understand how Tuesday had fallen in love with her. A good soul and exactly the right person to spend forever with her friend. Someday, she hoped she'd find her own Addie.

"Hey."

Wyatt stopped and stared. Her shoulders stiffened. "What are you doing out here?"

"Stretching my legs." Royal smiled and looked around. "Remember when we were kids and would have beer parties in the forest? Good times."

Royal clearly remembered things differently than she did. Maybe his crowd had come out here, but not hers, and somehow, she doubted he'd actually been part of the keg parties. Jocks had been the leaders when it came to the keggers, and nerds didn't hang with them. The hierarchy back in her day had been unforgiving. "I'm working." Her words were a little snappy, and while she might sound rude, she didn't care. She'd grown weary of his popping up every time she turned around.

"What are you working on?" His question seemed casual enough, but the undertone in his voice wasn't. Wouldn't actually surprise her to hear that the unusual-goat-killing news had already hit town. Didn't exactly explain his presence out here though. The way she saw it, his appearance in her path had more of a stalker vibe.

No need to go into details that could inadvertently encourage him. "I have a class coming up." Short and sweet. Dismissive, she hoped.

An attractive man, he probably thought his glowing smile with the perfect white teeth, the product of either good genes or expensive dental work, would work on her. Royal had been gone from here too long and didn't really get which way the wind blew. Either that or he had a serious case of denial. "Nice. When?"

Why did he care? He wasn't, and never would be, a student who would join in. Though he wore casual clothes now, she'd seen him in town in his expensive suits. Outdoorsman wasn't in his wheelhouse. "In a couple weeks. I have to go. Friends are waiting on me." She started to move past him on the trail but stopped again when he touched her arm. A surge of something she couldn't quite define raced through her. She stepped away.

"Sorry. Sorry. Just wanted to say if I can help with anything, let me know."

"Will do," she said without looking at his face. *Never* is what she thought as she started walking again. Faster.

❖

"No, no, no, no, no." Mari sat in her truck staring at her driveway. What should have been her empty driveway and yet, wasn't. She'd had an interesting day with Oliver, including meeting the fascinating wilderness teacher, Wyatt, and now this. Her heart sank and her stomach rolled in very threatening way. This was not how she wanted to end her day, and how in the world had Sherrill found out where she'd moved? One explanation: her old office. Of course, they'd tell her where she'd gone. The old add-insult-to-injury thing. She'd call and give them a piece of her mind if not for the fact she never intended to talk to them again.

"Hey, baby." Sherrill got out of a shiny new Range Rover and smiled as if everything in the world was perfect. Far from it, and since when did she drive a Range Rover? A Mercedes, sure. A BMW, absolutely. A vehicle that could be taken off-road, never.

"What are you doing here?" Mari slammed her truck door.

"Like my new wheels? I thought it was perfect for snow and rough terrain. Drives like a dream. Who knew?" She laughed light and cheerful, as though she had not a care.

"Not necessary where you live." It rarely snowed in Portland, and Sherrill wasn't one to spend her leisure time hiking, thus requiring a vehicle that could traverse rough terrain. Made Mari wonder, not for the first time, what she'd ever seen in her. Well, besides a killer body, beautiful face, and smooth words. All three things had managed to camouflage the psychopathy long enough to reel Mari in.

Sherrill held up her arms. "But necessary here." Her smile grew brighter. Mari had a sinking feeling that inside the expensive vehicle were a whole lot of suitcases and boxes. They needed to stay right where they were.

"You don't live here." Might as well get to it. Subtlety didn't work with Sherrill.

"You do." The smile didn't diminish. "I have to say, you picked a super-nice place. Big, too." The unspoken message didn't pass her by.

"Sherrill, we're not having this conversation again. You've wasted your time and money. My home, as in me, alone."

Sherrill waved a hand dismissively. "Nothing wasted when it comes to you, baby."

Mari took off her cap and ran her hand through her hair. Pretty sure it looked like a bird had built a nest in it. She slapped the cap back on. "I can't do this with you again. The divorce is final. It's been final for a long time. You have to move on and leave me alone."

Sherrill tilted her head. Her expression didn't dim. Since she'd seen her last, she'd changed the color of her hair. An interesting shade of red that didn't work as well with her skin as her natural blond. "Baby, you and I both know that piece of paper changes nothing. We're soul mates. Always have been. Always will be." She smiled, but now her eyes betrayed the casual mood she tried to present. Darkness rolled behind those eyes with the expensive fake eyelashes.

Mari bit the inside of her lip to keep from screaming. The intolerable work situation that had preceded her move to Montana was bad enough, but now this? She'd come here hoping to find a pleasant and ethical work environment and that the distance would finally push Sherrill to let go. The former was looking good. The latter not so much.

"You need to leave." A firm stance. With Sherrill, any hesitation opened a door wide in her mind. She took the give-an-inch, take-a-mile philosophy to doctoral levels.

Sherrill put her hands on her hips and raised her eyebrows. "Or what?" A dangerous edge in her words.

She could do dangerous edge too. "Or I'll call the sheriff."

Her laugh was brittle. "Oh, darling, that's so rich. You think that silly restraining order in Oregon will be enforced here? Or that it even matters to me? It's like you don't know me at all."

Sherrill was wrong on that count. She knew her well. "Leave, Sherrill." She took her phone out of her pocket and pressed 9-1-1. The sound of the call going through came across the speaker loud and clear.

Sherrill's expression turned ugly. There she was, the woman Mari had run from. "Fine. I'm leaving, but this isn't over." She wrenched open the driver's side door and got in.

Mari hit *End* on her phone after a single ring. Dispatch would call back, and she hoped by the time they did, Sherrill would be gone. Easy to explain the reason behind the call and the legal documents filed in Oregon to keep Sherrill at a distance. Hadn't thought she'd have to do the same thing here in Montana. So much for a clean break on all fronts.

Sure as the world, her phone rang just as Sherrill's car disappeared. She explained the situation to the emergency operator and assured the kind woman in the dispatch center that she'd check into a family-law lawyer in the morning. Had to be someone good in Hamilton who could help her file yet another no-contact order. There went her budget again, and here she'd thought her days of legal fees were over.

The more she thought about it, the more she decided sooner rather than later would be a good thing. It would be money well spent, though she'd have really liked to do something fun with the cash, like buy a new sofa. She sighed, looked down at her phone again, and hit Ollie's number. He picked up on the second ring, and it took her maybe two minutes to explain the reason behind her call.

"You phoned the right guy." His words were matter-of-fact, as though his employees called him every day about how to get legal assistance.

"I was hoping you might have a good recommendation." She walked into the house and locked the door behind her. In the kitchen, she pulled the small notebook and pen out of her pocket. Had to love cargo pants.

"There are a couple of good folks not far away, but I'd recommend you talk to Royal Fremont. Born and raised here, he spent time in Canada teaching law before coming back home. I know he's in the process of setting up a private practice. He's a good guy and, given his practice is new in town, should have plenty of time to meet with you."

"A teacher?" She felt like she needed someone with more boots-on-the-ground experience. Sherrill wasn't exactly known for her willingness to accept anything that didn't line up with her wants and needs. To say she had no respect for the rule of law was downplaying it.

"A lawyer and a teacher. I think you'll like him, and from what I've heard, he's good at both. There are a couple of others I can recommend, although you may not be able to get in to see them right away."

His logic made sense, and to take a chance on the new guy in town might be a good thing anyway. The new ranger in town working with the new attorney here. Symmetry. "All right. I'll give him a call in the morning."

"Not sure if he's got his office set up yet. I'd say, run by the café in the a.m. for coffee, and check with Tracy."

"Tracy?" A name she hadn't heard yet, not that it meant much. She'd been here a whopping twenty-four hours. A busy twenty-four hours but not busy enough to scope out downtown yet.

"She owns the Tacamara Café on Main Street. Makes the best coffee for a hundred miles and knows everybody. She'll be able to tell you how to track Royal down."

Mari smiled. She sure wasn't in Portland any longer. Hamilton wasn't tiny, though it wasn't big either. She'd grown up in a major city, and it would be some time before she acclimated to the small-town mentality. So far, she liked it. In a lot of ways, Sherrill's appearance excepted, it felt safe and friendly here. A sanctuary at a time when she needed it.

"Okay. That's a plan. I'll swing by her café before I come in to work. You want me to pick you up a coffee or anything?" Portland, like Seattle, had magnificent coffee shops, and it made her happy to think Hamilton was host to something similar. A little bit of the familiar amongst the mountains.

"Naw. I'll bring my Folgers from home. Now, if you're so inclined to grab me one of those apple fritters, you'll be my best friend forever."

She laughed, and the stress of finding her ex on her doorstep began to fade. "You got it. Apple fritters sound like heaven. I'll see you in the morning, and Ollie, thanks for everything."

"You're most welcome. I want to make sure you're safe and happy." The rattle of ice in a glass made her think he was enjoying a refreshing drink after a hectic day. A little practice for the upcoming evenings around the pool.

"Appreciate it." More than he could possibly know or understand. Stalkers were something everyone knew about. Unless one became a victim of one, they had no idea how awful the reality was. Nothing felt safe. She always looked over her shoulder.

"Well, gotta admit it's as much about me as you. I'm past ready to retire, and if you run screaming back to Oregon, I'm screwed. Do you have any idea how long the hiring process is?"

She laughed even harder, appreciating his honesty. "I'll try real hard not to run or scream." A return to her former home would never be in the cards. Too many she never wanted in her orbit again. The screaming? Couldn't be sure about that one.

Royal put the unsuccessful encounter behind him and spent a few hours working through the paperwork he needed to get his office up and functional. The lease, the utilities, the advertisement for staff. It had been a long time since he actually practiced law full-time and found it interesting to get back into it. Teaching had been a calling, and he'd enjoyed the years he'd spent in those classrooms. The interest of students did a soul good. The occasional more-than-interest from *those* students didn't hurt the old ego either. It happened a lot more often after the change. He never acted on it. Appreciated it just the same. Who wouldn't?

Like everything, though, teaching had a season, and it had come to an end for him. Now, the season called for the new challenge of a solo practice here in his hometown. Or solo until, or if, Claude passed the bar. Even then, given Claude's personality, it would likely retain more of a one-man shop. Since coming here, Claude had become obsessed with his plants, and even getting him to come inside took a lot of convincing. For a man who grew up with every privilege, he was settling into the rural life with ease.

For Royal, it felt good to return here and settle into this life. Except for the complications. He glanced out the window at where Inez weeded a flowerbed. She did have a way with the blooms. Less of a way with people, and ultimately, he saw that as the major problem. He should have realized his mistake before he uprooted her to the US. She wasn't the right one to have brought along. His fault and now his duty to correct.

"What are you contemplating so hard?" Claude walked into the home office with the big bay window looking out over the back acreage and plopped down in the chair on the other side of his desk. He stretched out his legs, bits of dirt falling from his shoes to the rug.

"This and that." Not the time to share his thoughts with anyone. He might ultimately need to call on Claude for assistance. If and when that happened, he'd loop him in.

"You mean what to do about Inez." Sometimes he had the sense that Claude could read minds. More like an eidetic memory, which was how the lazy student maintained perfect grades throughout undergrad and law school. He'd been born with more gifts than just generational family wealth.

"Among other things." No sense denying it. Chances were, he would end up needing Claude before it was all said and done.

"Come on, boss. I know you better than that. She's creating havoc, and that's a threat to us. Gotta do something before she gets us all in trouble. I mean, dude, she went to a freaking dope store. That shit could make her more unreliable than she already is."

"And that something to do would be what?" Claude tended toward rash action rather than a good, thought-out plan. He had drive, determination, and a brilliant mind. He was also a trust-fund baby who would never have to work a day in his life and consistently looked for the fast, easy solution to any particular problem. Royal didn't have any regrets about bringing him along for this journey, though he kept a close eye on him. Having Inez and Claude around made him feel a little like a parent of teenagers. Not a whole lot different from teaching. More than once, he'd ended up taking a more parental role with a struggling student.

"I think she's outlived her usefulness." He said it without any emotion. Matter-of-fact in a way that chilled Royal.

He narrowed his eyes as he studied Claude's face. Nothing reflected there. As bland as his voice. The words hinted at an unexpressed dark emotion. "Usefulness isn't why we're all together."

"Isn't it?" He raised a single eyebrow.

Royal wanted to respond with a heartfelt no. Couldn't do it. Too much truth in what Claude said, even if he didn't like it or the way he delivered it. "Not the issue here."

"Right." Claude drew the single word out.

Had to shut this down before Claude got too creative for his own good. Or the good of their household. "Just let it go. I'll take care of it."

"Good plan. I don't want her messing up a good thing."

There it was. Despite their closeness as a unit, Claude usually thought of himself first and foremost. "You like it here?"

"I do, actually. It's quiet and peaceful. Lots of open space. It's a nice change from the city. Didn't realize how wide-open spaces, fresh air, and fewer people would appeal to me."

Royal laughed, some of the stress of the day fading. "It's exactly what I wanted to run from when I headed off to college. Didn't think I'd ever come back, yet here we are. Must say it appeals to me too. I think city life can be draining, especially for those like us."

Claude glanced out the window before looking back at Royal. "Not sorry you came back then, eh?"

Easy answer. "No. I belong here."

"How about me?" Claude nodded toward the window.

"You're going to be fine. In fact, like me, you belong here. Her." He nodded toward the window. "I'm not so sure. Jury is still out."

"Jury's going to come back with an indictment. Better to end it before it becomes a problem. Before she becomes a bigger problem." A frown crossed his face. Didn't diminish his good looks.

"I won't let it get there." He stayed confident. Too much was at stake to be anything but. The solution would work. He firmly believed it. All Inez really needed was time to settle in. She'd get over her rebellion eventually.

"I think you're already there." Claude was holding on to his Inez theory as tight as a dog with a brand-new bone.

"One goat." While Royal didn't like what she'd done, it wasn't the end of the world either. Orchestrate a little damage control, and all would be well. Yeah. All would be perfect. It made sense in his head.

Claude made a dismissive noise. "One goat that has already garnered unwanted attention."

He ran a hand through his hair. That part was true. Made the damage control a little more complicated. Not impossible. "I'm already on it, and I'll handle it. I'll handle her."

Claude stood and stretched his arms over his head. "If you say so." He sounded bored now. Typical Claude. He lost focus in a hurry when it didn't serve his purpose. Royal once more questioned how much help he'd be in the law practice. Interesting cases, sure. Mundane cases, which made up the bulk of most private practices, probably not. Chances were better than average that Royal would essentially run a solo practice whether or not Claude became a part of the firm.

"I do." He kept his own words firm, as any good leader would. Claude did need to be reminded every so often of his status as alpha. Obedience wasn't optional.

Claude pressed his lips together and looked down at the dirt and grass on the rug. "Sorry about the mess." He left the office without offering to clean up said mess.

After Royal vacuumed, he finished the paperwork, then headed to the basement. The box remained where he'd dropped it earlier. The local hardware store had everything he'd needed in stock, and the cameras he'd wanted were also available at a local computer store. Saved him a trip to Missoula, which he much appreciated. Now wasn't the time to be away from home.

After he finished the work, he took his phone out and downloaded an app. Five minutes later, he could see his own image standing between the room with the deadbolt on the outside and the stairs. He smiled. Inez was going to hate her new room.

CHAPTER SIX

Wyatt hadn't laughed this hard in ages. Such fun to sit at the kitchen table drinking coffee and listening to stories of Tuesday trying to teach Addie how to be a dog handler, and Addie trying to teach Tuesday how to be a private investigator. Best morning she'd had in ages. Didn't realize how much she needed a morning like this.

"You two are a match made in heaven." Wyatt sipped her coffee again, grateful that at least this time she wouldn't spit it out on a laugh. Already had to wipe the table off twice.

Tuesday hadn't changed much since the first time they'd met. Still tall, with great blond hair and beautiful green eyes that, despite all the tragedy that had entered her life, glowed with happiness. Wyatt gave the credit for that to Tuesday's wife, Addie Caine. Like Tuesday, she was tall, but with brown hair and eyes so dark they leaned toward black. She too radiated happiness. Love did exist. For others.

Addie held up her coffee mug as if to toast. "Amen to that, sister. Out of darkness, light shall fall, and this lady is definitely my light."

Wyatt loved how Tuesday's smile lit up her face. "Back atcha, gorgeous."

A little bark from the backyard had Tuesday leaving the table. A few seconds later, Tripper trotted in. Wyatt ran her hand over his head as he leaned against her. He'd changed since she first met him as a young pup. These days he was taller and heavier, and his chin had turned almost all white. "Good morning to you too, sir." "He has great taste in people." Tuesday smiled.

Wyatt looked up. "You still working him?" Despite the signs of age, the regal German shepherd looked good. A natural athlete of the dog world.

Tuesday nodded. "Yeah. I pulled out of the team in Spokane after that POS shot me, but once we moved to Omaha, we got back into it. Great team out of Omaha. He's still as sharp as ever, although I'm on the hunt for a pup. Tripper will be training a recruit soon. Won't ya, buddy?"

"Training me too." Addie smiled. "I'm a damned good PI, but I have to tell you the human-remains-detection work is crazy hard. Until I met her." She nodded toward Tuesday. "I had no idea about the hundreds of hours they train, and it's all volunteer. Who knew? These people are saints."

Tuesday put a hand on Addie's arm. "Ah, thanks. It's definitely a calling, and don't sell yourself short. You're getting it, babe. You'll be a damned fine K9 handler in no time."

"Maybe, or maybe our boy here is doing all the work and making me look better than I am." Addie laughed.

Tuesday laughed too. "Yeah. He can do that."

"True story." Addie leaned over and ran a hand over Tripper's head.

It was good to have life, light, and laughter in her home. Wyatt had been here by herself for so long, she'd forgotten how nice it could be to have someone with her. "You two, I mean, you three, up for a hike?" Her go-to feel-good activity, and besides, she loved sharing the beauty of her world with others. Tuesday knew how wonderful it was, given she'd been here before and hiked the mountains with Wyatt. For Addie, it would be a new experience. She looked forward to introducing her to the grace and beauty of the Montana wilderness.

"Yes!" Tuesday jumped up. "Mountains, mountains, mountains!" Tripper picked up on her joy and gave a little yip before he went and sat near the back door. Nobody was getting out of that door without him.

Addie rolled her eyes as she inclined her head toward Tuesday. "She's done a mighty fine job of settling into the Midwest, but the minute we drove into the mountains, she lit up. I think she misses them a lot."

Wyatt understood that feeling well. She couldn't imagine living in the flatlands. "As well she should." Wyatt smiled to soften her words. As much as she loved where she lived, it wouldn't be very polite to insult Addie about her hometown. Besides, not everyone was a fan of massive mountain ranges and coniferous forests. Wyatt's aunt lived in Eastern Montana, where the terrain was flat and open, and she loved it. No chance of her ever moving back to the west side of the state.

Addie waved a hand in the air. "No worries, you two. I get it. The mountains are pretty amazing. Now, if I had to live here all the time, it might feel claustrophobic to me, but remember that I was born and raised in the Midwest. I dig the open feel of the plains."

The longer Wyatt was around Addie, the more she liked her. Smart, attractive, and reasonable. The hat-trick of great qualities. No wonder Tuesday had fallen hard and fast. "Okay then, let's roll." She looked over at Tripper. "You ready to run, young man?" Tripper barked and wagged his tail. She took that as a doggie yes.

"Let's do it." Tuesday motioned with her hand for Tripper to come to her. She slipped a black harness on him, hooked up the straps that went around his body to attach on his back, and then opened the door. He ran to her SUV and waited. "You want to ride with Tripper in the back? I can adjust the dog cover so there's room for both of you."

Wyatt laughed as she glanced in the window of the SUV and at the sling-type seat cover. "How about you follow me? Lots of parking where we're going." She didn't add that, as much as she loved that dog, and even if Tuesday moved the sling out of the way for her, sitting with him meant she'd end up covered in dog hair.

Tuesday smiled and nodded. Yeah, she got it. "Lead the way. Can't wait to get out there again. It's been way too long."

"It has." She'd missed her friend and could never quite shake the feeling that she should have been there to help her when her world had been turned upside down. Getting shot in the line of duty, discovering her brother was a serial killer, and, equally as shocking, finding out her mother and her brother weren't her biological mother and brother. Life-altering events like that called for the support of good friends. They had connected by phone during those wild times, but until now, not face-to-face. They hadn't talked about any of it since they arrived yesterday, and she didn't bring it up. Last Wyatt had heard, Tuesday and Addie were still trying to piece together the details of the mystery. Once they unraveled the lies and the cover-ups, the story might make a blockbuster movie.

The drive wasn't long and the parking area empty when they arrived. Not unusual for a weekday, although the area got used pretty much 365. There'd likely be more folks by the time they finished their hike.

"Did you bring any source?" Wyatt looked at Tuesday's truck. Source, a term used by HRD handlers, referred to items of human remains, from blood to teeth to cremains. It's what they used to train the dogs. In prior visits, Tuesday brought along the training aids to give Tripper a chance to do a little work. The more varied environments they worked in, the better the teams became, or so Tuesday had explained to her.

Tuesday shook her head. "I didn't this time around. Tripper's on vacation too. No training exercises until we get back home. He gets to run for fun today."

Surprised her. Tuesday and Tripper were always up for any opportunity to do some training. That they were here for relaxation only let Wyatt know how much had changed since the shooting and the move to Nebraska. Not a bad change either. Wonderful to see both of them relaxed and happy. All work and no play… "Good enough. We'll just enjoy the day. The weather couldn't have cooperated more for your visit."

"Perfect." Addie slipped on a small pack and tucked her water bottle into the side pocket. Tuesday had also put on a pack, only hers carried two water bottles. One for her and one for Tripper.

"Shall we?" Wyatt waved toward the trees. "Let's all fill our lungs with our beautiful, clear Montana air."

Tuesday breathed in deeply and smiled. "Ah, wonderful already. Let's do it." Her smile stayed on her face for an hour. Then it turned into a frown. They'd veered off the trail a while ago and meandered through the forest enjoying unspoiled nature and solitude. Fallen pine needles crunched beneath their feet, and they had to watch not to trip on downfall. "Did you see that?" She stopped and turned to Addie.

Addie stopped as well and frowned. "Yes." The single word was almost a whisper.

Wyatt wasn't sure what they were talking about. She did a full circle but didn't see anything unusual. "What? What am I missing?"

Tuesday slipped out of her pack and, from inside the main pocket, pulled out a GPS. For a few seconds she pressed buttons on the unit before looking up at Wyatt. "Okay, marked it," she said to Addie. To Wyatt, she explained, "Tripper's body language just changed."

She had a bad feeling about that statement. "He's gone into work mode." She wasn't asking a question. She laser-focused on the big German shepherd, and she saw it now. Tension and attention that hadn't been there minutes before.

Tuesday nodded. "He's in scent."

Wyatt had been around Tuesday and Tripper long enough to understand what that meant. Their morning adventure had just morphed from a leisurely hike in the forest to a search. No dead goat this time either, as Tripper had been trained to ignore animal remains. No, he had just detected the odor of human decomposition. Somewhere in the immediate vicinity, someone had lost their life. "Damn."

❖

Mari walked out of attorney Royal Fremont's office a lot lighter than when she'd gone in. Ollie hadn't been wrong about him. Smart, articulate, and not bad looking, for a guy. The office itself was a work in progress, partially furnished and with boxes stacked everywhere. She appreciated the chaos, given her house looked close to the same. A bit of kinship from the moment she stepped through his door. At home, she cringed every time she stared at the full boxes that the movers had delivered and neatly stacked. Eventually she'd be forced to deal with them.

Royal had put her at ease right away, and she not only liked him, but she also came away from the meeting full of confidence he'd be able to assist her with the Sherrill problem. She drove to her office relieved that, by the end of the day, a Montana restraining order would be in place. Hopefully, it would be enough to encourage a hasty retreat back to Oregon.

Best part, it wasn't even nine yet. She'd only be a little late for work on day two. Not a great way to start a new job, though Ollie had told her to take her time. He came across as that kind of guy. More concerned about her safety than a time clock. Not that she actually punched one. She wished they could spend more days together before he headed out to warmer climates. She'd have to make do with what she could get.

"Royal get you fixed up?" In the break room, Ollie leaned against a bright-orange counter that had to have come straight out of the 1970s. He held a large, insulated mug, and the scent of coffee filled the room.

"Cross your fingers. He'll let me know by the end of the day if the judge signs off," she told Ollie as she rummaged in a cupboard until she found a mug for herself. After she filled it with coffee, she took a sip. It was awful. Definitely have to do something about that.

Ollie nodded. "He'll get it done. Good guy. Glad he moved back. Great to have someone of his caliber in town."

"Hasn't been here long, has he? His office is only about half put together, and everything else is still sitting around in boxes."

Ollie smiled. "He's been back a few months. Grew up here and then went away to college. Until this year, he'd been MIA. His parents passed away decades ago, and he spent quite a few years in Canada teaching at the law school up in Vancouver, or that's what I heard anyway. He doesn't really bring it up."

"Really? An American lawyer teaching in a Canadian law school? Is that normal?" Seemed odd to her. Not that someone wouldn't want to live in the Vancouver area, because it was, frankly, stunning up there. She enjoyed the city every time she visited. Especially Stanley Park. An absolutely magnificent urban oasis.

Ollie shrugged. "Not sure. My guess would be his specialty is US law. Not a bad thing to have knowledge about both sides of the border. Particularly for the states and provinces like Washington and British Columbia."

Now, that did make a bit more sense. "Could be," she murmured as she sipped the bitter beverage that Ollie swore was coffee. She had her doubts and tried not to cringe as she drank. That she didn't put it down was a sad commentary on her addiction to caffeine.

"Don't worry. Royal was always a polite kid who came from a stand-up family, and if he says he can help, believe him. I'll vouch for him."

She laughed. "I get it. I get it. Good guy. He'll get it all squared away with my ex, and I'll be able to start my new job and new life a free woman." Oh, she hoped her words were true.

"Damn straight." The phone in his pocket rang. He pulled it out and barked, "Allridge." His expression morphed from interest to shock. "On our way." His hands were shaking as he ended the call and slipped the phone back into his pocket.

"What?" Her second day and, from Oliver's tone, something bad had happened again. The same feeling she'd had when Sherrill showed up dropped down heavy again.

He took in a big breath and blew it out slowly. "Wyatt and her friends found a body."

"Another goat?" It worried her that animals were getting this ferocious. She might be new here, but even she knew it wasn't normal. Something was out of sync amidst the pine trees, glacial lakes, and tall mountains. They were still waiting to hear from the vet on cause of death for the mountain goat they'd dropped off yesterday.

Darkness flowed over his features. "No goat." His words were soft but they landed hard.

"Oh, crap."

"Big oh, crap."

❖

Inez leaned against the office door. "Did you see the cops flying down the road, lights flashing? A regular police parade. Looked like the entire force turned out."

Royal glanced up from the box he'd been unpacking. Lots of books, even though he rarely cracked one. Online resources made legal research a whole lot easier these days. Funny how people came to a law office expecting to see books, and so books they got. Window dressing that collected tons of dust.

"I heard the sirens." Hard not to. It did sound like every cop from fifty miles around went screaming down the highway. Wasn't sure why she'd driven downtown to tell him though. Not like she came here to help set up the law office. Unlike Claude, Inez had not been one of his students. Rather than the law, she went for holistic healing and was a massage therapist recommended by one of his students. Her education had stopped once she graduated from massage-therapy college. He'd been encouraging her to set up shop in Hamilton, without success. Give her something to do besides sit around and complain that she was bored. A fail to date.

"We should go see what's up. Finally, something interesting appears to be happening here in the boonies."

He put his hands on his hips and stared at her. "Why do you fight this place so hard? You liked nothing better than our weekends up in the Northern Territories. Far more wilderness there than here, so why does this bore you? I'm baffled, and I sure don't understand your attitude."

She shrugged and played with her hair. "I don't know. Maybe I don't like the fact that I was forced to move, and I miss Vancouver. Stuff going on day and night. I never had a chance to get bored. If you wanted to come back to the States, at least you could have picked someplace like Seattle or Los Angeles, where there's more action. Your hometown is Hicksville, and it puts me to sleep."

Same old song and dance he'd heard dozens of times already. "You haven't given it a chance. Set up a practice and you'll meet tons of people. Life will get way more interesting as you get to know your neighbors. There are a lot of good people around here."

"I don't feel like working on people anymore, good or bad. They want their massages and then bitch and complain about the cost. Don't even get me started on the pathetic tips. After a while it gets real old, and I'm over it. As for this place, we've been here too long already, and I'd love to go someplace fun." She stopped twisting her hair as she gazed over his shoulder and out the window.

"Inez, I've heard all your complaints over and over, and I'll be blunt. I don't care. This is our home now, so get used to it and quit griping nonstop." At times he left diplomacy behind and leaned into his leadership role. Granted, he'd been the one to decide to return to Montana. It didn't mean that he hadn't discussed the decision in detail with both Inez and Claude beforehand. The conversations had been courtesy only. It hadn't been up for a vote, and it wasn't a democracy. Never would be either. Not the way it worked in their world.

"It's boring." Back to twirling her hair around her finger.

Old, tiring news. "Best advice I have for you is to find something to do. I'm done discussing this. You're a big girl. Figure it out."

A sly smile crossed her face. "I have been, and then you don't like what I find to do."

That look on her face hit his last good nerve. He slapped his hand on the desk. She had enough sense to jump, the smirk disappearing. "I won't put up with this from you. Get a hobby. Get a job. I don't really care. Just do something besides bitch and cause trouble. I'm not going to listen to this whining from you one second more, and I'm done cleaning up your messes." He almost growled the words.

Inez dipped her head and took a step back. "Okay." The single word was a whisper. About damn time he got her full attention.

A chime sounded out front. The door. Inez was as stubborn as she was beautiful, and despite the "okay" she'd just offered, dropping it wouldn't happen. It hadn't taken long after he'd first met her to understand how much of an indulged child she'd been. Not rich like Claude. Beauty had been her currency, and she'd wielded it like an expert. Accustomed to getting whatever she wanted when young, she carried that lesson through into adulthood. In the beginning, he'd found her entitled attitude mildly annoying. These days it moved quickly to untenable. Her impetuous ways could, and would, cause real problems for him if he didn't get her under control soon. He touched the key in his pocket.

When he'd considered coming back here, it had been a way to protect them all. Threats to their well-being became overwhelming, and coming here seemed like a perfect solution. The council had sounded the alarm, and he'd listened. The lives of their kind had been put in danger, and he saw his hometown as a solution to side-stepping that danger. He still believed it to be a wise move, with the exception of the wild child. He turned toward the door to see who'd come in. He'd deal more with Inez later.

"Knock, knock." Tracy from the café stood in his doorway holding a coffee.

"Hi." A nice distraction from constantly parenting Inez.

She smiled and held out the cup, which he took. "Thought you could use a caffeine kick." She glanced at Inez. "Sorry. I didn't know you were here, or I'd have brought you one."

Inez shook her head. "No need to be sorry. I'm not a coffee drinker. I do have to go find another hobby though." She waved her hand in the air as she almost ran out of his office. He resisted the urge to follow her.

Tracy's forehead furrowed as she watched Inez flounce away. "She has to go find a hobby?" She turned back to Royal.

He shook his head. "Long story."

She laughed and then swept her gaze over the boxes and piles of books on the floor. "That's a whole lot of books."

"Yeah. They're a big pain in my butt, especially since they're more for show than anything else. Do all my legal research through electronic sources these days. This—" He held out the coffee "—is wonderful and most appreciated."

"Glad I could make your day better. You sure have a lot left to do here. I remember when I set up my café. A million things to take care of, and I swear the unpacking took forever." She ran her fingers along one of the empty bookshelves. "This is going to be nice."

"I do think I'm going to like it." It was true. The office size was perfect, and the whole space had that small-town quaintness that appealed to him and, hopefully, his potential clients. Quite different from his office at the university. When it had become available about six weeks earlier, he'd jumped on the lease. Ready for a change in all aspects of his life. The foray into academics had been fulfilling, at least for a while. He wanted something different now and someone to share it with. He was moving in the direction of both.

"Surprised you came back. Most folks don't, once they get out of here. I mean, look at me and Wyatt. We never left."

He took a sip and studied her face. Got the feeling she came for more than the gift of exceptional coffee. "What's up, Tracy? Do you need some legal help?"

She shook her head. "No, at least not right now. Never say never, though." She shrugged and smiled.

"Then what is it?"

Tracy glanced toward the doorway and the reception area. "I saw the new ranger leave your office this morning. Is she okay?" There it was.

He set his coffee on his desk as he shook his head. Should have figured she would come asking that question. "Tracy, you haven't changed." A matter-of-fact statement with no judgment attached. It had been her way since childhood.

She frowned and stuffed her hands into the pockets of her jeans. "Hey. I don't think that's a compliment."

It wasn't. "Well, you always did have a finger on the pulse of the school back in the day. I think you have the same thing going on for the town these days." When they were kids, she knew everything about everybody, regardless of their class.

"I should be insulted but…" She shrugged.

"But I nailed it."

"You did. And?"

Once more, he shook his head. "Sorry. You'll get nothing from me. Client privilege." Tracy had to know he couldn't violate a client's confidentiality, and he had no doubt that she did. She was nonetheless the kind of person who never hesitated to try the information hubs, even in the face of lawyer ethics.

Now she laughed and held her hands up. "Doesn't hurt anything to ask. Worst that can happen is I get a no."

"It's a no."

"I got it." It wouldn't be the last time she tried. Of that, he had zero doubt.

He returned her smile. "I will give you *A* for effort." She wasn't the first to go fishing for privileged information, and she wouldn't be the last. A hazard of his chosen profession. Besides, he loved her coffee and didn't want to send her back to the café angry. Or have her so mad at him she stopped sharing the town gossip. While he wasn't, or would never, be at liberty to share anything with her, he was happy to listen to whatever she did know.

She waved a hand and turned. "I'll take that *A*. Always was a four-point student. Now, I gotta get back to the shop before my staff goes on strike."

"You that bad a boss?" That would surprise him if true. He couldn't recall anyone disliking Tracy.

"Naw. I'm the best, but it's time for a couple of them to call it a day. They can't leave if I'm not there."

Loyalty confirmed his opinion. Still a good soul. He held up the cup and tipped it toward her. "Thanks for the coffee." *And the reminder that I'm not in the big city anymore. Be careful about everything you say and do because the Tracys are watching.*

CHAPTER SEVEN

"A re you okay?" Tuesday put a hand on Wyatt's shoulder. Did she really look that panicked? It wasn't panic. More surprise than anything else. The occasional death of an animal by another animal happened. A dead woman was about the last thing she expected to see.

Not out of character for her to be concerned about Wyatt. Tuesday trained for this kind of tragedy, and those who did the same kind of work as she and Tripper all embodied an empathy greater than most. Admirable on many levels.

In all her years as a survival teacher, this was the first time Wyatt had come upon a human body. It was the wilderness, and things happened to people. Not unheard of. It had just never happened to her. "I think so." Honest answer. She didn't really know how she felt at the moment. Sad. Scared. Wary.

Tuesday nodded. "It's disconcerting the first time. Don't feel bad if it shakes you up. It's a very normal response." Tuesday made a motion with one hand, and Tripper came out of his down to stand next to her. His focus stayed on the human remains he'd led them to moments before. All business, with every trace gone of the previous joy he'd displayed while they'd been hiking.

"It doesn't look natural." Wyatt stared at what had been a beautiful woman with long brown hair and a slim, athletic body. Her blue eyes, not quite obscured by the hair stuck to her face, were dull and unfocused. Her mouth stretched open as though she'd died mid-scream. Blood had soaked into her light blue hoodie decorated with pink flowers down the sleeves, turning it dark, and her pants sported stains that would undoubtedly turn out to be blood as well. A metallic smell rose so thick in the air, it was no mystery how Tripper had caught the scent from hundreds of yards away. Chills raced up Wyatt's arms.

Addie stood next to Tuesday, hand on her shoulder. "Tuesday's right, Wyatt. It's hard to see someone like this. It throws you, and trust me when I say I know how it feels, because I do. It's how I felt the first time. You would think that my years as a cop would have prepared me for it, but nope. Surreal and horrible." Addie put her hands on her knees as she leaned closer to study the body. "Hey, anybody else think she looks like she was scared to death? I mean, the blood on her clothes tells us something violent happened here, but look at her face. Don't tell me that's not a death scream, and it's frightening as all get-out."

"Maybe. Or it could have been something like a heart attack." Tuesday put her hand on Tripper's head. "Extreme pain could do it." He leaned into her legs, his body remaining tense.

"Maybe. Doesn't account for the blood though, does it?" Addie didn't look or sound convinced, and given the evil she'd encountered in her search for her missing brother, Wyatt could understand her skepticism. She wasn't so sure a heart attack accounted for the extreme expression. Looked like straight-up terror to Wyatt. She shifted to her left and said, "Uh-oh. Pretty sure that's an entrance wound right there." She pointed to her forehead.

Tuesday leaned in next to Addie. "You're right. She's been hurt, badly, and it looks like a gunshot wound, but hard to tell for sure with all that hair in the way. We'll have to wait on the experts to make that call."

Wyatt didn't like any of it or the way it made her feel. First the goat. Now a woman. She couldn't stop looking around, as though something evil waited to jump out from behind one of the trees to tear them apart. She stopped herself for a second as she wondered why she'd thought of being torn apart. Probably the shock. She looked over at Tuesday and Addie. "What now? I mean besides calling in the authorities?" She had the numbers for both the sheriff's office and Ollie's office in her contacts.

"First things first. Addie and I can secure the area. It's a potential crime scene."

"Out here?" Wyatt didn't want to think of something like murder in her woods. Her playground since childhood. It threw a dark cloud on a lifetime of bright memories. She scanned the area again, narrowing her eyes. Evil did walk out here. The presence of it tickled the hairs on her arms. Damn.

Tuesday dropped her pack to the ground, digging around inside it until she produced a roll of bright-pink flagging tape. "Regardless of how she died, we treat this like a crime scene until law enforcement clears it otherwise. Standard operating procedure."

Wyatt would defer to Tuesday as both a former law-enforcement officer and a search-and-recovery professional. She'd been trained for exactly this scenario. Wyatt might be able to help people survive out here for days or even months, but when it came to an unattended death, she had no experience.

Wyatt took the flagging tape Tuesday handed her and began to string it around the trees. To preserve any potential evidence, she followed Tuesday's directions and made sure to make the marked-off area maybe twenty meters around the body. After she secured the flagging tape to the trees, she stood for a minute and once more studied the woman in the center. She avoided looking at her face. What she noticed now was how her pants were torn at the knees, as if she had fallen on rocks, and her blood-soaked hoodie was ripped in several places. One shoe was missing, and glancing around, Wyatt didn't see it anywhere within the large protected space. Something for the sheriff's folks to look into, though she planned to keep her eyes open as they trekked back to the vehicles. Possible an animal picked it up and carried it off.

She turned to Addie and Tuesday. "We need to head back toward the truck to call this in." She looked at her phone showing a no-signal message, and she hadn't thought she'd need her FRS radio. "No bars out here. I've marked the coordinates for the officers." She also had a good sense of the landmarks that would help the responders, who were, like her, familiar with this area.

Tuesday put a hand on Tripper's back. She didn't move to pick up her pack from where she'd dropped it on the forest floor. "Tripper and I will stay behind. Don't want to risk someone stumbling on this and disturbing anything before your cop buddies can get out here."

Buddies might be a stretch or not. Most everyone at least knew the local law enforcement, even if they weren't friends. "Okay. That actually makes a lot of sense." This is why she deferred to Tuesday. Might be her mountains and forest and rivers, but it was Tuesday's expertise.

"I'll stay with you." Addie stepped close to Tuesday.

Tuesday shook her head. "No. You go with Wyatt. I've got Tripper with me, and I'd feel better if you two went together. We don't know what happened here or if whoever did this is still around." She left that thought hanging for a couple of seconds. "We need to use whatever advantage we have."

"All the more reason for me to stay." Addie's expression grew dark.

"Again, I've got my boy. He'll keep me safe, and you two can do the same. You know Tripper is protective, and who's going to want to take on a hundred-pound German shepherd? Hopefully, once you can make the call, they'll be here quick. We'll be fine in the meantime."

Wyatt thought that Tuesday made some very good points. Not that she wanted to leave her friend out here alone any more than Addie did. Except, really, she wasn't alone. Tripper would warn of any danger and give his life to keep her safe. "Come on, Addie. The quicker we get to the truck, the quicker we get back here." She started running.

❖

Mari reached the door ahead of Ollie. "We better move fast. The sheriff's office has been called, right?" It wasn't unheard of for someone to die out in the wilderness. Sometimes for normal, natural reasons. Other times, not so normal and not so natural.

Ollie slipped into his jacket and slapped his cap onto his head, calm, collected, and in no apparent hurry. "Wyatt called them first. Then me."

They were on the highway five minutes later and rode together in silence. Two days she'd been here, and it had been a roller coaster the whole time. The one bit of peace she'd experienced had been the drive from Portland to Hamilton. Lots of hours of beautiful scenery and quiet introspection. She'd arrived at her new house rested and hopeful about this new adventure. In some ways, she'd thought that perhaps destiny had brought her to Montana. Pushed her into a new life she'd been too timid or too scared to take on without the giant shove. Now, she wondered if she'd been massively wrong. She'd been passed over for promotion, her feelings had been hurt, and she'd stomped her feet and run away. Not as much destiny as petulance, and the universe was showing her the error of her ways.

Especially given Sherrill's appearance. Hard to move on when the past punched her in the face. Hopefully, the attorney would make good on his promise and handle the situation today. Sherrill didn't like to play by the rules. She deemed herself above them. Mari figured a night or two in jail when she violated the restraining order—and it was a *when*, not an *if*—might do the trick. Sooner or later, her ex would have to come to terms with the fact that they were over. Way over and had been for a very long time.

Her thoughts circled back around as to whether coming here had been a mistake. That activity lasted until they parked next to a marked cruiser and she stepped out of the truck to see Wyatt waiting by hers. Something about her grabbed Mari's interest and wouldn't let go. She had an aura, or something like an aura, that drew Mari in. She wanted to know more about this woman who Ollie spoke so highly of. Maybe petulance hadn't brought her here. She really hoped not. Hated to think she might be that petty.

Disappointed her a little that Wyatt didn't wait for their arrival alone. Shouldn't, because logically, Wyatt would have a life that included friends, a boyfriend or, perhaps, a girlfriend. She hadn't been sitting up here in Montana waiting for Mari to gallop in on her white horse, even if she had a horse. Or knew how to ride one.

Another woman stood next to her. Tall, dark-haired, and intense. A girlfriend? A friend? The way they stood apart made her believe the latter, and that made her feel better, which then made her silently chastise herself for acting like a teenager with a new crush. They were out on the most serious of calls, not for a dating-app meetup. Wow, how messed up was she these days? *Get it together, Mari.*

"Hey." Ollie reached them first. "Lloyd make it yet?"

Wyatt shook her head. "No. Still waiting for him. As you can tell." She waved toward the cruisers. "Some of his deputies have made it already, but no Lloyd."

Ollie looked to Mari. "Lloyd Epps is our local sheriff. I'd have introduced you sooner or later, but it now appears it's going to be sooner. Good cop with some experience in murder, if that's even what we're dealing with. He spent ten years in Bakersfield before he came back home to lead our fine town."

"Tell us what you found." Mari looked at Wyatt, noticing the pale tint to her skin and the sadness in her eyes.

"Maybe we should wait for Lloyd." Wyatt broke away from Mari's gaze and looked to Ollie.

Ollie glanced toward the wilderness and then back at Wyatt. "Could be a bit, depending on where he was when you called. Our folks can get spread pretty thin. Too much area to cover, not enough cops to cover it. Anyway, give us the down-and-dirty version while we wait. Another animal attack?"

Mari hoped that wasn't the case. Strange as the attack on the goat might have been yesterday, she wanted to believe it to be an exception and not something that would happen again. Especially not to an unsuspecting human. The best-case scenario would be a health-related incident. A heart attack. A fatal asthma attack. An accidental slip and fall from a rock outcropping. Something that, though tragic, could be easily explained.

Wyatt shook her head. "I've been thinking about the woman and what Addie had pointed out since we left to come back to the truck. No accident. Not caused by a forest predator. Unless a bear has figured out how to use a gun, no, not another animal attack."

"Murder?" Mari had a hard time with the idea. Why on earth would anyone murder another person out here in such a majestic and beautiful place? It was an obscene thing to do. If day one had been unreal, day two was turning out to be otherworldly.

Wyatt nodded. "I'm not a professional on that front, trust me, but it sure appears that way. Sure doesn't look like a suicide. You agree, given you're the one who spotted the bullet wound almost obscured by the woman's hair?" She glanced at her companion, who nodded. "Oh, and by the way, this is my friend Addie. She's a private detective out of Nebraska."

"Are you out here on a job?" Ollie looked interested. Mari sure was.

"No. We're here for a visit with Wyatt. Nothing official."

"We?" Mari caught that single word.

"My wife, Tuesday is here too, along with her dog, Tripper."

Mari scanned the area, not seeing any other people around and definitely no dog. "Where are they?" She returned her attention to Addie.

"Tuesday and Tripper are with the body. Might make more sense to you if you know their background. They're a nationally certified human-remains-detection team, and Tripper found the body while we were out hiking. The scene is in the best possible hands right now. Not only are they an experienced search team, but Tuesday is also a former US probation officer. She will keep everything secure until it's turned over to law enforcement."

"Good to know." Ollie reached out and shook hands with Addie. "Appreciate the professional assistance. Could have been a disaster if a civilian had come across the body."

Mari followed suit and shook Addie's hand. "Are you from Montana too?"

Addie shook her head. "No. I'm based out of Omaha. Tuesday and Tripper are originally from the Spokane area. After we got married, I talked her into relocating to Nebraska. Teaching her the tools of my trade, and she's coming along nicely as my apprentice. She and Tripper are also members of our local search-and-rescue team. Their skills and certifications are up to date."

The day got even more interesting. First the meeting with the attorney, and now a private detective and a K9 team specializing in finding dead people. What were the odds of having just the right people in just the right place at just the right time? One would want to go buy a lottery ticket based on those chances.

"Here comes Lloyd." Ollie turned his attention to an incoming vehicle, siren and lights going strong. "It's showtime."

Normally Royal wouldn't have given the sirens and speeding police cars a second glance. Not an ambulance chaser before he accepted the invitation to become a law professor, and he sure as hell didn't plan to be one now that he'd returned to private practice. Not why he became a lawyer in the first place. Actually, not sure why he'd gone that route. Probably had something to do with his penchant for watching old television shows about maverick lawyers. How his dad had loved to watch vintage shows like *Perry Mason* and *Matlock*. He'd have done anything to make the old man proud, and if he'd lived long enough, Royal was sure he'd have been a happy dad.

Today, his notice of the sirens had nothing to do with wanting to drum up business for his new practice. Besides having no interest, it wasn't his area of expertise. No. Following them in his Jag had more personal reasons attached. At least he'd had the good sense to come into the office today in jeans, a T-shirt, and boots. If he pulled in behind the sheriff's office vehicles, maybe it wouldn't look like he'd been following them.

He saw a familiar face when he pulled in. Lloyd had been born and raised in Hamilton and came from a long line of law enforcement professionals. His father and grandfather had both been the county sheriff, so it was less than surprising to see his old schoolmate wearing the colors. Lloyd had still been around when Royal left town, and he'd heard through the grapevine that he'd done a stint as a detective down in California somewhere. San Luis Opisbo, Oxnard, Bakersfield. He couldn't recall exactly where, but somewhere with a lot more action than typically seen in these parts.

He parked the Jag and got out, walking toward the group of people near the forest-service trucks. Wyatt stood in the group of cops, her hands in her pockets and a frown on her face. He stifled the urge to rush to her and kept walking slow and easy. No one seemed to notice him, at first, anyway.

"Royal? What are you doing here?" Wyatt looked up at him and her frown deepened.

Only then did he notice Mari standing next to Wyatt. She gave him a quick nod. "Hi, Royal."

He glanced at Wyatt again and decided she didn't look pleased to see him. Disappointing. He'd have to work on that. By now she should be leaning into him, not away. "What's up? A lot of lights and sirens. Somebody hunting illegally?"

Lloyd turned to him. "What the hell are you doing here? This isn't any place for you, and you're sure not going to procure any business out of this." The look of distaste on his face didn't bode well for Royal.

He shrugged. "Thought I'd take a little hike. Get some fresh air before I go back to unpacking the new office. All sitting and no hiking isn't good for the body or the soul, you know?" Sounded good to him. A logical reason for him to show up here.

"And you didn't see any of this." Lloyd waved toward the vehicles.

"Well, sure, but it's a big place so I came on out to stretch my legs."

Lloyd frowned and shook his head. "Not today, Royal. It's bull, and you know it."

"Why?" The lawyer in him couldn't leave without asking questions. The wildness in him screamed to be let free.

"We're closing this area for the rest of the day." Oliver stepped in. "You'll have to find someplace else for your hike. You know as well as the rest of us there are plenty of other places to go stretch your legs."

"This is the closest and I'm already here." Pushing back was kind of fun. "I won't get in your way."

"No," Lloyd snapped.

Nothing ventured, nothing gained. He ignored the wildness that still wanted to run toward the faint scent of blood on the air. He doubted the rest of them noticed. He did. "Fine, but can you at least tell me why?" He tried to stay on the good side of law enforcement, but his reasons for wanting to know were solid even if he couldn't share them. That he also liked to poke the bear—the bear being Lloyd—couldn't be ignored either.

"There's been an incident, and we'll leave it at that." Lloyd turned his back to him. A silent dismissal. Bastard. Always had been, but he supposed that came naturally when your family held the keys to the town for a couple of generations. Not that he thought Lloyd a bad guy. From the word around town, he'd proved himself to be a good man. But the attitude ingrained in him irritated Royal. He didn't take dismissal well.

"Wyatt?" Perhaps he could lean on friendship to get her to spill. Important for him to know what they'd found out there. Besides, he wanted her to know he was here for her.

She shook her head. "Not now, Royal. Just go, like Lloyd says. Everyone will know soon enough."

"Come on, guys. Maybe I can help." Hopefully, it didn't sound like begging. A guy in his position didn't beg.

Lloyd turned back around to him. Eyes narrowed, he stared at him for a few seconds. "Royal, perhaps you don't understand how things work. You've been gone a long time. See, here's the thing. I'm the law around here, and what I say goes. I say go. Now. Or I'll have one of my officers escort you and your fancy little car back to town. Clear enough for you?"

Wyatt walked over and put a hand on his shoulder. Her touch was electric. "Go, Royal. Just go."

He ignored Lloyd as he put his hand over Wyatt's. Warm, comforting. His complete focus stayed on her beautiful, alluring face. He breathed in her sweet scent as it banished the intoxicating odor of blood on the breeze. "For you, anything."

A quizzical expression crossed her face, and it made him smile. He'd have plenty of time to explain it all to her later. After the Harvest Moon. After she became his—body, mind, and spirit. He walked back to his car without saying anything more.

Chapter Eight

"How far?" Lloyd directed his question to Wyatt as their small contingent hiked over downed trees, through tall wild grasses, and up a mild incline. Nothing too strenuous, although Wyatt could hear Llyod's breathing ramp up.

"About a mile in. If you're going to use your phone for anything, you might want to do it now. Service will start to be hit and miss." The sheriff and his deputies had their radios that would work even in the dead areas, but Wyatt wanted him to be aware just in case.

Lloyd stopped and pulled out his cell. The rest of them stopped as well and waited while he made a call. "Tell Randy to load up the four-wheelers and the side-by-side. We're going to need them out here yesterday." He ended the call and put the cell back into his pocket. "All right. Backup is on the way. Take us in."

Wyatt led, glancing down at the coordinates in the GPS Tuesday had handed her before leaving her behind to keep the site secure. The arrow on the screen moved closer to the point marked earlier. Even with the slower Lloyd, huffing and puffing, they managed to reach the taped-off trees and the waiting Tuesday and Tripper without delay. Tuesday sat on the ground, her back against a tree, Tripper next to her. At first glance he appeared calm. Second look told her that he remained on alert.

"And you are?" Lloyd stepped up to Tuesday, who stood and moved next to Addie. After she introduced herself and Tripper, he nodded and then turned to study the body inside the taped-off trees. "Can you tell me how you found her?"

More explanation from Tuesday, basically a repeat recitation of what she'd shared with him earlier. "Tripper and I are a certified human-remains detection team. Finding the dead is what we do."

"So, you were out here searching." Lloyd scratched his chin, fine salt-and-pepper stubble less a fashion statement and more like evidence of not taking the time to shave.

"Oh, no. Not all. We were out for a hike with Wyatt. We're here visiting from out of town."

"A hike?"

"Who wouldn't want to hike out here? It's gorgeous, and Tripper enjoys it as much as the humans do. What most people don't understand about an HRD dog is that he's never really off duty. Tripper will shift into work mode the second he catches the odor of human decomposition. That's what happened today, a routine hike turned into a search, and that's why Tripper led us to her."

Wyatt noticed that Mari paled as she listened to Tuesday, though she was focused on the dead woman. "Are you okay? Your first dead body?" She wanted to put a hand on her arm, give her comfort. She kept them at her side.

"I need to see her face." Mari's words were soft, almost strangled. An odd request, even if it turned out it wasn't her first encounter with a body.

"What's up, Mari?" Ollie looked at her now too, concern on his face.

"I think it's Sherrill." Wyatt barely caught the four words.

"Who's Sherrill?" Lloyd pulled up the flagging tape and stepped underneath it.

"My ex-wife." She put a hand over her lips as though afraid she might throw up.

Lloyd spun to stare at Mari, his brows pulled together. "Well now, that puts a whole different light on this situation. What's your wife doing out here?"

She dropped her hand and met Lloyd's stare. "Ex-wife."

Wyatt didn't expect that, not that she knew what to expect with a situation like this. She took Mari's arm and guided her around the tape until they were in a position to get a better view of the woman's face. "Are you sure it's her?" Maybe it just looked like her ex-wife. That seemed far more likely.

"Oh my God. Oh my God. Oh my God." Mari sank to the ground, and all doubt fled from Wyatt's mind.

Wyatt kneeled next to her, still holding her arm. "It's her, isn't it?" She might not have known the woman, but she could tell by Mari's reaction she wasn't mistaken.

Mari nodded. "I don't understand. What was she even doing in the forest? She isn't a nature lover and sure as hell wouldn't go hiking by herself. No way she should have been way out here."

"Maybe you were with her? It's not like the woods are unfamiliar to you." Lloyd continued to stare at Mari, his eyes narrowed.

Mari's head snapped up. "You are so wrong. You know what? I met with an attorney just this morning, the same attorney you sent away, to get a protection order put in place here in Montana. If I didn't want her in the same state with me, why in the hell would I go take a midnight stroll with her in an area I'm not familiar with? Just FYI, I've only been here a couple of days." Her voice still shook, but now she sounded angry. Seemed Lloyd had struck a nerve.

"Well, we'll check that out, now won't we? For the time-being, I need you out of here. Ladies, that goes for you too. We have work to do, and we don't need civilians messing up what looks an awful lot like a crime scene."

Wyatt helped Mari to her feet. "Come on. We'll all go back together. Lloyd." She looked to the sheriff. "Let me know if you have any questions for us."

"Count on it. I'm going to have questions for all of you, and especially you." He pointed to Mari. "We'll be calling you in for interviews once we're done here." He nodded toward the body. "Be available and don't leave town."

"I'll stick around, if that's okay." Ollie looked at Lloyd, who nodded. He directed his gaze toward Mari. "Talk to you later."

They left the sheriff's crew and headed back in the direction of the parking area. For the first five minutes, no one said anything. Wyatt finally broke the tense silence. "Your ex-wife?"

Mari nodded, darkness still hanging like a cloud over her face. "We've been divorced for almost four years, but she won't move on. I had a no-contact order in Oregon because of it, and yesterday she showed up on my doorstep."

"Oh, dear. That had to be awkward." Wyatt couldn't imagine having to deal with someone that persistent.

Mari blew out a long breath. "Ollie gave me Royal's name, and I met with him this morning to put another order in place here. I was hoping it would finally send her away. I thought when I made this move, I'd finally be free. Look how that worked out for me."

"Why do you think she was out here?" Wyatt had been rolling that question over in her mind. Mari had said her ex wasn't the out-doorsy type, and even more interesting, she'd just arrived yesterday. How would she have even made her way out to this area to hike?

Mari's voice held the same note of confusion. "It doesn't make any sense. She hated the woods. Always wondered how she fell for someone whose office was the great outdoors. She was more into big cities, Jimmy Choo heels, and Prada handbags. For some unexplainable reason, my hiking boots were a turn-on."

Tuesday spoke up. "I had time to study her body while we waited, and before you give me crap, I did it from a safe distance, meaning nothing inside the tape was contaminated by me any more than it had been when Tripper went in." Wyatt understood that part, because she'd seen him work before. He would have approached the body to confirm before he went back to get them. Once he brought them to her, they'd stayed back in order not to leave any trace. Part of their training had been to treat every find as a potential crime scene whether it actually was or not.

"Good to know." Wyatt didn't want Lloyd yelling at them any more than he was already prepared to do. Yelling was his default mode. Annoying to her. Off-putting to many others.

Tuesday continued. "She's been there long enough for livor mortis to be clearly visible from a distance."

"Meaning?" Wyatt understood that livor mortis meant her blood had settled. She didn't have a good understanding of the timeline involved in the process associated with human death. Tuesday would.

"Hard to say exactly. It shows up no more than an hour after death and sets about three to four hours later. It appeared set, so I'm thinking she'd been there at least four hours. Maybe hours longer. The ME will be able to determine with more certainty."

Wyatt's gut feeling told her it had happened hours earlier. "She was killed during the night, which means it wasn't a poacher or an accident. It really was murder."

Mari stopped and rested her hands on her knees. For a few seconds she thought she would toss her breakfast. Since the breakup she'd been begging Sherrill to leave her alone. Never, in a million years, did she think something like homicide would grant her that wish. Nor did she want it to happen like this. She closed her eyes and willed her stomach to stop rolling. The vision of Sherrill's lifeless face filled her mind. Obsessive in a very unhealthy way, yes, but deserving to be murdered, no.

"Are you okay?" Wyatt put a hand on her back, and the reassurance it gave her helped. For being that of a relative stranger, her touch filled her with waves of comfort.

She straightened back up and took a deep breath. For a few seconds she tipped her head up to the sky and let the sun warm her cold skin. "No." She could have lied. Didn't see the point. These women were basically strangers to her, yet she felt a kinship with them that demanded honesty. She might have made an error in judgment when marrying Sherrill. Trusting these three wasn't.

"It's normal to feel sick." This time Tuesday put a hand on her shoulder. Not quite the same sense of comfort. Appreciated just the same.

"I don't understand any of this." People changed jobs and relocated all the time, and how many of them had to deal with a nightmare like this? Not fair.

"Do you have to go back to the station?" Wyatt asked.

Going home sure didn't appeal to her. "I should. I suspect the sheriff is going to want to interview me sooner rather than later." Easy to find her if she waited for him at the office.

"Here's my suggestion. Given he wants to interview all of us, why don't we head to my house and wait there? I'll make some tea." Wyatt stood at her truck and held open the passenger door for her. Hadn't occurred to her until this moment that Ollie had driven them here and she didn't have a way back to town.

Tea was always good, though Mari thought Scotch sounded better. Like a whole bottle. "I guess that would be okay." True enough that the sheriff would want to question all four of them. If they were at the same place, easy to get statements. Of course, he might also be irritated because staying together meant they could coordinate their stories. Not that they had stories to sync because it was as they'd already told him. No coordination required.

After she slid into the passenger's seat, Wyatt paused before closing the door. "You don't need to be alone either. You've been here what, a couple of days, and now a shock like this? Let your new friends help you through it. We're here for you."

The sincerity in Wyatt's voice tugged at her heart. Sometimes it took years to make a good friend. Sometimes, it took simply meeting them. "That sounds good."

Wyatt's house wasn't far, and at the end of the long gravel driveway the two-story log home rose, rustic and beautiful. Welcoming. "This is lovely." Animals grazed in pastures beyond the house, and she glimpsed what appeared to be massive gardens too. None of it should surprise her, and it didn't.

Wyatt smiled and answered her unasked questions. "My grandparents built the original cabin, my parents expanded on it, and I've added my own touches. A family heirloom of sorts. I'm fortunate to have had such wonderful people in my life." Mari caught the quick sideways glance.

Inside, the house was warm and inviting, the kind of place people love to come to and relax. Tripper ran in ahead of them and jumped up on the sofa, curling into a ball and promptly going to sleep. "He makes himself at home." Tuesday smiled. "The big guy needs a nap after the unexpected work he did today."

"He did that the first time he came to my house too," Addie said as she put an arm around Tuesday's shoulders. "Knew right then and there the three of us were a match made in heaven."

"Might have been made in hell, given how we met." Tuesday rolled her eyes. "We'll tell you that story another day. It is a little hard to believe for a bunch of reasons. Believe me when I say we have a good sense of how you're feeling right now." Tuesday looked sideways at Addie.

"Truer words have never been spoken." She kissed Tuesday's cheek.

Mari could tell an interesting story lay beneath the casual words. Curious to know what it might be, except not today. Her brain buzzed already. Anything more and she might explode. "I'll look forward to it, as you said, another day."

"How about some tea?" Wyatt ushered her to a spacious kitchen with a large window that looked out over a green yard and the extensive gardens she'd glimpsed from the truck. There were at least a dozen, and she could see the new growth stretching toward the light. By the end of summer, she suspected it would produce enough food to keep Wyatt and a dozen of her friends fed for the year. Self-sufficiency on full display. She liked it.

"Got anything stronger?" Tea would be nice if it were a regular day without bodies of any kind, let alone someone she'd been married to.

Wyatt leaned against the counter and studied her. "I do, but I'm thinking regardless of where we are, you're still on the clock. Am I right?"

Damn. Someone with scruples, good sense, and an awareness of time. Yes, she'd love a shot right now, and yes, Wyatt was the voice of reason. In a few hours, when her shift officially ended, Scotch would be back on the menu. "Tea is great."

Wyatt smiled and got to work. A few minutes later, Wyatt set a steaming mug in front of her. Tuesday and Addie were in the backyard with Tripper, throwing a ball. The moment they'd opened the back door, he'd come flying in from his spot on the sofa. They'd explained that he needed a reward after finding a body, and the promise of his ball was all it took to get him up and running.

Sitting across the table from Wyatt, they looked at each other in silence for maybe thirty seconds. "What?" Mari asked. Questions seemed to roil behind Wyatt's pretty eyes.

"Where were you last night?"

Royal didn't appreciate being shooed off like some random lookie-loo. Then again, he did understand the law-enforcement process, and Lloyd wasn't wrong in asking him to leave. He'd just hoped that the good-old-boy mentality he remembered from his youth would come into play and he'd be allowed to at least observe. Apparently, Lloyd's time in California had him leaning more in the direction of modern policing, given he'd made it clear in a hurry that things had changed around here in his hometown. No observing. No leaking of information. No chance of accidental contamination. Oh, well. Nothing ventured, nothing gained, as his old man had liked to repeat.

Thing was, he really needed to see what they were all there for. Bad enough Inez had caused a stir with the goat. Should have introduced her to her new bedroom last night. His bad for deciding to give her another shot at appropriate behavior. Now he had an unsettled feeling the grace he extended to her had backfired. Claude sure didn't need to know. He'd never hear the end of the I-told-you-so.

Royal never had children, never wanted them, although he suspected teenagers had nothing on Inez. He needed to figure out how to handle her. Claude tended toward a more heavy-handed approach. He supposed the three of them all had their strengths and weaknesses, and that's why they worked so well. At least they had until they'd come here.

At home, he found Claude in the back tending to his raised gardens. The guy had a surprisingly green thumb that had kept them stocked with fresh, organic produce in Canada. The first thing he'd done when they moved here was build the raised beds, and all of them were green with new growth. It had been Claude's idea to seek out the monkshood to deter unwanted wildlife from his gardens. That it was also called wolfsbane appealed to Royal for no other reason than the name. He very much appreciated the organic produce that had them eating like their food came from a five-star restaurant.

"Hey, boss. You're home early." Claude put down the spade he'd been using to work the soil and eliminate any unwanted vegetation.

"Inez around?" He hadn't seen her when he walked through the house.

Claude shook his head. "She went into town a while ago and hasn't come back." He leaned on the spade with an unreadable expression. Did he know more than he was letting on?

Royal touched the soft soil Claude had been working. The scent of damp earth floated into the air. "She came by the office earlier, but I haven't seen her since. Need to talk with her."

"What did she do this time?"

"Did I say she did anything?"

"Do I look stupid? You have that office to get up and rolling, which means you shouldn't be back here for at least a couple of hours. I also heard sirens a bit ago. Somehow, I got the feeling they were singing her song. Am I wrong?" Claude picked up the short-handled spade and started to work the dirt again.

He wished he had a definitive answer. "Yes and no. I'm sick of unpacking boxes, and since I had one new client today, I figured I could give it a rest until tomorrow. So, yes, I should have spent another two hours at the office in town."

"Okay. Reasonable. What's the rest? What am I wrong about? The sirens?"

"I followed them out to the same area where Inez killed the goat."

"Shit. What did they find?"

He shook his head. "That's the fucked-up part. I don't know. I got sent packing in a hurry, and nobody was talking. Wyatt and some friends of hers found something. I don't know what."

"She created a mess out there. Again."

"I don't know." With Lloyd shutting him down, he had no clue, and it was driving him crazy. He needed to find out exactly what happened so he could figure out how to mitigate yet another of Inez's messes because, yes, he leaned in the same direction as Claude. Inez had done something. Again.

"I'm telling you, man, you can't let her have free rein. That bitch is going to get us all in trouble or, worse, killed." Claude stabbed the spade into the dirt a couple of times. "If it were me, I wouldn't give her the rope."

"You're not in charge."

"Maybe I should be." And there it was. The subtext he'd been hearing from Claude for weeks.

"Want to challenge me, young man?" He stepped into Claude's personal space. Nothing new in their world. Always one younger, maybe stronger, who wanted to take over. Sometimes it worked. It wouldn't for Claude.

"I'm just saying…" Claude stepped back.

Royal stood tall, squaring his shoulders. "Right here, right now." His hands balled into fists, and a hot flush roared through him. His heart started to race.

For a long moment, Claude stared at him. Then he saw the flicker in his eyes. He lowered his head.

Good decision. Healthy decision. "Say something helpful. Or, better yet, go find Inez and bring her back." His heart rate slowed and his fingers uncurled.

As he watched Claude, his head still down, the first move his to make, tires on the gravel driveway made them both turn. Inez's Honda rolled down the driveway fast, screaming to a halt. One would think she was being chased by the police, except they knew better. She always drove that way. Did everything that way. One hundred miles an hour before coming to a dead stop. She got out of the car, her long dark hair free and wild. "What's up, boys?"

Royal studied her face. No hint of remorse or fear. "What did you do last night?"

"Oh." She put a finger to her lips and smiled. Definitely no remorse. "I take it they found her already? My, my. I figured it would take them longer, being out here in the boonies and all that."

Royal narrowed his eyes as he stared at her gleeful expression. He wanted to take her by the back of the neck and shake the smile off her face. "I repeat. What. Did. You. Do?"

Inez laughed like a woman who had not a care in the world. "You told me to take up a new hobby, so that's what I did." Her eyes almost glowed. "I picked moonlight target practice."

Chapter Nine

Perhaps, Wyatt could have led into the question with a little more tact. Instead, it sort of flew out of her mouth without as much restraint as a five-year-old would possess. Sometimes, a solitary life made for less-than-refined manners. Could be she needed more time around people to get her politeness skills back up to speed.

Mari at first looked surprised, and then her expression settled into something softer, more accepting. The thing about it, whether she liked it or not, it would be the first question Lloyd would ask her, and maybe she got that.

She held the mug of tea between her hands and for a second stared into it before looking back into Wyatt's eyes. "I was home sleeping. Alone."

"He's going to ask, you know." Lloyd would need to know where Mari was at the time of Sherrill's death. On the surface, she also had motive. Skilled with a gun, she had method as well. Wyatt shivered. At first blush, it didn't look good for her new neighbor.

Mari nodded and grimaced. "Trust me. I get it. In his shoes, I'd ask the same thing. I'm not offended. It's just that right now, my mind is racing. How do I prove it wasn't me? I wanted Sherrill far away from me, but I'm not cold enough to ever wish her dead." Tears pooled in her eyes.

Wyatt understood. She felt something similar brewing with Royal. All the random visits. Finding flowers on her doorstep.

The smiles and flirty chatter. The invitations for coffee or a drink. Nothing she'd done had been leading, yet he kept coming. A stalker in the making, and if he kept it up, she'd be walking a mile in Mari's shoes and having some other attorney drawing up a restraining order against him.

"Of course you wouldn't wish that on her or anybody else. A good woman wouldn't, and I might have just met you, but I know a good soul when I meet them." After years of teaching, especially classes out in nature, she had a refined sense of people. She could read them in an instant.

"Appreciate that, and I feel the same way. I didn't think I'd make friends this quick. Sherrill's death makes me despair. Your friendship gives me hope." She continued to hold the tea between her hands as though it were an anchor.

"My life's work is seeing the good in the world and all that it can be. I'm interested in making it all sing, and that applies to people too." Might be hard for Mari to understand that a woman out here in the open spaces of Montana used such broad strokes with the world.

Mari's head snapped up, and a surprised expression crossed her face. "My phone." Mari patted her pocket. "My phone can at least prove I was at home."

She'd been intent on her connection with the natural world and hadn't given a thought to what the electronic era could do. "That's an excellent idea. Maybe your car too. It's pretty new, right? Unless I'm mistaken, they also have tracking software built in these days. It could prove your car didn't move out of your driveway."

Mari nodded. "I think so." Something like relief crossed her face. "I want them to find who did this today, and I'll do whatever to help. All I can really offer is that it wasn't me."

"I'm happy to do what I can too. Tuesday and Addie as well." She glanced out the window at her two friends, who had come for nothing more than a quiet visit in Montana, some great hikes, and drinks around the firepit. Now, they were part of what looked to be a homicide investigation.

Mari finally set the cup of tea on the table. "You don't even know me. Why would you and your friends put yourselves out to help a stranger?"

Valid question and one she'd ask if she were in the same boat. She patted her chest with one hand. "Because I feel it right here, and I put a lot of faith in feelings. The body and the spirit let you know when something or someone isn't right. Also, when something or someone is right."

Mari dipped her head. "I appreciate that, and I promise that your faith in me is not misplaced."

She valued the words and already knew the reality. "Any thoughts on why she'd be out there?"

Mari started to shake her head and then stopped. "It took an act of congress to get her to spend even a single night camping. In all our time together, I got her out once, and she complained the entire time. What she is, however, is a little bit of a player. Not terrible, mind you, but it wouldn't be all that unusual for her to hit the bars."

"To pick up some guy?" Given Sherrill and Mari had been married, it made her wonder. This town wasn't a hotspot for lesbian bars, which left the options fairly limited.

This time Mari did shake her head. "No. Guys were never her thing. She might toy with them, but she wouldn't have gone anywhere with a man. She'd have gone for a woman. The prettier the better. She loves, I mean loved, girlie-girls. Again, one of those things I didn't understand about her fixation on me. I'm not a stunner and definitely not a girlie-girl."

Wyatt would argue the stunning part. Maybe not classically pretty but attractive in a way that would make anyone, man or woman, look twice. Sure made her look twice. Or three times. Or…

She regained her focus. "Then that's where we start. We check the local bars and see if we can find out if she met up with anyone. I know most people around here, and maybe I can figure out if she left with anyone I know."

Mari's brows drew together. "Shouldn't we wait for Lloyd?"

Spot-on question. "Probably, but if I were a gambler, I'd place a big bet on Lloyd being out there for hours. You know, hours we can use to start our own investigation." The idea appealed to her, and she had the perfect two guests to help. After all, Tuesday and Addie had taken down a serial killer and no doubt could be invaluable in finding a killer in their midst now.

"You think it's a good idea?" The cloud still shadowed Mari's face.

Her better sense screamed *don't do it*. She said, "I think it's a great idea."

❖

It filled Mari's heart with hope that Wyatt showed such faith in her. She didn't feel entirely confident about doing a covert investigation on their own and going around the sheriff while he was out at the crime scene. While her training included investigation techniques, she wasn't a detective by any stretch of the imagination. She didn't join the forest service to become a cop. Certainly, some aspects crossed over into law enforcement, but, for her, it had been about a job that took her out into nature, her happy place.

Well, it had been her happy place until she saw Sherrill lifeless on the forest floor. Any job had its ups and down, a decided down pushing her to make the move to Hamilton. The down today fell into a completely different category, making it hard to think straight after seeing the woman she'd married discarded like that. It wasn't right regardless of how she felt about her these days. Any love had gone up in flames a long time ago, and she wanted Sherrill to be back in Oregon alive and focused on someone else. Not getting zipped into a body bag and transported to the nearest morgue.

"Okay, let's do it." Mari figured the sheriff would be pissed, and this could potentially cost her the new job. Weighing risk versus reward, she went with risk. At least it beat the hell out of sitting here for hours waiting for him to come question her. Their little contingent could spend a couple hours trying to get information on Sherrill's movements last night, and then when it came time to meet with the sheriff or one of his people, she'd have something useful to share. She hoped.

Wyatt slapped a hand lightly on the table. "That's the spirit. Let's go get them." She nodded toward the window. "And roll."

"I should probably change." She looked down at her forest-service uniform. What they were about to do would be as unofficial as it could get, and wearing her uniform would be a bad idea.

"We can swing by your house before we head into town. You bought the Simpson place, right?"

While she hadn't met the family, she did see their name on all the paperwork. "Yes." She started to walk toward the front door, wishing she had her own car. At least she could pick it up from the office once they got into town.

"Hey." Wyatt leaned out the back door. "I'm taking Mari to her house to change clothes. You want to go? We're planning a bit of private investigation work right afterward, and I'm pretty sure you two need to lead the charge. After all, you are the pros."

"We'll follow." Tuesday motioned to Tripper with her hand, and he ran to her side, all business. No words necessary. Someday, Tuesday would have to teach her how she did that.

"Great. We're out of here then." The storm door slammed shut as Wyatt came back into the kitchen. "Ready?"

She followed Wyatt once more to the truck. In the passenger's seat with her seatbelt fastened, Mari immediately thought about why they'd need a human-remains-detection team to come along to ask questions. Then it clicked. It wasn't about the HRD team at all. It was more about Addie, the private investigator. So, yeah, they should lead the charge.

Wyatt drove directly to her house without needing Mari to give her directions. It showed her strength as both a local and a wilderness-survival teacher. All she could manage after a few days was to find her way to the grocery store, the office, and the Bob Marshall Wilderness Area. With the size of their area of responsibility, not very impressive. Given there had been two incidents in two days in the same general area, she didn't plan to beat herself up either. If she made it through with her career intact, she'd orient herself to her new home much more thoroughly. Maybe Wyatt would help her.

She invited everyone inside, although they opted to wait in the vehicles. It might be a little insulting except for the reasons they were here in the first place. Wyatt knew she'd only moved here within the last week, and Mari felt certain she'd shared that detail with Tuesday and Addie. Pretty sure Tripper didn't give a hoot one way or the other. If she were to make an educated guess, they were giving her grace if the house were a mess of boxes and plastic-covered furniture dropped off by the movers. They weren't wrong, although it wouldn't bother her for them to see the mess. She rarely worried about those kinds of things.

In jeans, a fleece pullover, and a pair of well-worn brown leather Danskos, she rejoined Wyatt. "Okay. I'm ready."

Wyatt turned and looked at her. "You didn't bring a bag."

"What? A bag? Why?" Those were real detailed questions right there. More babble than coherence.

Wyatt put a hand softly on her arm, her eyes warm and lovely. "Given what happened to your ex, I thought maybe you might want to stay with us tonight."

She tilted her head as she studied Wyatt. "Stay with you…" They'd been drawn toward each other since the moment they met, yet staying with her seemed more than a little premature.

Wyatt held up a hand. "Yeah. I wasn't real clear there, was I? Seriously, though, how do you know you're safe here by yourself?" She clapped a hand over her mouth before slowly pulling it away. She appeared embarrassed. "Sometimes, I jump to conclusions. I don't know that you're here by yourself. Maybe you don't need us."

She smiled, and warmth flooded her. Made her feel like family had come along with her instead of being hundreds and hundreds of miles from them. "You're not wrong. I am by myself and have been for quite some time. As for my family, they all thought that staying in Oregon worked for them. They waved me good-bye

with the good-luck-in-your-new-job-and-give-us-a-call message."
She hadn't expected anything else. She also hadn't expected to
feel so sad leaving them behind.

"Then what do you think? Do you want to stay here alone or
come stay with us? I can tell you what I'd prefer, though I think
you can guess." Wyatt squeezed her arm, the warmth spreading
through her.

She started to say thanks but no thanks, because she didn't
want to come across as a needy woman. Seemed like an imposition
on her brand-new neighbor, if calling someone who lived some
miles down the road a close neighbor made sense. Her second
impulse and the one she leaned into had her grabbing the door
handle. "I'll be right back."

"Good."

❖

"Jesus fucking Christ." Royal couldn't help it. The urge to
strangle Inez almost had him hurdling toward her with his hands
going for her pale neck. He called on the same patience with her
that he'd had to use over and over with his students. His feet stayed
rooted to the ground, his hands at his sides, albeit curled back into
fists. He took a few deep breaths.

She smiled and shrugged. "Not quite as much fun as, well, you
know." She ran her tongue over her lips. "Still pretty satisfying."

"You're going to end up killing us all." Claude leaned against
her car and gave her a hard look. "You're a selfish bitch."

"Fuck you." Inez stuck her tongue out at Claude.

"Enough." The comment was meant for both of them. "We've
got to come up with damage control so they can't trace it back here.
How did you get her out to the wilderness?" His mind whirled as
he thought of how to undo the damage Inez had brought to his
doorstep. Kept bringing to his doorstep.

"I was careful. I'm always careful." She sounded bored.

They had vastly different ideas of what comprised careful.
"Where did you meet her?"

She shrugged and gave him a sly smile. "More like a pickup than a meet-and-greet. I have a way, you know?" She laughed softly and brushed hair off her face.

He drew in a breath. Getting things out of Inez reminded him of his student-teaching days in a middle school. All hormones, defiance, and angst. It had been hell. "Where did you pick her up?"

She put a finger to her lips and looked to the sky. "Hmm."

"Come on! You're not that dumb." Claude slapped a hand on the car roof.

Inez jumped and turned a burning look on him. "Knock it off. I don't appreciate you pushing me. Always pushing me. You're a bully. I don't like bullies."

"Well, maybe if you weren't such a cunt I wouldn't have to push you around."

"ENOUGH." Yes, just like middle-school kids, and there was a reason he'd ended up teaching in the law school rather than in public school. He'd figured out after those student-teaching days that he wasn't cut out for that life. He'd headed directly to law school and never looked back.

Claude and Inez turned to him, Claude appearing as unrepentant as usual, and Inez with her arms crossed over her chest. "Tell him to quit." She pouted and glared. "He's always mean."

He looked at Claude. Royal understood why the big man was irritated. He also got what Claude didn't. Inez would never respond well to harsh words and aggression. Not that she couldn't be aggressive. But within their group, she took it as a personal affront.

"Claude, let me handle this. Why don't you go finish your gardens." Working in the soil always seemed to calm him. For a guy who came from a family with more money than God, his fascination with the earth intrigued Royal. One of the reasons he'd brought him into the fold.

"Whatever." Claude spun and headed out back. "Just get her under control." The last comment had been muttered under his breath. He would know that Royal could still hear. He let it pass this once. More important things to attend to than his temper tantrum.

After Claude was out of earshot, he turned to Inez. "This has to stop, and by that I mean right this instant."

Her expression shifted to one of a child who'd been caught being naughty. "It was fun, and if I can't run for a little fun, then why not play an alternate game? She wasn't from around here anyway. Who's gonna care if she was used for target practice? You told me to find something else to do, and I did, so it's your fault really."

"Who's going to care?" Had she seriously just said that? "Oh, I don't know. Maybe the sheriff?" Really, Inez wasn't that stupid.

Another shrug. "I suppose."

"I suppose? Inez, are you listening to yourself? Doing all this isn't going to change anything. I'm not going back to Canada. This is our home now. You have to acclimate and stop putting us in jeopardy."

"Or?" She actually stomped one of her feet. Lord, how old was she? Twelve?

"Or things won't go well for you." Might as well lay it all out in black and white.

He could almost see the wheels turning in her head and expected another bratty response. Instead, her shoulders slumped and she said, "Fine."

This wouldn't be the end. She'd behave for the moment. How long that moment would last would be anyone's guess. An idea came to him as he studied her face. "I want you to register for one of the women's survival classes that Wyatt puts on." Brilliant, if he did say so.

Her face screwed up with an expression of distaste. "I don't need to learn survival from a bunch of broads who've never been in the wilderness. Jeez. I can't even believe you said that."

"You will take a class or two." The more he thought about it, the more perfect the idea became for several reasons. Sometimes he amazed himself.

"Why? I know how to take care of myself. It's a dumb idea and a huge waste of my time." Pouting again.

He ignored the childlike behavior and instead appealed to the adult in her. "Because you'll be able to find out what Wyatt knows about that woman you killed. It's bound to come up." Of course it would. A perfect example of why a woman would need to be skilled and capable in the woods alone. Seriously, it was a brilliant plan.

Her expression shifted from petulance to interest. "That's not a bad idea."

"It's a great idea."

She smiled. "I'll do it."

It wasn't a suggestion. She would do it because he told her to. He'd let her think her participation in the class was voluntary. He also didn't tell her that she'd be his eyes and ears when it came to his soul mate.

Chapter Ten

Wyatt waited for Mari to return, wondering the whole time if she'd overstepped. The offer to stay the night with them felt like the right thing. Under these circumstances, it seemed wrong to let her be alone in that big house. She wouldn't want to be alone if tragedy happened in her life. Besides, without knowing how her ex had ended up in the woods murdered and alone, Wyatt believed it better that Mari not be by herself. Until the killer was located, it could be dangerous.

Could also be that Wyatt's growing fascination with the new forest ranger had her extending an offer that she wouldn't normally. Lots of women had passed through her world as they dealt with any number of serious life events. That's why many of them came to her. They'd been hurt, abused, abandoned, or ridiculed, and they wanted to regain their confidence. Or, in some cases, to find it for the very first time. To prove to themselves they were capable and skilled all on their own.

Mari already gave her the sense that she possessed the skills and knowledge of a capable woman. Her confidence wasn't hard to see either. It would take self-assurance to move away from family and friends and start all over where she knew no one. At least that had been true until two days ago. Ollie clearly liked her and had already taken her under his wing. Wyatt viewed her as a friend and, by this time tomorrow, was certain Tuesday and Addie would too. Tripper liked her, and, honestly, that said more than anything. Always trust the dog.

It wasn't even five minutes later when Mari came back out and tossed a small bag into the backseat. "A few necessities. Hopefully, I won't need more than a change of clothes. You said Lloyd was good, and I hope he figures this out ASAP."

Wyatt wasn't convinced they'd be able to solve the crime quickly. Lloyd and his crew were good, but they were talking about a body in the middle of a forest with no surveillance cameras and, as of right now, no witnesses. Unless the killer turned out to be a dunce, it could take some time to figure it out.

"You can always come back for more." She put the car in reverse and started to back up.

"Sure. If I need more."

"Right. If you need more." *You will.*

"Where do we start?" Mari stared out the window at the long, straight highway leading into town.

Wyatt had been thinking about it while she waited and suspected that Addie would have a more detailed plan once they joined up. "We're going downtown and start there."

Mari nodded. "Makes sense. I'd begin with the most popular bar. Sherrill liked her martinis."

"Good to know." That fact narrowed things right down. Only one place fit that description a hundred percent.

"Dirty."

She laughed. "I know it's wrong to laugh, but oh those things are nasty." Out of the corner of her eye, she saw Mari smile.

"That's being nice. They taste like cleaning solution, but Sherrill thought them nectar of the gods. She could put them down like water."

"Argh. That almost makes me gag. Does let me know where our first stop is going to be. Tyler makes the best drinks in town, so if anyone could have mixed her a great dirty martini, he would be the guy. His place is also the go-to club in town. At least for the younger set. The older folks prefer something a bit different."

Her smile faded. "Let's start with this Tyler then. Her idea of fun usually included a lot of booze and loud music. Country, rock, popular—didn't matter as long as she could dance. She liked attention, especially from a younger crowd."

She had a hard time imagining Mari in a club drinking and dancing with her arms in the air. A drink, sure. A dance, sure, but more like a good liqueur, on the rocks, and a slow, romantic dance. Maybe she was wrong, but she doubted it. How in the world did those two meet and marry? Some day she hoped to hear the whole story.

Addie and Tuesday followed her downtown and pulled into the parking spot next to her. "She liked a good drink," she explained when they were all standing together. "And Tyler is the one to give her what she wanted."

Addie nodded. "Good call. A tourist ending up in the woods in the middle of the night probably wasn't sober. You agree?" She looked to Tuesday

Wyatt had not a single doubt when it came to Tuesday's opinion in this instance. A decade plus in search-and-rescue back in Washington had given her not only skills but a head full of knowledge about people who got lost in the wilderness. Not just the hows but also the whys.

"I would second that guess. Especially at her age. Younger people might decide hiking in the middle of the night would be fun. Patrons our age aren't as inclined unless it's an area they're very familiar with. Not the case here." Tuesday closed the passenger's door and tapped the back window lightly as she smiled in at Tripper.

Addie put a hand on Tuesday's shoulder. "Let's go talk to your bartender." She glanced at her smart watch and frowned. "You think he'll be available?"

She got what Addie meant. Mid-afternoon wasn't prime time for an establishment like his. In a couple of hours things would begin to pick up, and getting his attention would be tough. "He's also the bar manager, so quick answer, yes. He's most likely there and getting things ready for the night business."

Addie nodded. "Good."

"What about the dog?" Mari looked back at the truck, where the rear windows were down a couple of inches and a black nose poked through.

Tuesday nodded in his direction. "He's fine. He's accustomed to spending significant amounts of time in the truck. Have trained him for that since I got him at twelve weeks. It's part of search-and-recovery. A lot of time spent waiting while search plans are made, teams are assembled, and equipment checked. He knows the drill, and while the weather is pleasant, it's not warm enough I need to keep a fan running for him."

"Impressive." Mari glanced at the truck once more.

"He's a good man." Wyatt loved Tripper. Smart and skilled, he gave all dogs a good name.

Tuesday leaned toward Tripper and patted his nose. "Keep an eye out for any murderers."

Mari started to walk toward the door of the bar and stopped to stare back at Tripper. "Can he do that?" He'd already proved he could find the dead. Did the dog have even more refined skills?

Tuesday smiled. "Not that I know of, but hey. Doesn't hurt to ask. He's surprised me more than once."

"Impressive," Mari muttered and decided it wouldn't shock her if that dog found the guilty party for them. All she had to do was look into his eyes, and his intelligence shone through.

"Come on." Wyatt motioned them toward the bar. She stepped through the door and waved at a man sitting in front of a laptop there, long hair pulled back in a ponytail, a glass of lemon water next to the computer. The tables were empty, and only two sat at the bar nursing beers, one man and one woman, neither looking at the other. Music played softy through the speakers.

"Hey, stranger." He came off the stool and extended a hand to Wyatt. "Good to see you. What's this, friends? I didn't think you had any of those." He laughed at his own joke.

Wyatt rolled her eyes. "Such a funny guy. Should have been a Hollywood comedian."

"I try. I try." His smile lit up his face. Mari thought it a very friendly face.

"Tyler, these are my friends, Tuesday and Addie. They're visiting from Omaha." She waved toward the two women.

He raised his eyebrows. "Oh, wow, ladies. You're a long way from the great plains."

"We sure are but have to say, it's lovely here. I like your town." Addie shook his hand, as did Tuesday.

Wyatt turned to her and smiled. "This is Mari, Ollie's replacement."

Seemed like everyone around here knew Ollie, as that's all she had to say in terms of explanation. "Hey, Mari." He now extended his hand to her, his grip firm. "It's a pleasure. We're going to miss old Ollie. You have some big shoes to fill, though I suspect you already know that, and he wouldn't have picked you if he didn't think you were up to it."

Mari shook his hand, returning the friendly yet firm grip. "I've pretty much figured that out in the two days we've worked together. I'll do my best to make him proud. Nice to meet you, Tyler."

"Welcome to Montana. You'll love our mountains and the friendly folks who call these parts home. Great place to live and raise a family."

"Tyler." Wyatt interrupted the cheerful chatter before he went down a path Mari might not want to go. "We need to pick your brain." Time to get to the reason for their visit. The clock was ticking.

"For you ladies, absolutely. What can I do for you?"

Wyatt looked to Mari. "Can you show him a picture of Sherrill?"

Mari pulled out her phone and scrolled for a few seconds, looking for a picture. Given the divorce, she'd pretty much deleted all that had Sherrill in them. Except one, and honestly, she couldn't even explain why it hadn't gone into the trash like the rest. Taken at Multnomah Falls on a gorgeous sunny day, it was hands down the best picture she'd ever taken of Sherrill, and long before her borderline personality disorder showed itself in all its glory. She held it up for Tyler. "By any chance, did you see her here last night? She's a few years older than when this was taken, but she looks pretty much the same." Silently, she corrected herself... Sherrill looked older.

He squinted as he studied the image and began to nod. "Yeah, yeah, yeah. She came in last night." He looked up at the ceiling for maybe five seconds and then returned his gaze to Mari. "Martini."

She nodded. Sherrill had been here. "Dirty."

"Yup. Dirty. Not the requested drink of many folks around here as a general rule."

Addie stepped up. "Do you recall if she talked to anyone? Danced with anyone? Left with anyone?"

He laughed. "Sure do. Attractive women like that one get the guys going. Thing is, she blew all of them off. Even Shane." He gave Wyatt a look that told Mari there was a story.

Wyatt explained. "Shane is our local pretty boy who knows exactly how pretty he is. He'd be the first one to hit on a beautiful woman, hoping to get lucky, and more times than not, it works. Someone new, attractive, and drinking a martini would be a woman wearing a Shane target on her back."

Tyler laughed and slapped a hand on the bar. "Should have been here, Wyatt. Fun to watch. She shut him down in a New York minute. Poor guy didn't know what to do. It was freaking hilarious."

"I'm betting he pivoted and hit on another woman. Can't see him giving up that easy." Wyatt shook her head.

Tyler snapped his fingers. "You got that one right. Pretty boy didn't leave here alone, but he didn't leave with your friend there." He pointed to Mari's phone.

"How about women?" Addie was making notes in a small binder as she asked the question.

Tyler shook his head slowly. "Didn't really see anyone in particular. In Missoula, she'd have had more luck in that pool. Here, the field isn't quite as big. Not to say it's empty." He looked at Wyatt and smiled. She winked at him. Interesting.

Mari's initial optimism that the bar owner could provide them with a solid lead floated away. "Nobody?" She held on to a little hope that they'd come up with something useful. Something to give Lloyd that would put his investigation on the fast track.

He shook his head again. "Not that I noticed. If she did hook up with some woman, I didn't see it. A couple of drinks and she wandered out, or at least that's what I recall. Got busy around ten, if you know what I mean."

Addie nodded at the same time as Wyatt, who said, "Thanks, Tyler. Appreciate your help."

"Wait." Addie looked up from her notes. "Before we go, does your exterior have cameras? Security footage we could take a look at?"

He hopped off the tall bar stool. "Of course. We're not Missoula, but we're not out in the sticks either. We have the latest and the greatest tech, and we can take a quick look if that'll help."

"It might." Wyatt. "Let's see what you've got."

The camera idea pleased Mari. She'd not thought about it, yet it sure made sense, which then made her feel a little dumb for not thinking of security. Wasn't sure she'd make a credible detective. Good thing Addie and Tuesday happened to be around when this happened. They might not think so, but she sure did. Sometimes, it took a village. Couldn't ask for a better village.

Tyler led them into a back room, where they gathered around two monitors as he scrolled through the video feed to right before ten the following evening. Mari watched closely as they sped through the file. Nothing much of interest appeared until it hit eleven forty-seven. A flash of a light blue hoodie with flowers on the sleeve.

"Wait. Stop. Did you see that?" Wyatt tapped the screen. Tyler paused the video file.

"Sure did," Tuesday said as she and Addie leaned close. Mari peered over the top of them all, her view somewhat obscured by all the heads gathered close in front of the monitor.

On the screen, Sherrill stood close to another woman, her hand on her arm. "Who was that woman Sherrill was talking to?" It wasn't just a chat. She knew how her ex worked, and it appeared more like she was hitting on the woman rather than asking for directions. Her signature move was that hand on the arm. Warm, friendly, and hopeful.

"Who's that woman?" Wyatt tapped the screen. "I can't really see her face."

Tyler leaned in. "Oh, I know her. She comes in here frequently. Inez is her name. You know, Wyatt. She's Royal's cousin or something like that. She moved here with him from Canada."

"Royal's cousin?"

"Yeah. She's pretty hot. Can see why your friend would be interested in her."

"She's a lesbian?" Mari was pretty certain only another woman could entice Sherrill to go somewhere.

"Naw. From what I've seen, she likes everybody, and when I say everybody, I mean everybody. You feel me?"

Wyatt nodded. "I get it, yeah."

"You think she had something to do with it?" Tuesday leaned in and watched the screen as Tyler once more pushed *Play*.

Addie frowned. "Could be, although if you notice, they talked for maybe a minute, and then they went to separate cars. Both of them alone. You'd think if they took off together, they'd ride in the same car."

"Crap." Mari's hopes for something concrete faded.

Wyatt put a hand on her shoulder. "What do you think about the separate-cars thing? Would Sherrill ride with her or meet her?"

Wyatt's question was spot-on. Had Mari wondering about her own critical-thinking skills at the moment. More like wondering where they went. She should have thought of that too. "She'd be more likely to take her car and meet her somewhere. She's got a thing about independence."

"Well, then." Wyatt stood up straight. "I say we go talk to Royal and his cousin."

"Absolutely. That's our next stop." Addie was back to making notes. "Even if they didn't make arrangements to meet somewhere, she might have seen something. The direction Sherrill drove off in. What she said. Little details can seem unimportant and then turn into something that solves the case."

"She's hitting on her." Mari stared as they replayed the few minutes of interaction one more time before they left. The moves were there, and despite the less-than-clear quality of the video, the expression on Sherrill's face told her she'd been interested. A full-on hookup most likely.

"How can you be sure?" Wyatt looked at her.

She shrugged. "Years of living with the woman, years of stories in an attempt to make me jealous. I can tell when she's flirting even without hearing the words." It wasn't rocket science. Sherrill had made moves like that on other women right in front of her before they split up and divorced. A little embarrassing to admit, even to herself, that she'd stayed after witnessing the one who was supposed to love her more than anyone go after others.

"Okay then." Addie slipped her small notebook into a pocket. "Shall we go talk to this cousin?"

Mari nodded. "Definitely."

❖

Royal should have been surprised when two vehicles rolled down his driveway. He wasn't. The only surprising thing turned out to be that neither of them was law enforcement. Wyatt and Mari got out of one. Out of the second, the woman he'd seen out in the wilderness area before he'd been invited to leave and a second woman he hadn't seen before. No Lloyd and none of his deputies. Interesting.

He waved and smiled at Wyatt. Warmth flooded him as he gazed at her face. He swore she got more beautiful every time he saw her. The air carried her unique scent, and he breathed in deeply. He'd recognize her smell from a mile away. "Surprised to see you here. Pleased, though. I knew you'd ultimately succumb to my charms and come visit the farm." Wyatt didn't smile. His charm wasn't working on her. Yet.

"Not a social visit." No warmth in her words. He had his work cut out for him, not that things wouldn't take a one-eighty on the night of the Harvest Moon. He just hoped her feelings toward him would soften before that night. Would make it all go a heck of a lot smoother.

Instinct cautioned him to tread lightly with her and her friends right now. He could do that. Had been doing it for years. "Oh, so what's the not-social visit about?" He schooled his expression into one that he hoped conveyed the appropriate somber concern. The professional Royal, here to help.

"Your cousin." Wyatt stared into his eyes.

He looked away and scanned the faces of the other three women. Like Wyatt, all very serious. Told him more than he wanted to know. *Damn you, Inez.* He swept his gaze back to Wyatt. "Four of you come to ask about my cousin? Must be important."

"Yeah. Very. Is she around?" Wyatt's expression didn't waver from dark and serious. There would be no pleasant interaction today.

His attention to her never slipped. Connection had a way of doing that. Sooner or later, she'd feel it too, and he could be patient. How long had it taken him to recognize his forever mate anyway? She'd get there just as he had. The epiphany would happen. "She's inside. Strangely enough, she's in signing up for your next workshop." He hoped that would please her.

"We need to talk to her." Same snap to her words.

"We?" He glanced at the three women who, so far, had stayed silent as Wyatt took the lead.

"Mari, I think you two have already met." She nodded in the direction of his first Hamilton client.

He gave Mari a slight nod. "Yes. We have. I'm doing some work for her," he said to Wyatt before turning to Mari again. "I've got the paperwork drafted." He'd gotten that much done before racing out to discover Inez had once again created a mess.

Mari pressed her lips together as she shook her head. "No need to file."

Now, he frowned. "Why is that? I planned to go back into the office in a little bit and get it over to the court." She'd seemed pretty intent on sooner rather than later on the legal order. The about-face didn't track.

Tears pooled in her eyes before she spoke. "She's dead." She stuffed her hands in her pockets and appeared to steady her emotions. After she blinked a few times, the tears disappeared.

His teeth clenched for two reasons. First, because now he knew who Inez had picked up last night. Second, he caught the subtle movement between Mari and Wyatt. Almost as if they were a couple. That wouldn't do. Not at all. Wyatt belonged to him. Forever. He stifled the urge to scream, *Back off, bitch!*

He hoped his expression didn't betray his emotions. Shouldn't, as he'd perfected a most excellent poker face through the years. A lesson he'd spent plenty of time on when teaching his law students and in courtrooms before he took on the role of professor. Good lawyers didn't give anything away in their expressions. Good alphas didn't either. "Seriously?"

"As serious as a heart attack. It was Sherrill out in the woods this morning. The sheriff and his crew are working the scene as we speak. It was murder, plain and simple." Wyatt reached over and took Mari's hand. He wanted to rip them apart.

"Did you kill her?" Royal looked away from the clasped hands and directly into Mari's eyes. Deflect, deflect, deflect.

"Royal!" Wyatt stepped even closer to Mari. "That's uncalled for. Mari didn't kill her or anyone else."

He wasn't repentant. "Legit question." Put him in a courtroom, and he'd ask the same question a dozen different ways. So would any other attorney worth their salt, and if this ended up in court, Mari would find herself on the witness stand, so no apology necessary or offered.

"You're not the sheriff." Wyatt didn't sound impressed.

"Might need to be her defense attorney." Oh, he'd defend her all right. Make damn good and sure she ended up in the women's prison in Billings. Behind bars and hundreds of miles from Hamilton. Hundreds of miles away from Wyatt.

"Mari didn't do anything, but your cousin talked to Sherrill last night, and now we'd like to talk with her." Wyatt stepped up to him. He breathed in the fresh scent of her once more. His fingers tingled and his heart raced. If only he could take her face between his hands and kiss her deeply. He remained still and stared into her eyes.

"No." He kept his words on the issue at hand.

"What do you mean, no?"

"I mean no, you may not talk to my cousin. If Inez did speak with Mari's ex before she was murdered, nobody discusses anything with her without me as counsel."

Wyatt spread her hands. "Not seeing the problem, Royal. You're here. You want to sit in and listen, do it. We don't care."

"The problem is I haven't had an opportunity to debrief with her, and until that happens, it's a big fat no. Let me put it another way. No one talks to her except law enforcement, and only with me right there. If anybody interrogates her, it will be Lloyd or one of his detectives, not a group of women pretending to be investigators. You made a trip out here for nothing."

"I'm a private detective." The taller of the two women from the second car finally spoke up.

"And you are?" She had the air of someone whose pre-PI training was done inside of a police academy. She might be private now, but this lady was a cop at some point in her life. He could spot them a mile away.

"Addie, and this is my wife, Tuesday. Her human-remains-detection dog found Sherrill's body."

Only as she said it did he catch the scent of the dog in the air. He turned and looked toward the truck. Still in the vehicle, there it was, its nose poked through the open window. He needed to pay more attention. He shouldn't have missed the dog.

Lawyer Royal kicked in at full force. "Okay, Addie and Tuesday. Good work and good for you."

"So, we can interview your cousin?" Addie readied a notebook and clicked her pen. All business and ready to talk. She wasn't going to like his answer.

"That would still be a no. No badge. No interview." How dumb did they think he was, especially the one who declared herself to be a PI. If that were true, she'd know the lay of the land.

"Royal!" Frustration rang clear in Wyatt's voice. She would have to learn that his say was always the final say. Lawyer Royal. Alpha Royal. All the same. His word ruled, and in good time, she would understand.

"Still no," he said as he shoved his hands in his pockets.

Wyatt's eyes narrowed. He liked how she looked when she got fired up. Sexy as hell. "*Royal*. We've known each other for decades. I can't believe you're acting like this. You've been trying to get all chummy since you came back here, and now that you have a chance to make good on that attempt, get into my good graces, you shut us down."

He shrugged. "She might be my cousin." Sort of. Not really, but they didn't need to know that minor detail. "But I'd be a pretty shitty attorney if I let you interrogate her. Let's all be clear here. I'm not a shitty attorney."

"Ask her a couple questions. Not interrogate." Addie still held the notebook and pen at ready.

"Question. Interrogate. Potato. Patato. The answer remains a resounding no."

For a few seconds longer, they all stared at him. He stared back, and at last, they returned to their vehicles. He watched them leave, his gaze lingering on the back of Wyatt's head as she drove away.

CHAPTER ELEVEN

Wyatt left Royal's house with an uneasy feeling. Sometimes women signed up for her classes and would come to her bragging about their skills, only to crash and burn when it was time to demonstrate. Far too many over-estimated what they could really do and under what conditions. Royal's behavior felt a lot like those women's. He might be an ethical attorney looking out for a client, which might be true in some respects. He was also hiding behind his ethics, and she intended to find out why.

Sure, she hadn't known him well growing up, and yes, he'd been gone from the area for years. Since his return, he'd made a pest of himself, as though he might be interested in her. She made no secret about her life. In school, she'd known something about her was different, but it took going away to college to let her inner self shine. Her first girlfriend seemed to have been sent by the gods. Suzie had opened her eyes and her world. Pure, fleeting magic, at least in terms of their relationship. Suzie had been like a firefly. A joyful spark of light that appeared for a few seconds and then flew away. Thinking of her now brought as much pleasure as the first day they met. After Suzie, she'd never looked back

It also made her wonder more about Royal. Why wouldn't he let them talk to Inez? The surveillance video showed the two women conversing for maybe a minute. How could it be a problem if they asked her about that minute?

"I don't like that he wouldn't let us talk to her." Mari looked out the window. "What are they hiding?"

Great minds working alike. "I agree. In fairness to him, it was kind of a standard lawyer response." Not that she wanted to minimize his obstinance. She was only trying to think through the interaction logically.

"True, but seriously, if they talked for only a minute, what's the big deal?" Mari's fingers tapped on her thighs.

"My thought too." It irritated her that Royal had shut them down that way. They might have come up with something concrete. "Let's get back to the house and see if Addie and Tuesday thought of anything else while they were driving back. This is their world, so if anyone knows next steps in the investigation, it's those two."

"It seems wrong to give up." Mari frowned as she continued to stare out the windshield.

Ahead of them, Tuesday's truck headed in the direction of home. She hoped they were talking through next steps. "We're not giving up. We're pivoting." If anything, Royal's choice to block them from talking to Inez made her even more determined. Pissed her off too. They wanted to find a killer. An innocent person shouldn't have a problem chatting with them.

Mari looked over at her and nodded. "Pivoting. I like that. Hopeful. If you can call anything today hopeful." Sadness sounded in her words.

Wyatt took Mari's hand, which trembled slightly as she wrapped her fingers around it. "We'll figure this out. Lloyd is a good guy, and he might be sheriff in a smaller town, but trust me, it's no reflection on his skills. The guy's got game. He comes from a long line of lawmen, and he brought back some mad skills from his stint in California."

"You trust him?"

"With my life." Not a lie. Lloyd might get on her nerves on occasion with his cop attitude, but he wasn't a good-old-boy either. Smart and ethical, with an ability to keep an open mind. She had faith in him and the force he'd assembled. They'd find who did this. Eventually.

Mari squeezed her hand and nodded. "Okay. Then let's go huddle and see if we can come up with something four women without badges can do."

Wyatt squeezed back and hoped her sinking feeling that this was just the beginning would turn out to be wrong.

❖

Back at Wyatt's house, Mari paced. Thoughts whirling, she attempted to come up with some rational reason why Sherrill would be found dead in a Montana forest. In some respects, not a big stretch. Mental illness did some not-too-good things to the thought processes of those who suffered. Sherrill's stalking of Mari was only one small example of the challenges Sherrill faced every day. Her inability to control her urges, a second, and probably the one that got her out there on the pine-needle-strewn ground.

Except that no matter how she came at it, it wasn't exactly Sherrill's style to go for a moonlight meander in the woods. She loved fine hotels, expensive vodka, and sexy women. Not that Mari thought of herself as a sexy woman. Smart, yes, but she always believed Sherrill, despite her never-ending pursuit of beautiful women, had been attracted to her more because of her uniform, combined with her confidence. Mari had no idea how many one-night stands Sherrill had during the course of the relationship, both in and out of the marriage. For a long time, she pretended it wasn't happening. In the end, she couldn't ignore the truth.

But who could have gotten her out there and away from a nice soft bed and an evening of dirty martinis in a hotel room? Midnight strolls anywhere, like Paris, a definite yes, but out where her body now lay, a definite no. She voiced her thoughts.

Addie tapped her pen against the small binder that now lay on the kitchen table. "Sex. That's my educated guess." She picked up the mug of coffee Wyatt set in front of her and sipped. Out in the backyard, Tuesday threw a ball for Tripper as a reward for all his hours waiting patiently in the truck. He raced across the yard,

SHERI LEWIS WOHL

grabbed the ball, and returned it to Tuesday, dropping it at her feet, tail wagging.

She took the mug Wyatt offered her. "Thanks." The coffee was hot and fragrant. Nothing like the swill Ollie tried to pass off as dark brew.

"You need cream or sugar?"

She shook her head. "No need to mess up perfectly good coffee."

"My kind of woman." Wyatt smiled and touched her on the shoulder. She almost shuddered at the contact, though not in a bad way.

Mari sank to a chair opposite Addie. "She was always game for a good hookup. Thing is, I've never known her to take it outside. In a car, sure. On the ground?" She shook her head. "She didn't like to get dirty. Too unrefined for her tastes."

"She married a forest ranger. I respectfully dispute the unrefined notion. There's nothing more glorious than the great outdoors." Wyatt voiced the obvious. "Love is blind, I suppose."

"Not as much blind as defiant. I was a challenge she had to conquer." The thought had been flattering in the beginning. Later, she'd realized it was always a game to Sherrill. If she couldn't have something, or someone, she didn't let go until she got it.

"And possess." Addie was making notes again. "Typical of a stalker. Have to possess the forbidden fruit."

"I didn't get that part until I left her. She didn't really want me. Didn't want anyone else to have me either. She didn't share her possessions even if she'd tossed them aside for something new and shiny."

"You're not a possession." Bitterness sounded in Wyatt's voice. The kind of response normal people had in a situation like hers.

"To Sherrill, I was." That had been a hard pill to swallow. Through their time together, it had become more and more clear that she was a *thing* to Sherrill and not a soul mate to love and cherish. They had come from completely different worlds, and

• 142 •

though Mari didn't like to admit the truth, it had taken her a while to catch on. The love-is-blind thing applied in her case.

"She was messed up." Once more Wyatt put a hand on her shoulder, and it felt nice. Her energy rolled through Mari in a warm and comforting way. It was strange to have this kind of support from a woman, or maybe it was because, after Sherrill, she'd put up walls tall enough that no one could scale them. Until now.

Mari leaned into Wyatt's touch. "More than you can possibly know. Her problems could keep a good therapist in business for decades." She caught herself again. "Could have kept a therapist in business."

"What did I miss?" Tuesday leaned against the back door, Tripper drinking loudly from the water bowl Wyatt had set down for him. Mari thought more of the water went flying onto the floor than he actually drank.

Mari looked away from Tripper and his water bowl, and over at Tuesday. "We haven't made a whole lot of ground yet. Still brainstorming."

"I'm here to help." Tuesday poured herself a mug of coffee and sat next to Addie.

Mari didn't mind getting off the current flow of conversation. It reminded her too much of her own failings. Of how she'd been blind to the giant red flags waving right in front of her face. She liked to believe she was smarter than that. The evidence said she wasn't. "Four brains are better than three."

"Mari's right. Let's put our collective intelligence to work and think through what we know." Addie shifted to all business again. "At the bar for a drink or two. Talks to this Inez for a minute. Leaves the bar. We don't know if it was with Inez because they drove separate cars." Addie scanned their faces. "Where's her car?"

Wyatt stood up straighter. "Good point. No other vehicles were out there when we pulled in, so how did she get to the woods?"

Mari frowned. "She always drove, and I mean always, no matter how many drinks she'd had. Part of her control-freak nature. Here's the thing. If she did drive out there, then someone took her car. I say let's go find it." She stood and headed outside.

❖

Before Royal could go inside and confront Inez again, he had to go for a walk. Her mess could cause him real problems. Addressing her while furious wouldn't help much. A true leader thought things through and stayed calm and focused even in the eye of a storm.

He strode away from the house, covering the yard and striding between the rows of raised gardens. He left those behind as well, continuing to where the trees bordered the property. The late-afternoon sun was warm on his face, the air still. The wild grasses were green, the pine trees thick, the quiet complete. Problem-solving in the peace that came from nature worked well. His heartbeat slowed, and his breath came easy. As did clarity.

Ten minutes later, he returned to the house. Inez sat on the sofa, her feet up, a laptop on her legs. "Are you signed up for the next workshop with Wyatt?"

"Yeah." She leaned back and made a face. "I'm going to sing songs around the campfire with a bunch of urban women who think they're survivalists. Doesn't that sound like all kinds of fun? I can hardly wait." She stuck her index finger in her mouth and made a gagging motion.

For a woman her age, she hadn't gotten over childish behaviors. "You'll do it, and you'll like it."

She rolled her eyes. "Sure. It will be the best."

"You'll pretend if you have to."

"You're the boss."

"I am."

"You're a prick."

She was getting dangerously close to stepping over a line. He stared into her eyes. "Watch it."

She stared back. "Or what?"

"Do you really want to find out?" His voice went low, a hint of a growl. His heartbeat picked up again.

She looked away. "Fine. I'll show up for the damn workshop, and I'll play my part like I'm up for an Oscar."

"That's a start." His voice returned to normal.

Her head snapped up, her eyes back on his face. "What do you mean?"

"I mean you'll be moving to the room downstairs. Today." The time for his little surprise had arrived. She'd used up her last chance.

"Wait, what? That room with the lock on the outside?"

"That's the one."

"No." Not a particularly strong denial.

"Yes." His voice went hard.

"You can't make me move in there. It's not a bedroom. It's a cell." A hint of fear.

"Exactly."

"No." She didn't like to give up, and he'd anticipated her resistance.

"You want to test me? It's simple, Inez. Actions. Consequences." He had his hands in his pockets and stood leaning against the wall as if nothing in the world bothered him.

Something like real fear shone from her eyes. Finally, she was catching on. "I'll behave."

"You've already told me that, more than once, and now we can expect the police to show up, thanks to your fun and games. Again, actions have consequences."

She shook her head. "No, no. They don't have any way of knowing it was me. I don't leave any traces behind. I'm not that dumb."

"Seriously, Inez, did you miss the four women who showed up asking to talk to you? None of them are police, yet they were able to track that woman's movements back to you. If you think the police won't be right behind them, then you're a fool."

"But..." Her lips trembled.

"But nothing. You fucked yourself, and you may have fucked me and Claude as well. Not okay, Inez. Not in the least. We're in damage-control mode. A goat was one thing, but a human is on a completely different level. What else do I need to know? What else have you done that's coming back to haunt us?"

She was shaking her head and then slowly stopped, her gaze meeting his. For a second or two, she stared at him, biting her lip. Finally, she whispered, "Her car."

Ice slid down his spine. "What about her car?"

CHAPTER TWELVE

Before they could leave to search for Sherrill's car, Lloyd came knocking on Wyatt's front door. She showed him into the kitchen, and they all sat back down at the table once again. "Coffee?"

Lloyd took off his cap and laid it on the table, rubbing his face with one hand. "I could sure use one. Thanks."

"Can you tell me how she died?" Mari sat across from Lloyd, her hands clasped so tight her fingers had turned white.

Wyatt wanted to reach out and reassure her. It wasn't the time. Instead, she continued to get Lloyd his coffee, sitting next to Mari after she handed him the mug.

Lloyd looked at Mari for what seemed like half an hour and was probably closer to fifteen seconds, his gray eyes unreadable. "She was murdered." The three words dropped like boulders.

"Lloyd," Wyatt said in the same voice she used on students who were having a particularly difficult day. "We could pretty well tell that when we found her. What aren't you telling us?" She expected him to be a little reticent, but she'd hoped he would open up more than he had done thus far.

"Then why ask me?" An edge of irritation colored his voice. Okay, so she didn't blame him being tense. Murder didn't happen often around here, and it had already turned into a long day. Still, not their fault, and he didn't need to take his frustration out on them.

"Sorry. I meant to ask if you found anything that might explain why someone would kill her out there?" Mari appeared to gather her courage and was staring at Lloyd. Anxious, yes. Fearful, no. Good for her. He never hesitated to intimidate most people, and Mari was doing a good job of holding her own.

He shook his head. "I wish. Someone did a damn fine job of cleaning up. Shot her in the middle of the forehead and then disappeared like the steam from a boiling pot of water. No clues in the surrounding areas, no nothing that helps us."

"Things like that don't happen around here." Wyatt tapped her fingers on the table. People died, sure. Even an occasional murder of the more garden variety. Angry spouse, cheating partner, drug deal gone bad, unchecked mental illness. But a body dropped in the middle of the forest? New one to her.

"We've had some odd things in the last few months. Nothing major, just out of the norm a touch. Then you show up and…" He stared at Mari.

Wyatt found that implication insulting, and it wasn't even directed at her. She had to think Mari took it the same way too. "It's not me." Mari's voice remained calm and even. Good for her. Stand up to Lloyd and she'd gain his respect.

"It's not her." Wyatt added her own confirmation, not that she had any concrete proof, only what her heart whispered to her.

Lloyd ran his hand through his thinning hair. "I'd be lying and trying for a quick resolution if I said I believed it was you. My instinct tells me it's someone else. Or something else. Have to look at you though. You're the closest one to her, and from all accounts, your relationship was rocky. Police Work 101, look at the person closest to the victim. The vast majority of the time, that's where we find the killer."

Mari narrowed her eyes as she studied Lloyd's face. "Something else? That doesn't make sense. I mean, maybe with the goat, sure. Sherrill? What? A grizzly got ahold of a gun and accidentally shot her?" Mari, like Wyatt, clearly caught that "or something else."

He shook his head. "No. Nothing like that. You might not remember, Wyatt, but my mother was a member of the Crow Tribe of Montana. My whole life, she taught me to understand there is more to the world than what we can see and touch. Today, while we worked that scene, a crow landed on a tree. It perched there and watched."

"That's not so unusual." Wyatt looked at him, also narrowing her eyes. She couldn't quite get a grip on his thought process. This other-worldly thread wasn't like him, and she remembered his dad all too well. A good old boy who held on tight to only what he could see. For Lloyd to lean into the teachings of his mother seemed contradictory to his dad's way of policing.

He leaned back in his chair and swept his gaze over all of them. "Pretty sure it was my mother sending me a message." Matter-of-fact, serious. Definitely not his dad.

Before Wyatt could formulate a response, Addie spoke up. "I understand." Her expression cleared, and something like comprehension shone from her eyes. Why would she embrace that scenario so quickly? Wyatt had seen many things she couldn't quite explain, though she didn't usually jump to the unseen world to solve a problem.

Lloyd looked at Addie with a surprised expression. "You do?"

She nodded. "I have my own experience with seeing what others can't. I've learned to take nothing for granted and pay attention when something comes my way. Like you, I believe your mother sent you a message. What do you think she wanted you to know?"

Wyatt studied Addie now. She'd been polite, interesting, and helpful since the first time they'd met. She'd liked her right away and not just because Tuesday loved her. Now she saw her differently, an aura around her that Wyatt hadn't paid attention to before. As though otherworldly spirits stood with her and helped guide her toward the truth. Wyatt no longer wondered how Addie had become such a successful private investigator. Or how she'd finally uncovered the truth about her brother's disappearance all those years ago. She possessed that *something* that couldn't be taught or learned. It just was.

Lloyd put both hands on the table and took a deep breath. "That crow dropped a tooth."

"A tooth?" This conversation had taken a left turn somewhere along the line, and while Wyatt wanted to follow, she remained lost. Crows loved to pick up trinkets, shiny things that caught their attention. And they were known to bring gifts to humans. A dime. A lost earring. A discarded piece of foil. Odd as a tooth might be, she wouldn't think anything other than the crow liked it.

Lloyd nodded. "Mom's way of telling me to keep an open mind and look beyond the obvious."

"Obvious how?" Still not following. Judging by everyone else's expressions, they weren't either. Usually, law enforcement followed more of a straight line, one that didn't include gifts from crows or messages from an unseen universe. Lloyd had something in mind, but his route to it was far from straight.

"It was the tooth of a wolf. A big one."

Mari sat back in her chair and rolled through her mind everything she'd just heard. A wolf's tooth. She leaned forward and put her arms on the table. "I did my homework before I took this job, and wolves are out there. It's entirely normal for one to lose a tooth." She really wasn't getting how this would factor into Sherrill's murder.

His lips pressed together, Lloyd nodded. "True enough. Packs of wolves are part of the wildlife in our world and not that unusual anymore. The packs are growing all over."

"So, what? Why would that be a message from your mother? It's not unusual for crows pick up random things."

Tuesday spoke for the first time, Tripper leaning against her legs and looking as though he took in everything being discussed. Mari wasn't so sure he didn't understand it all. His eyes and expression said he did. "Fenrir."

Not quite what she expected to hear. Mari held up her hands. "Fenrir? And that means what?" Maybe it was the stress that had her questioning everything. She couldn't get a handle on where any of this discussion might be going, and she'd never heard of Fenrir, whatever that meant. Did anybody else get it, or was it just her?

Tuesday spoke up. "Beware of the wolf. In folk legends, Fenrir is a powerful werewolf that grows in strength and is intent on destruction. To quote Voluspa, 'Much have I traveled, much have I tried out, much have I tested the Powers; from where will a sun come into the smooth heaven when Fenrir has assailed this one?'"

They all stared at Tuesday, which made Mari feel a little better. She hadn't been the only one lost.

"What?" Addie smiled, though she looked as confused as Mari felt. "A werewolf? An old legend? And you memorized that?"

Tuesday shrugged. "I like dogs and am thus drawn to things that involve them, like folklore. Fenrir appears as a massive wolf that resembles a German shepherd. Naturally, I'm interested. Some things just stick with you. The legend of Fenrir is one of my favorite pieces of trivia."

For a few seconds no one spoke. Mari broke the silence. "Are you implying that we have a werewolf running around killing animals and shooting my ex-wife?"

Lloyd shook his head. "Not sure I'm ready to go that far yet."

"But?" Wyatt put a hand on Mari's shoulder, her touch soothing.

"But I'm going to heed the warning from my mother and keep an open mind." Lloyd's voice remained calm and even, his earlier stern words and attitude long gone. Mari was impressed by his demeanor, given both the murder and the bizarre theory Tuesday had just thrown out.

Lloyd left shortly after making his seemingly paranormal declaration. Mari stayed sitting at the table as Wyatt walked him out. She looked at Tuesday and Addie. "What do you two think? A werewolf? That's straight out of a horror movie, and this is, unfortunately, way too real. I like to think I have an open mind, but I'm not sure it's that open."

Tuesday went to the back door and let Tripper out into the yard once more. Then she returned and sat across from Mari. "I don't know. You're right. A werewolf seems pretty unlikely, except..." She looked over at Addie. "I've seen things during the last couple of years that have left me with a mind way more receptive to unseen forces than it had been before. I have to think that Fenrir popped into my head because the universe is sending us a message."

"Me as well," Addie said. "I don't tell many people, but I'm going to trust you. I have visions. Have had them for years. It's part of what brought me and Tuesday together. It's also how we ended a reign of death and destruction. I don't take anything for granted anymore. If messages are sent from beyond, I pay attention."

Mari listened and processed their words. Still had trouble getting there with them. Her whole career had been out in the wilderness and, to date, not one werewolf sighting. Not a single brush with anything paranormal. "Meaning, you believe it could be a werewolf."

Tuesday held her gaze. No mocking—straightforward and sincere. "Stranger things and all that."

"I'm a touch, feel, and see kind of person." Mari wanted to believe she had an open mind, and in many respects she did. Mythical creatures like werewolves, vampires, and ghosts were about as likely as a unicorn. She couldn't make the leap to get there.

"I was too." Tuesday leaned closer and took one of her hands. "Trust me. I was right where you are not that long ago. Sometimes, things aren't what they seem."

She believed it to be more real world. "Someone shot Sherrill. Not a wolf. Not a werewolf. A person with a gun in their hand and pointed in her face. Stalking me or not, she didn't deserve that."

Wyatt came back into the kitchen and once again put a hand on Mari's shoulder. She could get used to that. Tuesday let go of her hand and leaned back in her chair, still gazing at her.

Wyatt jumped in. "We'll figure this out. The killer will be caught. Look. Lloyd is a good investigator, and I know in my heart that we'll get the answers we're seeking. Whoever did this to Sherrill will not get away with it. He'll find the culprit and bring them to justice. You just have to trust the process."

Whether a human monster or a preternatural creature had killed Sherrill didn't matter as much as the fact she was dead. Guilt pressed like a mountain of boulders on Mari's shoulders. "I hate that she died because of me." The words were hard to get out when she felt like sobbing.

"How in the world can you think that? All of us here know you didn't have anything to do with her murder. Right?" Wyatt looked at Tuesday and Addie.

"She's right," Tuesday said. "Look. I'm a former probation officer, and Addie here is not only a PI but a former cop. We know bad when we see it, and you aren't bad. Someone else did this. Not your fault."

"Except it is." They were missing the big picture.

"How can you think that?" Now Wyatt kneeled next to her chair and took both of her hands. Warm. Comforting.

Mari stared into her eyes and willed the tears not to fall. "Because Sherrill was here only because of me. If I'd stayed in Portland, she'd still be alive."

Royal stared out the back window, a couple of deer running across the field, jumping over the fences as easily as he could step over a pebble. Beautiful creatures and plentiful here. He'd always been drawn to nature. Maybe what had come his way had been preordained. It felt natural enough. Not at first, if he were being honest. In time, though, he'd come to feel at home with it. Like wearing a favorite pair of slippers he never wanted to take off, and that gave him at least a whisper of understanding for how Inez felt.

Nature carried responsibilities he'd come to appreciate as the years rolled on. He gazed at Inez, who sat on the deck, her feet on the railing, a vaping pen in her hand, and smoke trailing out of her mouth. The fruits of her trip to the dope store. Normally, he'd tell her no, that it was dangerous for those like them to indulge in mood-altering drugs regardless of their legality. Nothing to do with that and everything to do with their unique nature. Right now, he didn't care. It didn't matter anymore. How much more damage could she do? A voice in the back of his head whispered: a lot. He ignored it.

Claude came into the kitchen. "You need me?"

He'd texted Claude after Wyatt and her friends left. Took him a while to think through all the options. He kept coming back to one, so he'd drafted another email to the council. This time, he didn't hold back, and their response had been swift.

Royal handed Claude a piece of paper. "You need to take Inez to the airport in Missoula. Here's her ticket information."

Claude read it, his eyebrows rising. "Back to Vancouver."

"The council will meet her at the airport."

Claude's smile was triumphant. "About time. Told you she needed to go."

"Can't risk her staying here any longer. Not after she killed that woman." He hated even saying that fact out loud. They were able to assimilate as well as they did because they didn't take chances, and they sure as hell didn't kill people. Inez had messed up. He'd really wanted to make it work with her. She belonged to him, yet at some moments in life one had to accept the truth rather than continue to hold on to wishful thinking. He leaned into the former today. Bringing her into the fold had been a critical error, and now he had to make the hard decision to remove her. He never made these decisions lightly.

"Should have done this weeks ago. I've been telling you—"

"I don't need a lecture." In fact, it pissed him off when Claude jumped in with his arrogant told-you-so declarations. Royal supposed growing up pampered and wealthy did that to people. He wouldn't know about that. He'd worked for everything his entire life, including where he'd landed in the council's hierarchy. He'd earned his position. Claude should consider himself lucky to be here at all, should remember that, without Royal, he'd be nothing more than an over-educated rich kid.

"Sorry, man. When do you want me to head out?" His words were respectful, his expression smug. About the best he could hope for.

He decided to ignore Claude's arrogance. Perhaps once Inez was safely back in Canada, Claude would mellow. Not likely, but he could hope. "Now. I want her gone before the sheriff figures out what Wyatt has already. If she's not here, he can't question her. Better yet, if she makes it back to Canada, then it gets even more difficult for them to question her. They can try to extradite, if they can find her." There were packs in the far north that might take her in. Good places to hide and less chance to get into more trouble.

"Got it." Claude walked to the back door and opened it to lean out and shout, "Get your ass moving, princess. We're out of here." The scent from her vape wafted in through the open door.

Inez shot him the finger but still got up and came inside. She gave Royal a sour look. "I knew you were going to kick me out the minute you threatened me with that cell downstairs. I'm already packed."

Every once in a while, she surprised him. The packing, not the grumpy expression. "Someone from the council will meet you at the airport in Vancouver."

"A babysitter." She frowned. "I'm not a little kid."

"No babysitter, more like a probation officer. You're running out of grace, Inez, and, trust me, they are not going to be as lenient with you as I am. What's the old saying? You just shot yourself in the foot."

"Ha-ha. To be clear, both of my feet are fine because I'm a damn fine shot." The defiance in her eyes wouldn't play well with those who awaited her appearance in Vancouver. Inez would find out soon enough that she should have behaved here. She wouldn't be pleased by the plans the council had for her or the place they'd be taking her. The action she longed for would be far, far away.

"You need to get to the airport now. Your flight leaves in three hours. Do not miss it." He used the same tone of voice on her that he did with students who fucked around in his classes. Whether professor or leader, he leaned into his authority. Sometimes being a buddy wasn't in the cards. "Do I make myself clear?"

She gave him a salute before she turned to Claude. "I have to pee, and then we can go. Grab my bag, will you, pretty boy?" She didn't wait to hear Claude's response.

"Sometimes, I really hate her," Claude said as he turned in the direction of her room and the bag she said she'd packed.

"Only sometimes?"

Claude laughed. "Got that right, chief. Most of the time she gets on my last good nerve."

"You have a good nerve?"

"Ha-ha."

Claude had never been a fan of Inez. Royal had hoped that, given time, their mutual strengths would mesh, and they'd find the kind of harmony that would make them all stronger. That plan had crashed and burned pretty much from day one. Optimistic by nature, he'd kept hoping. The hope died with that gunshot. Defeat didn't taste good.

"Hurry and get her there on time. Just don't drive so fast you get pulled over." If she missed the evening flight, there wouldn't be another until tomorrow. He wanted her out of Montana and out of the United States before everything blew up.

"Copy that." Claude returned a minute later with the bag. Inez blew past him and out the door. "Call you on the way back."

"Please do." He wanted confirmation that trouble was flying north.

The silence after they left was marked. For a couple of minutes Royal stood in the doorway to Inez's room. Where did she hide the gun? She might be on her way out of the country, but the gun better still be here. No way to take it across the border, and she should know that. Not to say she wouldn't try anyway. Inez had a little bit of the same entitlement attitude that Claude did, as though rules meant for the masses didn't apply to either of them. Trying to take a gun on any flight, whether domestic or international, wouldn't go well. Could mean jail for her. He wanted to believe she wouldn't be that foolish and make their troubles even worse.

He searched the drawers of her dresser. Nothing. Next, he checked under the bed and in the closet. Again, nothing. Two scenarios came to mind. She either was stupid enough to try to take the weapon with her on the plane or she got rid of it somewhere. How he hoped she'd opted for the latter. He left her room and went out into the backyard. He took off his shoes and stood barefoot in the grass, searching for the calming waves of the earth to steady him.

Running a hand through his hair, he breathed in and out. He didn't realize how much chaos Inez had brought with her until she wasn't here. Even with the threat of the missing gun, a bit of peace settled over him. Not naive enough to think she was home free by returning to Canada. Relieved nonetheless that things here would be quieter for the time being. Bringing in the council and sending her away bought him the time he needed. What happened to Inez after that, he didn't much care.

CHAPTER THIRTEEN

Mari lost it. She rested her head on the table and cried. Her shoulders shook, and tears dropped to the floor.

Wyatt's heart hurt for her, and, in a way, she understood how Mari could feel the murder was at least partially her fault. She was wrong though. The only one to bear responsibility was whoever had killed her ex-wife. Period.

"No. No. No." Wyatt scooted a chair next to her and put an arm around her shoulders. "You are not responsible in any way for what happened to her."

"She followed me," Mari said through tears.

Wyatt continued to hold Mari, hoping that in some way it gave her a measure of comfort. "That's on her. She chose to turn up here and harass you. Remember that fact. No. It doesn't mean she deserved to die. It only means she didn't have to come here, and her decision to follow you is one hundred percent on her."

"I feel so guilty." Mari sat up and wiped her eyes. She didn't move away from Wyatt. "She had no business out in the forest."

"Wyatt's right." Tuesday sat on the other side of her. "People make their own choices, and the consequences of those rest with them. You didn't ask her to follow you to Montana. Hell. You didn't want her to come. Remember free will. And that means none of this is on you, and you sure as heck didn't drag her out into the forest to get shot."

Across the table, Addie tapped her fingers. "You can also be damn sure we've got your back. We know you had nothing to do with the murder, and we'll walk with you every step of the way to prove it."

Mari swept her gaze over everyone's face, her eyes still damp and filled with sorrow. "Why put yourself out for a stranger? You don't really know me. I'm a stranger."

Wyatt tapped her chest. "We know you here. There's a lot to be said for instinct. Right, ladies?" She looked over at Tuesday and Addie, who both nodded.

Addie jumped in. "Tuesday and I have both dealt with the worst society has to offer, and those experiences have left us with finely tuned bullshit detectors. They're not going off with you."

"True story." Tuesday touched her shoulder. "No strangers here. You're one of us now. New friends are as important as old ones." She smiled as she looked over at Wyatt. "Not that I'm calling anyone old."

Wyatt laughed, and the tension in the room faded. She tapped the corners of her eyes with her index fingers. "Hey. I earned these wrinkles fair and square."

"Right." Addie rolled her eyes. "Talk to me about wrinkles in a few more years." She touched the side of her eye and then put a hand on her hair. "And the white hairs sneaking in."

"I don't see any white." Mari smiled, and a bit of the darkness left her eyes.

"Get a little closer. I hide it well. Give yourself another five, ten years, and you'll be here too."

"If I look as good as you do, I'll take it." Mari sat up taller, her eyes puffy, but the tears were gone.

"So." Wyatt took both of Mari's hands, grateful to feel the trembling in them lessen. "What's our next move?"

Addie looked out the kitchen window before turning back to them. "Dinner."

"A most excellent idea." Wyatt got up, went to the refrigerator, and started pulling out vegetables, lemons, and a bag of fish fillets.

"Given everything today, I shouldn't be hungry, except I am. Go figure."

An hour later, Wyatt pulled the steelhead out of the oven, the scent of lemon and butter wafting through the kitchen. She loaded the platter with the fish and set it on the tray, along with roasted potatoes and steamed veggies. Then she carried it all out to the patio table.

"Having any luck with the fire?" Addie, Tuesday, and Mari stood around the firepit, and they stepped aside to reveal a healthy blaze.

"We got it." Mari waved toward the flames. Made Wyatt happy to see all traces of her earlier despair gone. "All ready for a fireside dinner."

"Let me get the wine, and we're set." Wyatt returned to the kitchen and grabbed the bottle of dandelion wine out of the refrigerator, along with a marrow bone she'd pulled from the freezer earlier.

Wine poured, plates filled, and Tripper happily chewing on the bone, the women sat in chairs around the fire and balanced dinner plates on their knees. "This is great." Mari smiled and waved her fork toward her plate. "I'm guessing all you too?"

Wyatt smiled. They hadn't known each other long, yet Mari already got her. "Nine-pound steelhead that, yes, I caught, and my grandmother's recipe for the dandelion wine."

"I've never had it before." Mari held up the glass toward the setting sun, making the wine look golden. "The wine, I mean, not the fish. I like it."

"Me too." Tuesday smiled. "Trust me, a lowly dandelion would never have made it past *Mother.*"

Wyatt understood Tuesday's tone of disdain when speaking of her mother. Or the woman she'd believed to be her mother until recently. Long-buried secrets had been uncovered when Tuesday and Addie solved the secret of Addie's missing brother. One of those secrets had turned out to be that the woman who'd raised Tuesday wasn't her biological mother. Tuesday had been relieved rather than appalled. The two had never been close, and that was putting it nicely. They were still searching for the identity of her birth mother.

"If I'd known it tasted this good, I'd have been trying my hand at this." Mari smiled and took another sip. "I had a yard full of dandelions because I refused to put chemicals on my lawn. Drove the neighbors nuts, but the bees were pretty delighted about it."

Wyatt gave her a salute with her glass. "I'll be happy to give you wine-making lessons."

"Is there anything you can't do?" Mari looked around. "I mean, seriously, look at all of this. Amazing."

Wyatt loved her life, and Mari's admiration didn't hurt one iota. A shed full of split wood ready to fuel her stove for the winter. A freezer full of meat and a pantry stocked with preserved foods. Should the world crumble around her, Wyatt would be well-fed and warm for quite a long time. She glanced over at Mari. Room to keep at least one other person in comfort too. "There's lots I can't do." Not modesty, truth. She always had more to learn, and she loved that fact. Kept life interesting.

Mari made a sound. "Doesn't look like it to me."

"I can attest that she could use some work on a thing or two." Addie took a sip of her wine and smiled.

"Oh?" Mari appeared interested.

Addie set her glass down and looked at Wyatt with a sly smile. "Oh, yeah. She sucks as a detective. We've tried to teach her, but she's a resistant student."

Tuesday chuckled and patted Addie on the arm.

Wyatt frowned at her, though she didn't appear to mean it. "Hey. I resent that. Did I or did I not get us to the bar today? And your lessons were over video anyway so they don't count. Learning to be a PI requires face-to-face instruction."

"Oh yeah, the bar. All luck, and if you recall, it was Addie who suggested the video." Tuesday patted her shoulder.

"Humph." She picked up her own wineglass and sipped. These moments of levity did her heart good. She hoped they helped Mari too.

They ate, laughed, and, for a little bit, didn't think about the tragedy that had brought them together tonight. Wyatt figured it still lingered in Mari's mind, as it did in hers. No way it couldn't. Too close to home for all of them. Well, maybe not Tuesday and Tripper. For them, finding the dead was a calling. She figured Addie, in both her careers, had seen her fair share too. For Wyatt, human death was confined to the natural cycle of life. In other words, the loss of her parents and grandparents—the normal events that everyone had to deal with eventually.

Murder was new, and she had to believe the same applied to Mari. A divorce didn't mean that Mari no longer cared about Sherrill. That she'd moved on didn't either. She didn't see the ugliness in her that attached to people who couldn't move forward after heartbreak. The ones who believed in retribution and prolonged pain. Rather, the pain she saw in Mari now spoke of her being a good and kind person. Someone with empathy and an ability to forgive. Made her want to help even more.

The plates set aside and wineglasses topped off, they all sat in silence, staring at the fire as the sun set to the west. Wyatt turned the glass in her hand, the sweet scent of the wine wafting up, the flames flickering off the golden liquid. If not for murder hanging over their gathering, it would be a beautiful evening.

"Tomorrow, we look for her car." Addie stood and turned toward the woods at the farm's edge.

"How do we know what she was driving? She'd have rented a car in Missoula, right?" Tuesday leaned forward, wineglass in her hand, elbows on her knees.

"Not exactly," Mari said. "She drove from Portland in a brand-new Range Rover, kind of lighter gray or silver."

"Excellent. That shouldn't be too hard to find. Not everyone can afford one of those babies. I think they're close to a hundred thousand." Tuesday sat up. Tripper crunched on his bone. She leaned toward him. "Don't you dare break a tooth." She ran a hand over his big head.

"Hey." Addie still stared out into the darkness. "Do you see that?"

Wyatt walked over and followed the direction of Addie's gaze, all conversation about the expensive vehicle Sherill had been driving disappearing. What the hell? "Is that a wolf?"

Mari joined them. "Sure looks like it to me. Is that something you see a lot?"

Wyatt shook her head, staring at the wolf. It didn't move from where it stood in the shadow of the trees. Almost as though it stared right back at her. "No."

The wolf, not quite hidden in the darkness, stood stock still. Wyatt looked over her shoulder, where Tuesday had taken ahold of Tripper's collar even though he stayed right by her side. Any other dog would have raced into the forest in pursuit of the threat. Not this guy. Once again, he massively impressed her.

"What's it doing?" Wyatt had never seen a wolf this close to the house before. Could the fire be bringing it in? No. That didn't make sense either. She'd used the fire pit many times without attracting a single animal. Besides, a wolf or any of the forest creatures would be more likely to move away from a fire, not move toward it.

"Staring." Mari stated the obvious.

"Why?" Addie asked.

"You think it's hungry and eyeing your livestock?" Mari asked an excellent question.

Wyatt glanced toward the pastures. The goats were skittish. No surprise there. They'd sense the wolf, and it would make them nervous. A predator had a way of affecting likely prey. She looked back at the wolf. While a fair distance away, she felt certain of one thing: it stared right at her.

❖

Uneasiness flowed through Mari. The way the wolf stood motionless, its gaze steady, struck her as odd. Stalking wasn't out of the realm of possibility, but near an open flame? Pretty unlikely unless the animal was sick or injured. That didn't appear to be the case here. It was displaying too much control, its behavior very odd.

She glanced at Wyatt, and her facial expression made Mari grab her hand. "Are you all right?" It was her turn to show comfort and compassion.

Wyatt squeezed her hand as she shook her head. "I'm okay. I just don't like it." She nodded in the direction of the wolf. "It's acting so unusual."

At the edge of the forest, it suddenly lifted its head and howled for a few seconds, then turned and ran into the darkness of the woods behind it. The four of them, well, five, counting Tripper, continued to stare as though they had night vision and could follow every strike of its paws on the hard-packed earth. The pop of a log in the firepit caused Mari to jump and spin, her heart racing.

"Well," she said as she let go of Wyatt's hand. "That was pretty interesting." Her heartbeat slowed to normal as the logs popped a few more times, sparks rising into the air like tiny fireflies.

"Interesting in a creepy way that makes me want to bring all my livestock into the house." Wyatt sat and picked up her glass of wine. She drained it. "Never had one come this close before. Since I can't bring the animals into the house, I may have to look into a guard dog. Tuesday, I'm betting you know some good breeders and can help me train it."

Tuesday let go of Tripper and patted the top of his head. He stood and stared in the direction the wolf had run, though he didn't move from Tuesday's side. "Yes and yes. For now, we have my boy. He'll hear if anything comes close and let you know," Tuesday said.

Wyatt nodded. "Appreciate the good work, Tripper." She leaned over and patted his head too. "I have more bones in the freezer, and they're all yours if you keep us safe, buddy."

"Maybe everyone goes in the barn tonight?" Mari didn't think they should leave anyone outside. Wyatt had a small barn, and though she hadn't been inside it, from here it looked big enough for the animals she kept on the farm.

Wyatt nodded. "That's a grand plan."

"We're going to walk the perimeter." Tuesday stood and tapped her leg. Tripper jumped up, leaving the bone. No words appeared necessary. He knew the drill.

"You think that's wise?" Mari didn't. Something wasn't right with that wolf, and she worried about it hiding in the darkness, waiting and watching. It could do some serious damage to Tripper and to any of them if they got caught in a fight.

"We'll be fine." Until Addie spoke, Mari hadn't realized that while they'd been staring at the wolf, Addie had gone out to her vehicle and returned with a handgun in a holster now clipped to her belt. She patted the grip. "You two get everyone inside, and we'll make sure our visitor has left the immediate area. If not," she patted the gun again, "I'll take care of him."

"Come on." Wyatt held out her hand to Mari. "Help me get them in." She nodded toward the pasture.

Mari took her hand and thought once more about how much she liked doing it. Something she could get used to. Was she really that starved for affection that she grabbed onto someone who showed her simple kindness? Though it felt like a true connection, she suspected she was reading more into it than existed. A trauma response combined with arriving here with basement-level self-esteem after the major job snub. As confident as she typically was, that whole situation had hurt her at a deep level, and it would take some time to heal. In the meantime, she had to get a grip on her emotions and not embarrass herself. She liked Wyatt and didn't want to lose her as a friend by misconstruing an offer of friendship as attraction.

Getting her thoughts in line, she let go of Wyatt's hand. "Let's herd them in."

They made a good team. Within fifteen minutes, they had the animals in the barn with food and water, and the door secured. They were back in the kitchen when Addie, Tuesday, and Tripper walked in. Tripper sat at the door, a restored antique with glass panels top to bottom, staring out into the night.

Mari looked at Tuesday. "Did he find something? He seems intent on continuing his guard duties."

Tuesday shook her head. "No. The wolf isn't nearby any longer. Tripper didn't so much as twitch as we walked the edge of the woods. Whatever that wolf was doing, he apparently finished and went back to wherever he came from."

"He?" Mari hadn't been able to determine whether it had been male or female. Granted, it had appeared quite large, which hinted at male. Without closer inspection, she couldn't be sure.

This time Tuesday shrugged. "It felt male. Could be wrong. Just going with the gut."

Mari glanced at Wyatt. She got gut. "Probably right. Maybe it was a dad trying to warn us away from its den. Mama and pups could be nearby, and he wanted to let us know to steer clear."

Wyatt spoke up. "No." They all turned to look at her. "I routinely hike out there, and trust me, if a wolf den was nearby, I'd know. Nothing this close in."

"Maybe they moved in recently." That possibility still made the most sense to Mari.

Wyatt shook her head. "Not likely. They wouldn't make a den this close to humans. They'd be way farther into the woods. And, again, I'd have seen signs of them. I know this area better than most, and I'm telling you, no den out there. I don't know what that guy was doing, but if you weren't here with us already, I'd be calling the forest-service office to report."

"With you," Mari told her. She also knew she had to be honest with them and not overstate her knowledge and expertise. "I'll have to read up on the wolf stats, but I tend to agree that it seems odd how close he came. I'll do some research."

Wyatt looked out the window. "I say we get some rest, and tomorrow we can revisit everything."

"I should probably go home." Mari turned toward the front of the house.

"That's a no." Wyatt put a hand on her shoulder. "You stay here. That bag you packed was for a good reason."

"I should be safe." *Should* was the operative word, though she kept that thought to herself.

"Sure. Like Sherrill was?" Wyatt hit a bull's-eye.

"Not the same?" Mari didn't put herself in harm's way as a general rule, and sleeping at her home didn't seem like harm's way.

"How do you know? Maybe it wasn't about her. Maybe it was about hurting you."

She stood stock-still as Wyatt's word hit her like a brick to the head. "But I haven't done anything to anyone." Mari said the words, but a chill filled her, and suddenly, she wondered if she'd ever feel warm again.

❖

Might have been stupid on his part, but he wanted to see Wyatt. No. That wasn't even close to what he'd felt. It had been more that he *had* to see her. Remind himself of the future that awaited on the other side of the Harvest Moon. Once that happened, all the trouble since moving here would evaporate. His world would fall into place as it was destined to do.

With Inez touching down in Vancouver in a couple of hours, his confidence about the new order grew solid. Claude, while sometimes acting like a spoiled child, or rather regressing to the spoiled child he'd always been, made a positive impact on them all. Smart and handsome, he had a way of attracting attention, which worked for Royal. Eyes on Claude kept eyes off him. He wanted to fly under the radar long enough to get his house in order. Closer now that Inez wouldn't be around to attract unnecessary attention.

Despite the risk he took earlier by going to Wyatt's, the run had been invigorating. Unlike Inez, it had been a while since he'd let loose and enjoyed nature as he was meant to. Worth the chance he'd taken, both to see Wyatt and to feel the earth, the wind, the moonlight. It all left him feeling at home and alive.

Now invigorated, showered, and in clean clothes, Royal let the good vibes fill him. Glancing at his watch, he figured Claude should be rolling in any time, while Inez would be safely on a plane to Vancouver. Claude had a different relationship with Inez than he did, and he was interested to hear what she'd told him during their trip to Missoula. He suspected she'd open up to him more than she would ever do with Royal and, likely, had spent the entire time bitching about him. A bit like he was the parent and Claude was the trusted sibling. Not totally inaccurate, even though they weren't related by blood. And like siblings, they could fight and squabble and scream at each other, but still protect each other and share everything.

He took a glass of iced tea to the living room and sat in one of the comfortable chairs. His feet up on the ottoman, he watched out the window, waiting for the shine of the headlights from Claude's car to slice through the darkness. Tapping the screen of his phone, he frowned at the time. Claude should be close, if not actually back here by now. Full-on dark had taken over, the sky filled with stars and a bright moon.

Royal had directed Claude to drive straight to the airport and then to return straight home. To call him when he was headed back. He usually followed directions better than this. Not completely accurate, but accurate enough that Claude could follow directions very well. He could also deviate on a whim. He supposed it also came from his spoiled upbringing. From the stories Claude had shared with him, he'd been a lonely child with little to no supervision. Made Royal a bit sad. His own parents, though now gone, had been attentive and fun. They'd encouraged him to pursue his dreams and didn't even blink when he announced his move north. Different country though not far enough away he wasn't able to be here when the end came for each. Royal wasn't sure Claude ever saw his parents. For that matter, he wasn't sure they were even still alive. He never talked about them, at least not in the present tense.

A sweep of lights at last cut across the darkness outside. Another glance at the time on his phone. At least double what it actually took for a round-trip to Missoula. A lot of interesting watering holes between here and there though, and it had been a bit since Claude had let loose. Since coming here, he'd primarily focused his energies on building the massive gardens and doing a tiny bit of studying ahead of the upcoming bar exam. He supposed

Claude deserved a little fun, especially in light of the stress Inez put on them because she was bored. Because she could. For a few reasons, he would miss her. For a lot more, he wouldn't.

Claude walked in whistling. "Trouble is gone. Thank God for small favors." He bowed as if he were the lead actor in a successful play accepting the applause of his dedicated fans.

"You got her on the plane?" Inez didn't follow him through the door, so an unnecessary question. Still felt like he had to ask, that little niggling sensation telling him not to take anything at face value.

He shrugged. "Didn't see her get on a plane."

"But you did drop her off."

"I did, indeed, as requested. Problem solved."

A whiff of relief floated over him. He wished it felt more solid. "The council will take it from here." He had faith in the elders of the council. They'd seen it all. Inez wouldn't be as much of a challenge for them as she'd been for him.

"I'm going to turn in." Claude started to head toward his bedroom, but Royal stopped him.

"Where have you been?" Casual as Claude might be, things weren't adding up. He'd made a stop or three somewhere along the line. Important to know where and why. Didn't need any more surprise problems.

Claude looked at him for a moment as though formulating a response. The pause didn't sit well with Royal. "Had a little fun on the way home," he finally said as he leaned against the wall, his hands in his pockets. Mr. Casual with nothing to hide.

"What kind of fun?" Wariness washed over Royal.

"A drink. A couple of dances." He came up from the wall and did a twirl as if dancing with a woman. His smile was bright. "Your boy has moves."

"And?" He knew Claude well enough to sense when he was holding back. He might very well have stopped for a few dances. There was more.

He pressed his lips together before he finally said, "Might have gone for a little run along the way."

No wonder the rock in his stomach didn't disappear. "I told you to get her to the airport and then come straight back." He'd keep the part about going for a run earlier to himself.

"I came straight back, just a little pause in the middle. Besides, I'm not stupid, and I was careful. Unlike Inez, I don't try to draw attention to myself. I mean, no more than I can with this handsome face." His thousand-watt smile returned.

Not completely accurate. He loved the attention of women and had no problem acting like a male peacock. In the past, he'd confined the peacock posturing to bars. "At least tell me you didn't go for your run anywhere close by."

Claude waved a hand dismissively as he walked away. "You worry too much."

Chapter Fourteen

The scream launched Wyatt. She ran down the hallway to the room where Mari was sleeping. Or had been sleeping. She found her sitting up, the bedside lamp on, her hair wild, eyes blinking.

"What's wrong?" She sat on the edge of the bed and grasped Mari's arm. The trembling in her body vibrated against her hand. She wanted to embrace her until she grew calm once more. She didn't and waited instead for Mari to share with her what had dragged her from sleep.

Mari pulled in a long breath and let it out slowly. "A nightmare. I'm so sorry I bothered you. God. I probably woke up Tuesday and Addie too."

As if on command, Tripper ran in and jumped up on the bed, the weight of his big body causing the mattress to bounce. Tuesday and Addie followed and now stood in the doorway. For a moment Tripper stared into Mari's face, his dark eyes intense, and then he licked her, jumped back down, and joined Tuesday and Addie.

"Are you okay?" Tuesday asked. "We heard your scream. Tripper seems to think all is well now."

Mari nodded. "I'm really sorry I woke you all up." She ran a hand through her tousled hair. "A bad dream. Please go back to bed and, Tripper, thanks." She smiled at the dog, who wagged his tail before turning and disappearing down the hall, his nails tapping softly on the hardwood floors.

"Yup," Tuesday told her. "You've been cleared by the resident security expert."

Wyatt nodded briefly. The tension she'd felt in the room when she first stepped through the doorway had faded. Whatever demons had filled Mari's mind and pulled her violently from sleep had lost their power in the time since they'd come to her aid and the warm light of the lamp had pushed away the shadows. She waited until she heard the click of the bedroom door down the hallway. She was alone with Mari, in her bed, and how her heart pounded. Probably should leave and let her rest in peace and quiet. Instead, she pulled her feet up onto the bed and leaned back against the headboard.

"Tell me." Her shoulder bumped against Mari's and stayed there.

Mari leaned her head back and stared at the ceiling for maybe ten seconds. She didn't pull away. "You're going to think I've lost my mind."

"Try me." She nudged her briefly.

"Dreams are wild, and I'm thinking this one likely came out of the conversation about Fenrir. Tuesday's paranormal theory crept into my dreams."

Wyatt took Mari's hand, squeezing gently. "After today, the last thing I'd think is that you've lost your mind. Way more stress than any one person should be asked to handle, and yet you've done it with grace. Just tell me about it. From the sound of your scream, it wasn't a dream. More like a nightmare. Let me help you work through it," she urged again.

"Okay." Mari relaxed against her a little closer. "Started out with Sherrill running in the woods, laughing. Reminded me of the woman she used to be before mental illness changed her. Before she became a stalker. She was running and laughing, as if everything was right with the world. Then she was on the ground, dead."

"I'm sorry." She was too.

"That's not all." Mari turned to look at her, her eyes intense. "You were there too."

"What? Me?" Did Mari think she had something to do with Sherrill's death? No. How could she? Pretty clear she'd been here with Tuesday and Addie when Sherrill was murdered. Then again, it had been a nightmare, and so often they resembled the real world. Or how someone interpreted the real world anyway. Made her wonder what Mari thought about her.

"Definitely you, running through the woods."

Didn't sound too bad so far, at least in terms of her appearance in the nightmare, and Mari's words held no tone of reproach. "I have been known to run out there." She'd never claim to be a real trail runner, yet at times she needed to hurry. She was fit enough to run at least a mile or two without pain or injury.

Mari was shaking her head. "It wasn't that kind of run, and that's the odd thing about you appearing in my dream."

"Okay? So, what was it?" Wyatt frowned. Maybe being thrown out of deep sleep made it take a while for her to get the whole picture.

Mari stared into her eyes. "You were running from a really large wolf."

That didn't sound too bad or too far away from reality. "That's definitely possible. There are some packs in our mountains, and trust me, I would run from a wolf, screaming like a banshee the whole way. If I couldn't chase him off, I'd be really noisy and make myself as big as possible."

"There's more."

"More?"

"He caught you and bit you on the shoulder. It wasn't seeing Sherrill dead that made me scream. It was the wolf taking you down and sinking its teeth into your flesh."

As Mari said the words, a tingle in Wyatt's left shoulder made her shrug as if she could shoo the sensation away. "That would not be good."

Mari's hand covered hers. "Not quite the end of the nightmare. After the wolf bit you, it morphed into the shape of a man." She shuddered as if she were seeing it all again.

Okay, that was weird, and maybe, as she'd said, Mari's subconscious had grabbed onto their earlier conversation about Fenrir. Not that she actually believed in werewolves. Wyatt leaned more toward accepting the reality behind folk legends rather than believing in mythical creatures. Given she'd spent her entire life in this area, growing up in the wilderness and becoming an expert on it, she'd have come across evidence of something like a werewolf if it actually existed. Wolves, sure. Some had even mentioned dire wolves, though she doubted that one too. Dire wolves had gone extinct at least ten thousand years ago, so if someone told her they'd seen one, she'd ask them how high they were when it happened.

"Like you mentioned, I think the conversation about Fenrir fed your dreams. Toss in all the stress, and it makes sense. Just a dream that bordered on nightmare." She put an arm around her shoulder and hugged her.

Mari leaned into her. "I suppose you're right. A perfect storm. Still, it seemed very real. Not like any dream or nightmare I've ever had before."

Mari didn't sound convinced. "Trust me. Your mind is working overtime because of stress and grief." Wyatt's own grief over the loss of her parents had disrupted her life for months. They had died naturally, which made things a little different. She'd grieved nonetheless, and sleep had been elusive for a while.

"Guilt, maybe," Mari said. "Stress, perhaps. Grief, not really, and that makes me feel worse than anything. Shouldn't I feel sad at her death? I mean, I do somewhat. I also feel relieved, and that can't be right. What person is relieved when another loses their life?" Her voice caught, and Wyatt hugged her tighter.

"You're entitled to feel whatever you feel. It's that simple. Give yourself some grace. Now, I'm going to let you get some rest, if you can." Wyatt swung her legs off the bed.

Mari put a hand on her shoulder. "Please don't go."

❖

Mari shocked herself when she asked Wyatt to stay. The words spilled out of her mouth without much forethought or restraint. Now that they were out, they felt right, even if she also felt like she was imposing even more on her than she already had. She should be at her own home rather than leaning on a neighbor she barely knew. What decent person did that kind of thing?

Except, when she looked into Wyatt's eyes, something inside her fluttered, and a voice in the back of her mind whispered, "Trust her." Pragmatism remained one of her strongest and best qualities. Mari had a way of seeing the big picture and acting in a logical manner. This request didn't come from any big picture, and it certainly wasn't logical. It was pure raw instinct. She didn't want to be alone, and she wanted only one person to be at her side. It didn't hurt that Wyatt had come to her rescue looking like a dream, the good kind, with her dark hair long and loose, and wearing shorts and an over-sized T-shirt. Others might go for sexy sleepwear, but for Mari, Wyatt's shorts and T-shirt were spectacular.

"Sorry. Sorry. Sorry." She back-pedaled even though she didn't want to. No more imposing regardless of how beautiful she looked.

"About what?" Wyatt turned to stare into her eyes. Her hair framed her face, her eyes unreadable.

Time to be a considerate houseguest. "It's not your responsibility to push away the darkness my mind conjures up. You've already opened your home to me, your friends have given their time and expertise to help me, and none of you really even know me. To say you've all gone above and beyond isn't even touching it."

Wyatt took her hand and brought it to her lips. The sensation made her shudder. Wyatt's gaze didn't move from Mari's face, and she didn't look away. "I know you." She put a hand up to stop her from responding. "Hear me out. Yeah. I get that we just met. You're not wrong there at all. Sometimes, the universe works in strange ways and brings us the people we need when we need them."

"You and me." Geez, did she really sound as breathy as she thought?

"You and me." Wyatt's eyes were intense.

"Stay with me." It was all she could get out.

Wyatt leaned near and kissed her cheek. "All night."

"Thank you," Mari whispered.

"No thanks required." She kissed Mari lightly on the lips.

Beneath the covers, warmth spread through her. Still wasn't enough. She reached over and took Wyatt's hand. No words were necessary. The touch was enough to bring her peace, and she drifted off into deep and dreamless sleep.

"Well, well, well." A voice in the doorway brought Mari upright and blinking as she oriented herself. Oh yeah, Wyatt's house. Wyatt in her bed. She looked over toward the sound of the voice, where Tuesday stood in the open doorway, a big smile on her face.

"Not what you think." The warmth in Mari's cheeks didn't track with her words. Why did this feel like the time Mom caught her kissing Tori Everett?

"Of course, it isn't." Her voice was light, without any trace of malice. She even sounded like Mari's mother on that long-ago day. "Look, you two sleepyheads. We've been up for an hour, had our coffee, and now we're taking Tripper for a run."

Wyatt sat up and pushed the hair out of her face. Even more beautiful than when she'd raced in last night. "Where?"

Tuesday's smile was mischievous. "Where do you think?"

Wyatt was shaking her head. "Lloyd won't be happy."

"Hey, it's a public area, and you know how it is when you live with a working dog. They like to work. Can't imagine my boy will find anything, but it does him good to work. Happy dog. Happy house."

"Call me if…"

Tuesday gave them a little salute. "Will do." She turned away from the bedroom and disappeared from sight, followed, a few minutes later, by the sound of a vehicle driving away. Addie and Tripper must have been waiting for her in the truck.

"That wasn't too awkward. I'm so sorry." The warmth in Mari's cheeks hadn't abated. Leave it to her to put a kind-hearted host in what appeared to be a compromising position. They hadn't done anything other than sleep. It just looked otherwise.

"Ah." Wyatt waved her hand in the air. "Nothing to be sorry about. No reason two women can't share a bed if they want to."

That made her smile. "True. It's not like we were doing anything except sleeping."

"This time." The two words were soft and filled with promise.

Mari snapped her gaze to Wyatt's face. "This time?"

Wyatt shrugged, all traces of sleep gone from her face. "If you tell me you don't feel it, I won't bring it up again. Cross my heart." She drew a cross on her chest with her index finger.

For a long moment, Mari said nothing. She debated whether to lie. Too weird to feel this drawn to someone so quickly. Not her style, which made her wonder if she could trust her feelings. It had taken a very long time for her and Sherrill to get close and...the truth that hit her hard now was that she'd never felt the kind of attraction to her that she felt toward Wyatt. Maybe it was just the situation and heightened emotion that came with it. Maybe not.

She went for the truth as she believed it to be. "I feel it."

❖

The call brought Royal out of a deep sleep. Not having to worry about what kind of mess Inez might be creating had resulted in a peaceful night. That Claude had done a runner didn't even bother him as much as it normally would. Unlike Inez, Claude was good at staying under the radar. Maybe it came from his wealthy upbringing. He tended to be cautious of people's true intentions toward him. Did they like him for himself? Or did they like him for his money? Royal had been drawn to Claude for his brain. Smart, clever people were fun to have around. Good looking never hurt either.

His appreciation for Intelligence was part of what drew him to Wyatt. She was quite bright, and the way she could work the land was nothing short of amazing. Everything about her was perfect for his wants and needs. Royal always got what he wanted. Inez excepted. Might have been catfished on that one. Oh, well. Live and learn.

He grabbed his cell off the nightstand. "Yeah." Gruff and not very friendly. That's what folks got when they dragged him from needed rest.

"She's not here." Teresa Thompson from the council was all business. No hello. No sorry I woke you. Just the immediate business.

The fog of sleep pushed aside, he sat up. "What do you mean she's not there?"

"I mean, she never got off the plane. Did a little checking, and she never boarded in Missoula. Where the hell is she, Royal?" The irritation in Teresa's voice sounded loud and clear. The members did not appreciate inconvenience.

Dread ran through him, deep and dark. "I don't know, but I'll sure as hell find out."

"Apprise me as soon as you locate her. There will be repercussions."

"I understand, and yes, I will call you as soon as I know what happened to her and where she is." He ended the call with Teresa and rolled out of bed, fully awake, his mind racing.

Dressed, Royal headed downstairs, calling out as he went. "Claude!"

In the kitchen, Claude leaned against the counter drinking coffee. "What's up, big guy?" Calm and serene as ever. Not a care in the world.

"Where's Inez?" The question was bitter on his tongue. God, he'd had enough of the bull.

Claude shrugged and put his mug to his lips before he bothered to answer. "Sitting front and center before the council would be my guess. Naughty little girl, sent to the principal's office." He made no effort to hide his smirk.

He rested both hands on the counter and barked, "She never made it."

Again, Claude shrugged. "And I should care, why?"

"This isn't a joke." Bad enough that Inez was still causing problems. He didn't need Claude to be such an asshole. A little help would be appreciated.

Claude turned serious. "And I just don't give a rat's ass about Inez. I've told you for a long time she was trouble and shouldn't have been brought in. Case in point. She can't even do a simple flight north without causing problems."

"You dropped her off." His mind whirled with thoughts about what she might have done after Claude left her at the airport.

He glanced out the window. "Yeah. I dropped her off."

"She didn't get on the plane." She could have gone inside and called for a ride or even rented a car. She could have headed into Missoula for a night of fun and games.

"Doing what she's told has never been her modus operandi. Couldn't control her while she was here. No reason to think anyone could control her once she left." Claude took a long drink before he put his mug in the sink. "I'm headed out to the gardens. I think some rabbits have been raiding my plants. Will have to do something about that. Rabbit stew sounds kind of tasty."

"I don't eat rabbit." Royal had standards, and a small, beautiful creature wasn't one of them. "Block them, but don't kill them."

"Beg to differ with you, boss. It's important to save the crop. Could be a long, cold winter, and I don't want those little bastards messing up our food supply."

"Just figure it out without any of the rabbits showing up on the dinner table." Sometimes, Claude's obstinance got irritating. Always believed he was the smartest one in the room. Not always true.

After Claude went outside, Royal finished two cups of coffee and left three messages on Inez's phone. He would be able to sense if she was nearby, and she wasn't. Little else he could do to track her except wait until she reached out. She would. That was the thing about them. They were not solitary creatures. Ultimately, she would either finish her trip north and appear before the council, or find her way back to ask for Royal's forgiveness.

With nothing else to do, he supposed he might as well go to the office and at least get something useful done. He grabbed his keys and headed toward town. Maybe a mile away, he changed his mind, did a U-turn, and drove toward the wilderness. The thought of sitting in the office unpacking box after box did not appeal to him. Something more proactive did.

No other cars were in the lot when Royal pulled in. He looked around as he headed toward the forest. No one, silence except for the rustle of the wind in the trees and a couple of squirrels jumping from branch to branch.

After he'd walked for about ten minutes, he stopped and stripped, folding his clothes and tucking them beneath a couple of thick bushes. He took a real risk by doing this in broad daylight. At the moment, he didn't feel like he had a better choice. This was one of those days where the choices that presented themselves were bad and worse.

Risky or not, it felt good to make the change and run free. The power that roared through him was impossible to get any other way. Made him understand, somewhat, how Inez and Claude felt when he shut them down and prevented them from doing what came natural to them. They loved it maybe even more than he did. They'd been willing and enthusiastic pupils right from day one.

He swept his gaze left and right as he ran. Something whispered to him to stay vigilant, alert, and ready. Uncomfortable with the motivations of both Claude and Inez, he hoped a good hard run would clear his mind and settle his emotions. Then he could go into the office, finish unpacking, and figure out what to do about the MIA Inez.

When fatigue started to slow his stride, he did an about-face and headed back in the direction of the bushes where he'd left his clothes hidden. The change and the run had helped. Things were coming together in his mind, his focus growing sharp, and he decided he had a good plan going forward. At least that's what he'd thought until he came to a skidding stop. Could he have spoken, he would have screamed, no, no, no!

A hundred yards in front of him, two women and a dog were staring down at a body.

CHAPTER FIFTEEN

The kiss came as naturally as breathing. Soft, sweet, and heart-fluttering, the silver lining to a really dark cloud. Would have been perfect if not for the ring of her damn phone, still in her room down the hall. The soft chiming of the ring tone flitted through the air, as disruptive as the blare of an air horn.

"Sorry, sorry, sorry." Wyatt didn't move. Whoever was calling could damn well wait. This kiss couldn't, and it filled her heart.

"That might be important," Mari said as she swung her legs off the bed and stood, a tiny smile on her lips, her eyes soft.

A cool breeze replaced the warmth that had wrapped around Wyatt seconds before.

"I doubt it." She didn't want anything to disturb this special moment. What she wished for was to go back to those kisses.

Mari stood next to the bed and studied her with hands on her hips. Could she be more gorgeous? "As wonderful as that was, the real world is waiting, and it hasn't been very pretty the last couple of days."

You're pretty, she wanted to say. She said, "You're right." The chimes stopped, and she figured if someone really needed her, they'd leave a message. "I don't want to hear from the real world right now. I want to continue with this one, where it's just you and me."

Mari smiled. "Can't argue with that."

"Except?" She'd heard the question in her voice.

"Except we can't ignore anyone right now. Go." Mari leaned near and kissed her on the cheek. "Go find out what the world needs from you today."

She sighed. "I don't really want to." The way things had been going, it wouldn't be good news on the other end of that call. Waking up next to Mari made everything brighter, and how she wanted to hold on to that feeling.

"I know, and I'm right there with you. I managed to get enough sleep, thank you very much." She smiled at Wyatt. "I'm ready to take on the quest for answers again."

"Damn answers."

"Come on, grumpy. We'll face the day, and we can revisit this once we get the world straight again."

"Promise?" Would they be able to recapture the magic of a few moments ago? It had been so beautiful and heart-warming, Wyatt wanted to bottle it and hold it tight.

Mari gave her an exaggerated bow. "You have my solemn promise."

"Well then, I'll hold you to that, and now I'll go see who had the nerve to call me this early." She padded down the hallway to her bedroom, where the covers on the bed were still tossed aside from when she'd raced out last night. Her cell lay on the charger on the bedside table. She frowned as she read the missed-call notification. Did Tuesday need help? Flat tire? Accident? They hadn't been gone long enough for anything serious to have happened, she hoped. Tuesday picked up on the first ring.

"What's up. You lost already? So sad for someone with your skill set." The glib tone she used masked the concern that had her shoulders tense. Tuesday would appreciate the joke, her navigation skills right there with Wyatt's. Or even better, if she were to be honest.

"It's bad." Tuesday's voice was filled with tension, and Wyatt's heart dropped. A rock settled in the pit of her stomach.

"Tell me," she bit out.

"Tripper found another body."

"What!" She sank to the bed. No. It wasn't possible. She had to have heard her wrong.

"Wyatt, I'm not kidding. We were out maybe ten minutes, and he came back to me. He'd gone into full-on work mode and was letting me know he'd found human remains. Addie and I followed." Tuesday's words confirmed that she did not hear her wrong.

"Man? Woman?" This was insane. Things like this didn't happen around here.

"Another woman."

She put the call on speaker as she grabbed jeans, a sweatshirt, and her boots. "I've got to call Lloyd. Do you have your GPS with you by any chance?" Dumb question. Tuesday didn't go hiking without appropriate equipment. She'd spent too many years of her life searching for people who got lost and didn't have even basic survival items with them, like flashlights, a compass, or even a basic GPS unit.

"Never leave home without it." Tuesday confirmed what Wyatt already knew.

"Send me the coordinates, and I'll get them to Lloyd. Stay there to make sure no one disturbs anything."

"Just sent them to you, and we're setting up the perimeter as we speak."

She looked down at her phone, the ping of a text coming in. "Got it. It won't take Lloyd and his crew long to reach you, so hang tight."

"Oh, shit." Tuesday almost yelled.

"What?" Wyatt didn't like what she heard in Tuesday's voice. "What is it? Someone bothering you?"

"No. It's worse than that." Was it fear she heard in her words?

"You better tell me so I can get you help." The rock in her stomach turned into a mighty boulder.

"Tripper came racing in again." She had a bad, bad feeling as to where this was headed

"Meaning…"

"Meaning, he's found another body."

❖

Mari stood in Wyatt's doorway and listened. Probably rude to do so. Couldn't stop herself, bad manners or not. She'd heard the tone of Wyatt's voice before she'd put the call on speaker, and it had drawn her here. At least she'd pulled on pants and a shirt before racing down in her socks. Wyatt waved her in when she glanced up and noticed her.

"You got all that, right?" Wyatt ended her call with Lloyd and leaned over to tie her boots.

"This can't be real, can it? First Sherrill, and now two more? And that's not even factoring in the poor goat. Something bizarre is going on out there."

"Evil is more like it." Wyatt stood up and slipped a hoodie over her head. Her expression was grim, and who could blame her?

"I better call Ollie." She raced back to the spare room and slipped on her boots, then picked up her phone. It took three rings before Ollie answered.

"Glad you called." His voice was gruff. "We have another problem."

"I know."

"You know?"

"I'm with Wyatt. Tuesday called about the bodies that Tripper located, and Wyatt called it in to the sheriff."

"This is messed up, Mari, and I'm sorry this is your introduction to our area. This isn't how I wanted to go out or how I wanted you to step in. I honestly don't know what's going on around here. Trust me when I say this is not normal."

"Not your fault. Things happen."

"You mean shit happens because, Ranger, this is definitely shit."

"I'm heading out with Wyatt." She slipped her arms into her jacket as she talked.

"Good. Lloyd asked that we both meet him there."

"On my way."

She ended the call with Ollie and found Wyatt in the kitchen, waiting by the door. "I'd make coffee, but I think at this point, I'd throw it up."

Mari nodded. "Same here. Let's roll. I talked to Ollie, and he's going to meet us out there."

Wyatt started out the door and then paused. She turned back to Mari. "Tragic as this is, one thing jumped out at me."

Mari wasn't following. They didn't know anything yet beyond two dead bodies out in the forest. "I've got nothing."

"It's about you."

"Me?" What the heck was she getting at? How the discovery of more bodies would have anything to do with her was almost insulting. She didn't hurt Sherrill, and she sure as hell didn't hurt anyone else. Surprised her that Wyatt would come at her like this.

Wyatt put a hand on her arm. "What I mean is that something terrible is going on around here, and people are dying."

Her intent wasn't getting any clearer. "And that means what about me?"

"Sorry. I'm going at this the long way around. What occurred to me is that the bodies they found this morning prove how random the violence is. It means that you have zero to feel guilty about when it comes to Sherrill's death. Someone is killing people for reasons we may never understand. It has nothing to do with you."

Mari put a hand on her cheek as Wyatt's intent finally came into clear focus. "I love the way you think and how you're looking out for me. It is starting to seem like wrong place, wrong time for Sherrill and that perhaps, just perhaps, she did put herself in the path of a killer."

"I hear some hesitation in your voice."

"I may never completely get over feeling guilty." Couldn't help it. She would always come back around to the fact that if she hadn't been here, Sherrill wouldn't have come either.

"Why not? Clearly, a psycho out there is doing this, and you're not the reason he or she picked your ex."

"On the face of it, you're right. Not me. What is on me is that she followed me here, which is how she put herself onto the path of a killer."

"No. I'm not letting you carry that misplaced guilt, and if it takes me forever, I'm going to keep working on you until you see the truth."

"The truth."

"Yeah, the truth that Sherrill's murder was tragic, period. No one's fault except the psycho who ended her life. End of story."

Mari leaned in and kissed her. "You'll work on me forever, eh?"

"If that's what it takes."

"I'll hold you to that. Now, we better haul ass."

Fury had him running faster than he could ever remember. At least neither the women nor the dog noticed him, since the trio's attention had been focused on the body. Not that they'd had any clue it was him. Nobody would, part of the beauty of it. By the time Royal had pulled on his clothes, returned to his car, and made it back to the highway, the scream of sirens cut through the air. Lloyd and his crew passed him going at least ninety, probably more.

His emotions ranged from rage to sickness and back to rage. He'd be pissed at Claude, thinking he'd dropped Inez in the wilderness area, except the navigation in his car showed that he had driven to the airport in Missoula. He'd checked after the call this morning. So, what in the actual hell was happening out there?

Sure, he understood the goat and, maybe if he stretched a little, that woman, Sherrill, but this one? It couldn't have been Inez who killed her and left her body in a stand of small pines, could it? He pulled over to the side of the road and dropped his head to the steering wheel. His eyes closed, he recalled what he'd seen in the woods. Struck him now that the body wasn't fresh, something he should have realized the moment he'd picked up the odor of death. It's what had actually brought him to that spot. Damn. Inez could have killed this one too. Every time he turned around, he found himself faced with a new mess.

He brought his head up and stared out the window. Task one, find Inez. Here he'd thought he had taken care of the problem enough to keep himself and Claude safe from inquiring minds. Long enough for Wyatt to join them, become his forever. Now, nothing felt safe.

Best not to sit here like a lump. It would draw attention, and that was the last thing he wanted. Important to blend into the background, although being the new, albeit old, guy in town made it inherently difficult to stay in the shadows. Something or someone shaking up the status quo always captured the interest of those in a smaller community. His return to the fold would garner the attention of the community, particularly those who'd known him and his family in the past.

Royal pulled back onto the highway and drove to his office downtown. Rather than go right into it, he walked down to the café instead. "Good morning, Tracy."

"Hey, Royal. How's your morning so far?" Her smile was as bright as the neon-orange shirt she wore. The café smelled like coffee and fresh cinnamon rolls. On any other day, both might entice him. Today, the last thing he wanted. He had come for something else.

"Okay." He returned her smile, though his wasn't quite as bright, the effort too much under the circumstances. "Just got passed by the entire police department, I think. What's happened now?" He didn't look at her as he picked a napkin from the dispenser and a packet of sugar he'd never use.

"Oh, man," she said as she shook her head. "Don't know what's going on around here but sure feels like we've got a serial killer on the loose. Here of all places. Can you believe it?"

Now he looked at her. "What? A serial killer? Are you sure?"

"Yeah. Wyatt's buddy with the cadaver dog found two more bodies, and there was the one yesterday. It's like open season on women out there." She set a go-cup of coffee in front of him. He didn't mention that he hadn't ordered a coffee. "I bet one of those true-crime shows will show up here."

"Holy…" He hoped his expression displayed the right amount of amazement, which wasn't that difficult given he was genuinely shocked by the news of two bodies. He'd only seen the one.

"I know. We rarely have murders here, and now we've had three in a little more than twenty-four hours. How bizarre is that? You might want to reconsider your move back to this town. Feels like you were safer in Canada. I know it'll be a long time before I feel safe enough to go out there again."

Probably a good plan on her part. That orange shirt would make for a handy target. They'd see her coming by a mile. "You might be right about that. Figures I'd move home, and everything goes to hell in a handbasket."

She smiled at him again. Flirting. "Well, might be good for business." She winked.

He smiled back. Let her think he might be interested. Easier to keep the information highway open if he played nice. "Too bad I'm not a criminal lawyer, although I taught a few classes in criminal law. I might be able to wing it if I had to." He winked at her this time.

"Around here, it's just details. A lawyer is a lawyer. They'll come to you for help, and I'll be happy to send them your way."

"Nice to have such a great PR person." He held up his coffee in a salute and hurried out the door. Enough with the small talk. Too many things on his mind at the moment to continue to play games with Tracy. A little encouragement was one thing. If he took it too far or let it go on too long, she might get the wrong idea. He wasn't interested in her and never would be. Only one person mattered, which is why he needed to figure out what had happened with Inez and if she had anything to do with the bodies out there. Time was clicking away, and it was critical that this mess be cleared up before the Harvest Moon.

Once at his office, he poured the unwanted coffee down the drain and tossed the empty cup in the trash. At his desk, he leaned back in his chair and tapped his fingers on the arm rest. Helplessness had a scream rising in his throat. An alpha male always had control, and not knowing what to do was about to drive him insane. He always had a solid plan. In some respects, he still had one that he intended to follow through on, regardless of what was happening out there in the Bob Marshall Wilderness Area. It would be foolish, however, to ignore the deaths and the complications they created. If the trail led back to his hearth and home, well, that would be a big fucking problem.

He leaned forward and stared at the phone for a few seconds. Nothing ventured, nothing gained. He picked up the receiver and punched in the number he knew by heart. "Hey."

"Don't have time to chat, Royal, so make it quick." The tension in Wyatt's voice was thick. The upside was that she recognized his voice right away. Sometimes it took baby steps.

"I just heard. Your friends okay?" Always the thoughtful guy.

"You heard?" A note of surprise in her voice.

"Small town." He didn't need to explain much beyond that.

"And you went for coffee." She caught on quick.

"Yup. Are your friends okay?" He asked again. Not that in reality he cared one iota about her friends. Sounded good though, and if it kept him on her good side, that's all that mattered.

"They sound fine on the phone, but honestly, it's pretty messed up. I'll know more once I get out there and can talk with them. Nothing like this has ever happened before, and it's creepy. I love it in the woods. I take women from all over the country into them, and now every time you turn around, there's a body. It makes me sick."

"I'm sorry, Wyatt. I wish I could do something to help you feel better. I have faith in Lloyd and his people. They'll find him." He thought he sounded convincing. What he really thought was that Lloyd would struggle with the investigation, and Royal was all for it. He didn't trust that the kills were clean and wouldn't ultimately lead back to Inez.

"You think it's a guy?"

Good, she picked up on his intentional choice of words. "Just statistics. Not saying it couldn't be the work of a woman." Didn't want to promote the theory of a female killer. "Statistically speaking, it's likely a man. Did you hear anything about the victims?" With the seed planted about a male killer, he moved on to trying for information on the victims. The more he knew, the better he could calculate his own next moves.

"All I know so far is two women. Lloyd and his crew are on scene. Mari and I are on our way to meet them out there."

"I passed them as I was coming into the office." No need to share that he'd been on scene too. She wouldn't believe him anyway. "Your friends?"

"Still there. Talked to them for a couple minutes before Lloyd deployed them to search the surrounding area. He wants to make sure there aren't any more victims."

"God, I hope not." His heart sank at the thought that there might be more. How could he have been so oblivious to what Inez had been doing?

"Makes two of us."

"Let me know what I can do for you. How's Mari? This has to be a nightmare for her." Covering all the bases. He wanted to know about everyone involved in this. Kind of like a game of chess and keeping an eye on all the pieces as each move was made.

"All things considered, she'd doing all right, and don't worry. We've got her back." Confidence. Interesting.

"Again, if I can help, just know I'm here." He kept his voice upbeat. Let her know that he had Wyatt's back as well. That part wasn't feigned. He would always be there to support her.

"Thanks. We all appreciate it." The words sounded routine, without any real emotion behind them. As if he weren't important to her. He'd have to work on that. "Look. I have to go. We're almost there."

We're almost there. "No worries. Take care."

He ended the call and sat back in his chair as he stared out the window where dark clouds gathered. A storm brewed, and to him, it wasn't unwelcome. If ever there was time for damage control, it would be now, and a storm to wash away traces of anything incriminating worked. What it didn't help with was his first critical task: to find Inez.

Chapter Sixteen

Except for answering Royal's call, Wyatt didn't say anything as she drove. Neither did Mari. She hadn't been exactly honest with Royal. They weren't as near their destination as she let on. She just hadn't wanted to talk to him. As much as she could, she'd tried to remain civil. When her patience ran out, she'd had to cut him off.

Now, she glanced over at Mari. Still silent. She put a hand on her shoulder. Hard as a rock. The softness she remembered from the night before had disappeared. "We'll figure this out."

For a second, Mari still didn't speak. She looked out the side window before turning to Wyatt. "You ever feel like your life is spiraling out of control and you can't do anything to stop it? That you reach out to stop the spin, but it all slips between your fingers and begins to go faster and faster?"

It hurt her heart that Mari couldn't let go of the unearned guilt. It wasn't fair. "I'm going to keep saying it. None of this was your responsibility."

"To recap, my marriage breaks up. I'm passed over for a promotion that should have been mine, but no. It goes to a less qualified candidate who happens to be a pretty blonde with big boobs. The hiring panel was all male, by the way. Then my ex, the stalker, follows me and gets herself killed. Top it all off with an apparent serial killer in my designated area. If not directly, I'm responsible by default."

"Nope. Not directly. Not by default either." She could dig her heels in when needed.

Mari continued to look at her. Wyatt could feel the intensity of her gaze, even though her own was focused on the road. As much as she wanted to get out there, she tried to keep within the speed limit. Enough problems without driving dangerously. "Nope? I'm at the center of all of this. How can it not be on my plate?" No bitterness in her words. Sounded more like genuine curiosity.

Wyatt didn't believe any of it belonged to Mari, though she could appreciate her logic. "Maybe on your plate because of your job. Not your responsibility. The two are mutually exclusive."

"I can tell you're a hell of a teacher."

Wyatt raised an eyebrow. "And why is that?"

"Regardless of how awful something is, you see the bright side and move right straight to how to fix it. What's the phrase? Improvise, adapt, and overcome. That's you."

Wyatt couldn't argue. It was standard operating procedures for her. "Maybe."

"No maybe about it. You are that person. Here I am whining about my poor half-empty glass, and you're urging me to see it as half full. You make things better. You make them right."

"Okay, fine. I'm a fixer." She couldn't live her chosen lifestyle and not be a problem solver. Things happen all the time. Some good. Some bad. Lots that need work. She loved figuring out how to fix a problem. Mari had also pegged her accurately. She'd decided a long time ago to see the glass as half full. Not that she was always successful. Most of the time, yes, and that was good enough.

Mari put a hand on her arm. "So, tell me. How do we fix this? How do we overcome? I feel like I'm screwed here. Damned if I do and damned if I don't. I'm going to remain suspect number one."

She didn't believe that. "When it comes to Sherrill, maybe."

Out of the corner of her eye, she saw Mari shaking her head. "No maybe. You know as well as I do, they'll be looking at me. They're not going to pass me over just because Sherrill wasn't the only one murdered."

"A good cop would, but they've still called you out to help, which says a lot about Lloyd not believing you had anything to do with Sherrill or the other two. I don't believe he'd have done that if he honestly thought you were involved."

"That's the thing. I didn't have anything to do with any of this."

"You know that. I know that. Pretty sure Lloyd knows that too. In his defense, he has to tick off all the boxes before he can totally clear you, and I'm guessing he has most of them checked off, or, again, Ollie wouldn't have called you to meet them out there." Her logic was solid.

"I guess." Judging by the sound of Mari's voice, Wyatt thought she was getting through to her at last.

"No 'I guess' about it. Unadulterated truth. Ollie believes in you, and so do I."

"You really think so?"

"Absolutely, and once you accept that fact, you'll see it too."

"So put on your hat, and let's go see how we can help Ollie and Lloyd find this killing bastard."

"You think it's a guy?" Mari put her forest-service hat on first and then slid on a pair of sunglasses.

"I don't want to come off as sexist, but yeah, I do. Feels like this level of violence comes at the hands of a man. Besides, you heard Royal. He's on the same sheet of music. A man's doing all of this."

"Statistics on that subject are moving toward women catching up." Mari wasn't giving up without a fight. Wyatt liked that about her.

"Somehow that doesn't surprise me. I think women have always had the capability. Like everything else, it's taken years to start leveling the playing field. Would prefer that the leveling stay with things like electing a woman president, equal pay for equal work, and more representation in high levels of government, corporations, and education."

"No picking and choosing."

Wyatt shook her head. "I get it. Wishful thinking. But still holding on to it being a guy out there killing."

"Not a werewolf?" She glanced over at Mari, who gave her a slight smile.

"Hey, it's a legit idea. Fenrir might have come out of legend, but you know as well as I do that legends have a basis in reality. Not a werewolf. Maybe one big-ass wolf."

"True." Mari turned to look at her. "Not sure I can make a leap to werewolf in any event."

"Big wolf?"

"Sure. I can go with big, hungry wolf."

Wyatt gave her a little nod. "At least with the goat."

"True. Pretty sure a wolf, regardless of its size, wouldn't have a gun. Someone very human killed Sherrill."

Wyatt glanced at Mari. At the mention of her ex, the light went out of her face. She wanted to hug her, reassure her it would all be okay. Also didn't want to base whatever this was between them on lies. She didn't know that it would all be fine. One mutilated goat, one woman shot in the head, and two more dead by unknown means. Okay didn't seem to be on the horizon any time soon for the residents of her town, new and old.

"Lloyd will find him." If she said it enough, it would be true.

"Him, again. You're set on the killer being a man."

Wyatt was and would continue to believe that assertion. "I could be wrong, and if I am, I'll be the first to admit it. Thing is, my gut is screaming 'him,' and, in my mind, I'm seeing the hulking shadow of a man. That's my story and I'm sticking to it." She didn't voice that in her mind she also saw the hulking shadow of a wolf.

❖

Mari wished she could capture some of Wyatt's confidence. Under normal circumstances, she could hold her own. *Thank you, Mom and Dad, for giving me the foundation to be that way.* Since making the move to Hamilton, she'd felt her own foundation shake as though an earthquake roared beneath her feet. Could be she needed her parents to make a quick trip to Montana to bolster that foundation. Or, she could be a big girl and recover it herself. Probably needed to lean into the latter.

She glanced over at Wyatt and resisted the urge to lean into her. Not right to draw her into the mess that had become life of late. All Wyatt had been so far was thoughtful, steady, and encouraging. It helped, and to ask for more, rude. The truth about it for Mari: her circus, her monkeys.

"I've never had to deal with a killer. Certainly never one who killed someone I know." She didn't add, and once loved. That love died far in the past, and she hoped Wyatt understood that reality. Given the night and morning, all signs pointed to the reality that, in fact, she did.

"You'll handle it. I have faith in you." Wyatt flipped on a blinker and waited for a passing car before she turned left off the highway.

"Except you don't really know me." Say what she might, that was the truth. Feelings aside, they barely knew each other.

"Hey, we slept together." Wyatt gave her a little nod.

Mari laughed. "We did, quite literally."

"I'm careful about who I sleep with." Wyatt's words turned serious. "With or without you know what."

Out the windshield, the turn-off for the wilderness area came into view. "You know what" would have been amazing though inappropriate right at the moment. Down the road… "Same."

"So, we both agree that our instincts are telling us we're cool."

Was it instinct or was it something else? Mari would be lying to say her life wasn't somewhat adrift lately. As much as she appreciated the job here and the promotion it represented, it wasn't how she'd imagined her career or her life would work out. The divorce, Sherrill's stalking, getting passed over in Oregon— all had brought her here. Should have been a good thing, not days filled with death and despair.

And a beautiful, talented woman who made her mind whirl and her heart thump. A Charles Dickens quote popped into her head. "It was the best of times, it was the worst of times." Sure felt like that right now. Again, she glanced at Wyatt. Would the best of times wipe out the worst? She could hope.

"Oh, yes, I'd say we're cool."

"We're on the same page then. I like that. So, how about you go out there and do what you do." She pointed ahead of them where the parking area loomed, crowded with marked vehicles and a lone truck that Mari recognized as Tuesday's. "Addie, Tuesday, and I will help as we're allowed and do what we do best. Our power in numbers will be the extra needed to solve this problem sooner rather than later."

Wyatt stopped the car when a deputy blocked the road a hundred yards from the parking area and held up a hand. He walked around to the driver's side window and leaned down. "I can't let you in, Wyatt. You'll need to turn around and go back." His face was serious, his voice firm.

Wyatt didn't blink. "Jason, I've got Ranger Whitaker here. I'm sure Lloyd told you she'd be coming."

Mari leaned toward Wyatt and brought up a hand. "I'm Mari Whitaker. I'm working with Ollie."

Tall and maybe thirty-five tops, he nodded, and the tightness in his face relaxed. "Yeah, okay, all right. Lloyd and Ollie mentioned she'd be coming. Nothing about you, Wyatt. That means you can drive her in, but then you need to come back right away. No civilians on site. Not even you."

"I can help. You know I can. Your mom has taken three of my classes."

He nodded, his expression still serious. "She has, and she loved them. Doesn't change anything out here. You know as well as I do this isn't my call, and Lloyd said no civilians. That means you." He hooked his thumbs in his belt and stared down at her. All business.

Mari put a hand on her shoulder. Wyatt's calm demeanor contrasted to the tension Mari felt beneath her palm. "It'll be fine. Drive me in, and we'll go from there." Her voice was soft.

Wyatt nodded. "Okay, fine. I'll drive Mari, drop her off, and be back in a few." He stepped aside, and Wyatt drove on in.

When she pulled into the parking area and stopped, it became clear that the deputy had called ahead to the sheriff. Lloyd waited for them on a four-wheeler, his expression grim.

After a glance at Wyatt, Mari got out and walked over to where he sat in the saddle of the off-road vehicle. "Here, as requested. I take it you've decided I'm innocent as far as Sherrill's murder is concerned?" She took a calculated guess sprinkled with a whole lot of hope. Anyone who really knew her would be adamant about her innocence. Violence wasn't her thing.

He drew his brows together. "Mostly."

"Mostly?" Good. Not quite good enough.

He stared into her eyes, his expression neutral. A guy skilled at giving nothing away. Probably did well playing poker. "Let's just say that everything I've investigated thus far appears to put you in the clear."

"I didn't do it." She would say it as many times as she needed to. Sooner or later, Lloyd would be forced to see the truth. Well, that and possibly the technology that could verify her location at the time of the murder. Or, rather, murders.

He shook his head. "Here's the thing, Ranger. I don't think you did it either, which is why you're here. What you and Ollie know about the wilderness may be useful. Time's wasting, and we don't have the bandwidth to get into this now. Hop on and let's go. Bigger fish to fry out there." He waved at Wyatt and said loudly. "You can leave."

Wyatt leaned out the open window. "Lloyd, you know I can help."

"No, you can't. Go home, Wyatt." His words were firm, the message between the lines: *Don't argue with me.*

"What about Addie and Tuesday?"

"You don't need to worry about them. They're searching. Now go home." He turned the key on the four-wheeler, and it roared to life.

Mari almost tumbled off when he made a quick turn and headed into the wilderness, leaving Wyatt far behind.

"Searching?" she said over the sound of the engine while gripping the handles on either side of the seat. The ground was uneven, and he drove fast over the bumps. Mari hoped she didn't go flying off the back.

"Yep. Might as well use them while they're here. That dog is pretty damned good." He yelled over the roar of the four-wheeler.

"You think there might be more bodies?" she asked just as loudly.

"I hope to hell not, but I'm not taking any chances that some random hiker might come upon another one. The dog has found three so far. We'll see if he finds more."

She shuddered. "God, I hope not."

A few seconds later, his radio roared to life. A voice, scratchy over the airwaves, called out, "Deputy Harris to Sheriff Epps."

Lloyd brought the four-wheeler to a stop and reached up to the radio clipped on his shirt. "Go ahead, Kenny."

The radio crackled once more. "They found another one."

Royal heard a couple more sirens in the distance. "Damn." Rationally, they could be sounding the alert for any number of reasons, except his heart told him they were uncovering evidence of Inez's dirty work or, as she'd describe it, a good night's fun. As much as he wanted to protect her, and he still did despite everything, there came a point of no return, and she'd hit it. He couldn't protect her any longer because she put all of them in danger. Never before had he made such a tactical error. He blamed himself more than he blamed her. His take on people was typically accurate. When it came to Inez, epic fail.

No time to dwell on it though. Nothing he could do except damage control at this point. Thank the gods he happened to be an expert at that. His lawyer brain equipped him with most excellent tools, and Claude could, and would, assist. He was good that way. Also had an excellent eye for detail and would fill in the blanks if Royal skipped something. Until the Harvest Moon, it would be just the two of them, and they'd both have to be strong to deflect any suspicion that might come their way.

After he'd put away one box of law books, he hung up the *Closed* sign in the front window and then walked out, locking the door behind him. Something important awaited him.

Hanging out around his office, unpacking, and answering calls, might be important, but it just didn't appeal to him at the moment. After the moon, when life settled into its new normal, he'd pay more attention to business. Besides, he'd always had a few clients he did work for even while he'd been teaching, and their accounts were enough to make for a decent enough income to carry him through. That and his investments during the years left him in good financial shape. The cost of living in these parts was far less than up in Vancouver, which meant he had a fair amount of freedom. He'd miss the beauty of the Canadian city, its constant hum of activity, interesting people, and stunning views. With enough time, he'd get over it. The Hamilton area had its own charms, and since returning, he'd been reacquainting himself with them, and the longing for the forests and the mountains and the rivers of the north grew less and less with each passing day.

It didn't take long to reach the turn-off. The driveway was long and well-maintained. Another encouraging sign. The universe had been sending them hard and fast since he'd arrived back here. He liked to believe he had an exceptional ability to tune into the unseen world, as befitting someone in his position. Nature spoke to him as it should. He also believed that all his years at the law school had taught him to listen as much as he spoke. Perhaps even more. Much could be learned by staying silent and listening to the wind.

The house came into view. No cars. Good. He got out and walked around to the corner of the backyard. Royal surveyed the area and decided that the utility shed would be his best spot to do what he needed to without being seen. He jogged over and, in the shadows, stripped off his clothes. He folded his shirt, pants, and boxers, then laid them on top of his shoes. A breeze whispered across his skin, and the scent of wildflowers flowed through the air. Beneath his skin, his muscles rippled, lengthened, and sang. He dropped to the ground, the damp grass cool against his palms. Only for a moment. A few seconds later, the change complete, he ran, his paws barely touching the earth.

Her smell was everywhere. Beautiful, intoxicating, and all his. He'd make sure that nothing happened to the woman destined to be his forever mate. His nose to the ground, he followed her path from earlier this morning, her scent strong even though it had been hours since she walked here. Every little bit, he paused, lifted one of his hind legs, and marked. When he had marked the entire perimeter of the property around her house, he returned to the shadows and lifted his head. Again, muscles rippled, and bones moved. The wolf retreated, and once more he stood on two legs, naked and breathing hard. Sweat ran down the smooth skin of his chest. The run had been great, the mission to apply a layer of protection successful.

Now, all he had to do was get dressed before anyone returned. Would be hard to explain what he'd been doing should Wyatt or her friends come upon him. In a few days, Wyatt would have a full understanding, but for the moment, he wanted to keep his true nature quiet. Not wanted, had to. Some things couldn't be explained. Shown, yes. Explained, no.

He'd learned early how important it was to blend in and stay quiet. Their survival depended upon anonymity. Every year he got a little better. He shared that skill with those who came after him. Those he brought in and, thus, was responsible for. Protecting Claude and Inez, as well as those who didn't come with him to Montana, came as natural as breathing. Family of choice.

One more thing to do before he left. Royal leaned into his car and took a deep-red rose with a long stem from the passenger seat. He left it on the front mat, where she'd be sure to see it. No other color rose would do. Red said it all. Love. Power. Blood.

As he pulled out onto the highway, his phone rang. An unfamiliar number. He hit the button on the steering wheel. "Royal Fremont. How can I help you?"

"Mr. Fremont, it's Mari Whitaker."

Ah, the new ranger with the stalker ex-wife. Correction, the dead stalker ex-wife. "What can I do for you, Mari? If you're wondering about the bill for the protection order, don't worry about it. In light of what happened, there won't be a charge." He could eat a couple hours' worth of work, especially considering Inez was responsible for the end result, not that he'd tell her or anyone else that particular detail.

"I appreciate that, but that's not why I'm calling. We need you to meet us at the morgue."

"The morgue? For?" He frowned as he listened to her while concentrating on the flow of traffic. Traffic had picked up from earlier in the day, the rush hour, such as it was in this area, getting its start.

"We need you to come and identify a body."

What the hell? "I'm confused. Identify a body? Why would you need me?"

"Additional bodies have been discovered, and we're in the process of getting them moved to the morgue before they're transferred to Missoula." Her voice was tense and not at all like the woman he'd met in his office.

"Okay, Mari. You're going to have to give me more here. We're not talking about your ex, are we?" His stomach did a flip. Trouble needed to take a detour a long way away from him. Calling him to the morgue wasn't on his dance card.

"No, not my ex." She said the four words softly.

"Then who? Who could I possibly help you identify?" She had to have been filled in on his decades away from here and his relatively recent return. Of course, it didn't elude him that the murders coincided with his return. It wouldn't elude Lloyd either. A drop of sweat slid down his back.

"Your cousin, Inez."

Chapter Seventeen

Wyatt waited down the access road for a couple of long hours, hoping they'd allow her back in. Didn't happen. She tried texting Lloyd after the first hour and got a two-word reply: *Go. Home.* Punctuation included. Damn. Her second try at hour two got a similar response.

Thing about it, she lived in the community and had been there her whole life. These were friends and family. She depended on them, and they depended on her. Many could have turned their backs on her when she came out, and while a few did, most did not, including Lloyd. He took it in stride, like a good and kind person. So, when he told her to go home, twice, she respected his authority and went home.

At the house, she stopped in the driveway. No need to bother parking in the garage. She had a hunch she'd be making another trip or two before the day ended. For a few seconds, she leaned her head against the steering wheel. "Deep breaths," she whispered. "Deep breaths." She hated not knowing. She hated that she couldn't be there for her friends. They were competent and skilled, and that's what she had to content herself with. They'd fill her in once they returned, and that would have to be good enough.

Wyatt got out of the car and walked toward the front door. What the heck? She hurried toward the steps and looked down at the mat. "Oh, come on." She picked up the single rose, a small tag hanging from it with a heart and a single letter, *R*. What part of lesbian was he not getting? Even if she were into guys, Royal wouldn't be in the running. He just didn't do it for her. Zero chemistry.

For a couple of seconds she stared at the rose—beautiful, full, and fragrant—one likely picked up from the counter at the big convenience store off the highway. A real romantic. Then she raised her arm and threw it as far as she could, screaming as she did, "Leave me the fuck alone!"

Sinking to the front step, she put her head in her hands. Five deep breaths in, blowing each one out slow and even, her pulse settled, and her emotions quieted. Had to stop letting Royal get under her skin. Willful ignorance on his part and pretty sad for a smart guy. He couldn't seem to accept she wasn't interested in him and never would be. Oh, well, she'd keep telling him no, and sooner or later he'd have to give up. She wouldn't give him a choice. There were plenty of single women around, and he could jolly well go after one of them.

She glanced over her shoulder at the bedroom window. Maybe he'd catch on if he spent much time around her and Mari. Couldn't help it. Something about Mari spoke to her, and it felt like the time to listen. She wasn't getting any younger, and the dating pool around here leaned toward the meager side. Not that she had hook-ups on her mind. She met interesting women all the time when they came to her classes or she traveled to teach at seminars. Big, tall, beautiful, plain, out-going, shy. All types came to her to learn how to be strong and self-sufficient. Yet not one of them had drawn her in like Mari. Had to mean something, right?

No sense standing around feeling frustrated and useless. Better to use the time to finish the prep work for her next class. No idea when Tuesday, Addie, and Tripper would be back. Not sure if Mari would come back at all. With Lloyd seemingly giving her the all-clear, it seemed unlikely she would. Maybe she'd call her later and extend the invitation again. Couldn't hurt, and besides, she still believed they were all a little safer in one place. Mari could use the support, and with the work that her friends had been drawn into, they would likely appreciate the company of kindred souls. Stronger together. Yeah. She'd call Mari later.

She got up and went into the house, planning to work on the class details, answer emails, send out equipment lists. That would keep her nice and busy until it was time to feed the animals and start prepping dinner. She'd taken out some elk steaks earlier and would pick some fresh greens from the garden. A bottle of blackberry wine might give them all a bit of relaxation. Couldn't hurt, and the other three women would likely be tense and uneasy when they returned.

The ring of her phone interrupted her work. Tracy. "Hey. What's up?"

"Have you heard?" There was excitement in her voice.

"Heard what?" Not sure she wanted to know, given how things had evolved the last few days. They had already gone from bad to worse, and she had a sinking feeling they were about to go from worse to catastrophic.

"More bodies." She delivered the news in a breathy voice. Tracy did love the dramatic. She'd have made a very good actor if she'd been inclined to relocate to Hollywood.

Wyatt sank into the chair and closed her eyes. "Have you heard details?"

"You know I have, sister. Three in total. All women."

She put the phone on speaker and laid it on the table with shaking hands. "Oh, crap."

"Crap, indeed. That's not even the worst part."

What could be worse than three women dead? "Tell me." Wasn't all that sure she did want to know. Afraid not to know.

"You know Royal's cousin, the feisty brunette?" Excitement rang in her voice.

"Yes." A rock settled in the pit of her stomach.

"She's the third one they found out there today." She delivered the news with what sounded like an ah-ha flourish. Definitely could have been an anchor on the six o'clock news.

"Were they shot?" She feared the answer.

"Nope, and that's the freakiest part of all. Looks like some animal killed them."

She sat up. Animal attacks? She'd been leaning toward serial killer and a gun. Now her thoughts tilted in another direction. "How do you know all this?"

"Easy. Me and Kenny are tight, if you catch my drift." A little chuckle.

Of course she'd be involved with Deputy Sheriff Kenny Harris. Handsome, personable, and single. Exactly Tracy's type. "I don't think that's appropriate pillow talk."

"No pillows needed, and he didn't tell me any of it outright. More like I'm able to read between the lines. Don't want him to get in any trouble, so I can confidently say he didn't share any official information with me." Her voice turned indignant, as if Wyatt had insulted her critical-thinking skills.

"You amaze me."

"We all have our skill sets." Once more congenial. Apparently, Wyatt's perceived insult had been forgiven.

She ended the call and stared at her phone for at least a full minute. Wyatt's body buzzed, and thoughts raced through her mind. They kept coming back to one: werewolf.

Training kicked in when Mari got out in the field, and she assisted the sheriff and his staff as best she could. With an excellent feel for what did and did not belong in nature, she quickly spotted disturbances. Her focus sharpened as they worked, and the hours flew by. No time for anything beyond the investigation. It wasn't until Ollie was driving her home that it all came down hard on her. Her shoulders tightened, her stomach rolled, and a pounding started behind one eye. "That was messed up out there." She stared out the window as they buzzed down the highway, the mountains in the distance murky in the shadows of the setting sun.

Three bodies. Not a single one with a bullet wound. Beyond the location, nothing linked Sherrill to the rest. The other three displayed clear signs of an animal attack. It would take the skill set of a medical examiner to determine the precise cause of death. Sort of. Everyone out there today could see the massive wounds on each victim's neck. Fangs had latched on and held on until life faded. That was her take.

"Messed up is a nice way to put it." Ollie kept his eyes on the road. "I'd have gone with FUBAR."

"FUBAR?"

"Fucked up beyond all recognition." She might not have known him long, but that phrase struck her as out of the norm for him. He didn't seem like the kind of guy who used profanity often, if at all. That he did now spoke volumes.

She turned to look at his profile. Weariness showed in the slump of his shoulders. "You're going to be glad to get out of here, aren't you? I have a suspicion making sense out of the mess out there may be a long and drawn-out process." How could it not be? Four human deaths and one suspicious animal death all in the space of a few days didn't lend themselves to a quick and easy resolution. Something, or someone, evil was making themselves known to the residents of this quiet Montana town. Almost made her want to pack up and head back to Oregon. She could do something else with her life. There were other jobs besides the forest service.

Or not. She loved what she did. Bodies excepted. Working outside and breathing in the fresh air of the forests and rivers and lakes nourished her mind, body, and spirit. Nothing like it. She'd go crazy if she found herself inside day in and day out.

Ahead, the turn-off to Wyatt's house loomed. The urge to tell him to take her there was strong enough that she almost blurted out for him to make the turn. Wyatt's presence calmed her, and she could use some calm right now. She stayed silent and gazed back at the highway in front of them as Ollie drove toward her own home.

"Never thought my swan song would come with bodies." His words were quiet, sad.

"Who could see that coming?" She sure didn't view it as her welcome to the new job either.

"Don't want to dump this in your lap, especially after—" He glanced at her again. "Well, after, you know." The sadness in his eyes didn't escape her.

She put a hand on his arm. "No one ever expects something that awful to happen. Sherrill was a royal pain in the ass, and clearly, she had serious issues, but a bullet to the head in the middle of a forest? No. She didn't deserve that. I wish she'd stayed in Oregon, found someone else to stalk."

Okay, that sounded petty and wasn't her typical style. Typical didn't describe anything that had happened since she made the drive up here, and maybe that explained it. Or not. The hand-off of the job from Ollie to her should have been easy and efficient. Meeting neighbors should have been easy and friendly. No bodies. No suspicions leveled at her. No attraction to a beautiful neighbor. So far things going right with this change in life were nowhere to be seen.

"Life happens as it will." He turned philosophical as he pulled up to her house. "Most of the time, it's good. Then there are times like these. I learned a long time ago just to take it as it comes. Might not like it. Can't control it or change it. All we can do is choose how to deal with it. Give yourself the grace to feel whatever emotions come your way for a little bit and then let it go. Don't allow any of this to drag you down. You got this."

She opened the car door. "Thanks for everything. I'll see you tomorrow. Hope you can get some rest."

He nodded. "You and me both. With any luck, tomorrow we'll both be rested, and all we'll have to do is clean out my office so you can move in."

"That sounds perfect." She held up her hand, fingers crossed.

"You get some sleep. It's been as hectic for you as for me. We both need a healthy dose of R&R."

"I'll try." She didn't hold out any real hope that either one of them would sleep much tonight.

Mari watched him drive away and only then walked up to the front door and put her key in the deadbolt. Dark and quiet inside. Lonely. She'd been living alone since the divorce, and it had never bothered her to come home to an empty house. Today it did. She missed the sound of dog nails clicking against the hardwood floors and the cheerful banter of friends. Funny how quickly she considered Addie, Tuesday, and Wyatt to be friends. For someone who liked to take her time getting to know people, these three had been immediate pals. It was as if they'd known each other for decades rather than days. She supposed it was like that sometimes.

Now, she stood in her kitchen and leaned against the counter. She wasn't motivated to do much of anything. Hard to get moving after today. Death had a way of doing that. First Sherrill, and now the one woman who might have been able to help them was as dead as her ex-wife. Had to be related, didn't they? Or maybe she wanted to believe there was a connection to make some kind of sense out of this situation.

Taking off her boots, she set them near the back door and headed down the hallway. A shower might help clear her mind and soothe her rattled nerves. Being in her profession meant that sometimes death came knocking. She'd been lucky that those events had been few and far between in her years with the service. The last few days appeared to be making up for lost time.

The shower did help. Her shoulders loosened up and her mind calmed. The unease in her stomach finally faded. In a clean pair of joggers and a sweatshirt, she returned barefoot to the kitchen. She sighed at the boxes piled up against one wall. Unpacking would keep her occupied. She grabbed the top box and set it on the counter. A second after taking her favorite mug out of the box, her phone rang. The number registered even though she hadn't put it in her contacts list yet. She smiled.

"Hi."

"You make it home?" Wyatt's voice held a note of concern that warmed her.

"I am. Showered and in clean clothes. Just digging through boxes."

"Are you okay?"

The way Wyatt checked on her pushed away some of the darkness. "As much as I can be, given the bodies piling up. It's a mess out there. I really wish they'd let you stay with me." She'd been focused and helpful, doing the job Ollie and Lloyd asked her to do. Didn't change the fact that she'd have liked Wyatt there too. Her presence gave her strength. Steadied her.

"Tuesday and Addie filled me in as much as they could."

"How are they? Tripper was amazing, and the work they did, fantastic. They didn't have to stay and search, but they did when Lloyd asked for their help. Without them, who knows how long those bodies would have continued to lie out there." She shivered as the sight of the corpses flashed behind her eyes. Doubted she'd ever get over seeing them.

"Actually, the girls are on the road." A bit of sadness sounded in Wyatt's voice.

"What?" She glanced out the window, the darkness dropping inky deep. Tuesday and Addie, along with Tripper, had worked all day. They had to be exhausted. "Why would they leave now?"

"Addie got a call on a case she's been working, and they had to rush back. Cleared it with Lloyd and they'll return when needed for the investigation. You're right though. All three are amazing. Tripper is a special dog. The way he and Tuesday work together is nothing short of magical."

"It's going to be quiet there tonight." She thought of the house that just last night had been filled with warmth and friendly conversation. Not now.

Wyatt cleared her throat. "That's kind of why I'm calling."

Mari held her breath. "Oh yeah?"

"If you're feeling like company, do you want to buzz over for dinner? I have all this food I've been working on and nobody to eat it except little old me."

Any remaining tension faded. "That sounds perfect because I'm hungry, and I don't have anything around the house but tons of boxes."

❖

Royal had been on the phone since he returned to the house. He'd identified Inez and, after the few seconds it took to compose himself, requested a look at the wounds. At first, they told him no. Animal activity, they'd explained. Not pretty and not something family would want to see. His lawyerly powers of persuasion worked, and they'd pulled back the sheets to reveal the extent of her fatal injuries.

The medical professionals were not wrong. Definite marks of an animal having at her flesh, ripping and tearing, stealing the life from her body. He knew something they didn't. The wounds were not inflicted by an animal native to the area, although he didn't enlighten them. Need to know, and no one outside of himself and Claude needed to know. Not exactly correct. The council would need to know, which is why he'd spent the last two hours on calls.

"I'm sure," he said for probably the tenth time. "I know what I saw, and it was one of us."

Teresa's voice held more anger than tension. "Claude?"

"No. Not us as in me or Claude. Someone else has come. An interloper working my territory. Have you talked to anyone in the States who could shed some light on this?" Though the council in Vancouver covered the West Coast of the United States, there were other divisions she could query. The council located in the city of New Orleans tended to be one of the busiest. For some reason, that area attracted many of their kind, though his personal tastes ran more to the forests of Canada and the Pacific Northwest. He was comfortable around wildcats, bears, and moose. Alligators and vipers were not appealing nature mates.

The conversation went on like that for at least another twenty minutes. Claude walked in as he ended the call and set his phone down. He looked up at him. "You catch any of that?"

Claude gave him a small nod, his expression guarded. "Enough. I take it you found Inez."

"Dead."

This time Claude shrugged. "You know that sooner or later it was going to happen. She took way too many risks. Bound to catch up with her at some point. Basic math, my man."

Wasn't sure he agreed totally. Yes, she pushed the bounds. No, the consequences didn't need to be fatal. "She didn't deserve to die." The death of any of his pack was personal. They were his de facto children, and any good parent would grieve the loss.

"She killed that woman. I say it's an eye-for-an-eye situation. She had it coming." The coldness in his voice chilled Royal.

She'd drawn first blood, and karma had a way of evening things out so, again, despite everything, Claude wasn't wrong in that respect. Inez had made tactical errors. First, killing the goat. Second, shooting that woman. Could have killed any of the three other women they'd found out there today, based on the initial timelines for their deaths. They'd shared that information with him at the morgue, albeit reluctantly.

But how had she ended up dead, clearly killed by one of their own? A werewolf. He hadn't killed her. Claude hadn't killed her. Who? What werewolf had moved unknown into the territory he'd claimed as his own. It simply wasn't done. They had rules. Centuries and centuries worth of rules.

"You're right that she took too many risks," he admitted. "She enjoyed living on the edge, and it was one of the things I liked about her." As much as it irritated him, he'd also appreciated her free spirit. Before and after he'd ascended to Alpha, he been a more cautious guy. Wild abandon had never been his thing. Through Inez, he'd experienced it vicariously.

"Not me. Didn't appreciate her large and loud personality. I like my women quiet. She'd likely still be with us if she hadn't refused to cooperate and had assimilated into our new community. Not that hard to do. She's the one who made it hard, and that's on her."

"You're really saying you like your women submissive." No shocker there. For a man barely thirty, Claude had a bit of a nineteenth-century attitude toward women. He liked them, but he believed himself better than those of the female persuasion.

"I'm a smart, talented guy. A rich guy. Those three things alone deserve appropriate admiration. I don't think of it as submission as much as appreciation for the hierarchy." His words were casual, the meaning beneath them quite serious. He believed every word that came out of his own mouth.

"You know that makes you sound like a horse's ass." Royal went blunt. Not in the mood to pull punches or stroke egos.

Claude raised a single eyebrow as he crossed his arms across his chest. "I prefer stud."

Royal shook his head. They were headed toward a no-win conversation. Way more important to concentrate on damage control and finding out who else was in their area. When he'd decided to come back here, he'd done his homework. No other packs made this area their home, and he'd formally filed for leadership. Now, he wondered if the intel had been wrong or if another alpha was challenging him. He'd floated that thought with Teresa, and she had nothing to share. At least not today. His claim appeared to be solid and valid. She left him with her plan to query all the other territories for packs relocating. He'd see what she came up with by this time tomorrow.

"We have to find out who else is here. Someone is hunting in our territory." In the meantime, he and Claude could put their research skills to the test.

"I'll make some calls." Claude reached into his pocket and pulled out his phone. As he walked out of the room, he put it to his ear.

For at least a minute, Royal stared after him. Three of them had made the trek to Montana, a small but mighty pack. Several of the others who'd been with them in Canada had decided to stay behind, and he didn't fault them for that decision. Though he stood at the head, he'd made the move optional. Somewhat, anyway. The choices were come with him or join a different pack. Three joined established packs and stayed in Canada, while the three of them started over here, where he thought they'd be safer. Things had gotten very dangerous up North, where an influx of visitors threatened the lands they'd enjoyed for centuries. Appears he'd made a bad call. Compared to what they'd faced in Canada, turned out to be far more dangerous down here.

Should he and Claude return to Canada? He walked out the back door and stood on the grass staring up at the moon. He'd loved it in British Columbia, and he'd enjoyed his years teaching. A million positives. He breathed in the fresh night air, filling his lungs. He lowered his gaze to the shadows of the trees just beyond Claude's beautiful gardens. No. He couldn't go back to Canada. At least not yet. Three had made the move down here, and it would take three to cross the border again. Just a few more nights, and then, and only then, could he consider leaving Montana for the second time in his life.

CHAPTER EIGHTEEN

After dinner, Wyatt and Mari sat in the living room, side-by-side on the sofa, feet up on the ottoman. Wyatt had poured them each a glass of wine, although both glasses sat untouched on the side table. "Tell me." She reached over and put a hand on Mari's cool fingers.

Mari didn't move her hand away. "Here's the thing. I've seen bodies before. I've never seen anything like this. It wasn't like with Sherrill." A shudder went through her.

Wyatt squeezed her hand gently. "I've heard." Tuesday had called while on the road and given her what details she could. A professional even if out of her home area, Tuesday kept the vast majority of the search details confidential. Nothing she told her wouldn't have already buzzed through town.

Mari's gaze snapped to her face. "The sheriff called you? We were given the keep-it-zipped instructions before he cut us loose. Sort of seemed pointed toward me too. I think he's caught on to us being friendly."

Wyatt shook her head. "No. Lloyd didn't share anything with me. I got most of what I know from Tracy, and Tuesday told what she could without violating any confidentialty issues."

"You know, I haven't been here very long, but I sure know who the go-to person is. How does your friend know everything? I'm kind of impressed."

"Not wrong. How she does it, I don't have a clue. I've always thought she should have been a deputy for Lloyd instead of a business owner."

"I think I like it better the way it is. Her café is the best." She hadn't been able to patronize the café much yet, but what she'd ordered so far rivaled the big cities' fare.

"She's good at everything. I hate her." Wyatt said it with a smile. She'd always loved Tracy and always would. Such a good soul, gossip aside. Besides, could you really call it gossip if it was actually true?

Mari laughed and picked up the wineglass to take a sip. "This is good. You make this one too?"

She nodded. "Grew those blackberries myself and used my wizardly skills to turn them into the nectar of the gods."

"Tasty." She set the glass back down and stared at it for a long moment. When she looked back up to meet Wyatt's eyes, her expression was dark. "Did Tracy tell you about the animal marks?"

Back to murder. So much for the magic of her blackberry wine. "She did." It hurt her heart to think how scared the woman had to have been as an animal tore at her flesh. The screams she imagined echoed inside her head.

"Your thoughts? I mean, you've lived here all your life, and you know those woods like the back of your hand. If anybody has valid thoughts about what could have happened, it's you." Mari tucked a leg up beneath her. Her face was a little pale, making the shadows under her eyes stand out. Between the nightmare last night and a day investigating three deaths, easy to understand.

"You probably don't want to hear what I'm thinking."

"Try me." Mari picked up the wine again and held it between her hands, as if she needed something to hold onto rather than wanting a drink.

Might as well just spit it out. At worst Mari would think she'd lost her mind and, in reality, might not be that far from the truth. "Fenrir."

For a few seconds, Mari stared into her glass, her eyes narrowed as if she weighed deep thoughts on the matter. She looked up and into Wyatt's eyes. "The werewolf. You didn't think I was listening, did you?"

For a second, she'd wondered, though had no plans to admit it. "I knew you were listening. I didn't think you were taking it seriously." For that matter, it had struck her as too far out too. Until it kept happening. If the wolves went homicidal, surely it would have happened before. And since when did wolves become serial killers? It didn't make sense.

"Maybe not, if I'm being honest." Now she sipped the wine as if admitting that the truth came hard. More like admitting to listening to a serious discussion on a killer werewolf was the hard part.

"I'm good with honest." In fact, Wyatt preferred it. Could be brutal but still beat lies.

Mari scooted a couple of inches closer. "Things are weird enough it might take thinking outside the normal channels. Someone killed these women, and despite the gunshot versus the animal attacks, I'm not convinced that it isn't all related. Too much of a coincidence, even if the manner of her death is different. Not sure a werewolf would use a gun though." She talked fast, maybe trying to convince herself as much as Wyatt.

Actually, what Mari said put a couple pieces in place for Wyatt. "Think about it. Why not? Wolf one moment, human the next. Could be he used different tools because the situations were different."

Mari shifted in her seat. "Didn't think about it like that. Does make a weird kind of sense."

"Totally agree." Wyatt grabbed her glass and took a healthy swig. It went down smooth and soothing. Maybe they could figure this out yet.

Mari was shaking her head. "Hunting werewolves. Didn't see that one coming when I moved here."

Wyatt set her glass back on the table. Her thoughts shifted away from werewolves, away from death. "How about me?" She looked at Mari.

"You?" Mari raised her eyebrows.

She reached over, took Mari's hand, and brought it to her lips. She kissed her palm. "Yes, me."

Mari shuddered again. Wyatt wanted to believe it was for a different reason. "No. I definitely didn't see you coming."

"Is it a good thing?"

Her smile was warm, inviting. "Very."

She kissed Mari's palm again. "Stay here again tonight."

"I should go home. Tomorrow is going to be brutal." Not much force under her words.

"I agree. It will be. A good night's sleep will help."

"Your guest room is comfy."

"If that's where you want to sleep." She held her breath.

Mari threw her head back and laughed. The sound was music to Wyatt's ears. "Despite everything, you make me feel like there's hope, and I can tell you, that's something that's been missing from my world for a long time."

Wyatt took Mari's face in her hands. "One thing I believe, deep in my heart, no matter how much darkness wraps around us, is that hope lives. All of what's happening is dark and dangerous. Evil is out there walking, and people are dying. But we will get through this. Evil will be stopped, and when the light comes back out, we'll still be here. Together."

Mari stared into her eyes. A shadow passed over her face. "How can you be so sure?"

She didn't miss the unspoken part. If Sherrill didn't make it, how could Wyatt be so certain that they would too? She patted her heart. "I know it here."

This time Mari put a hand on Wyatt's face. "You have such faith."

"And you don't?"

"I want to say yes. I can't. I mean, the fact that I'm here is proof how unfair life can be. The universe threw a whole bag of lemons at me, and I hate lemonade."

Wyatt pulled her close, wrapping her in a warm hug. "But the universe brought you to me."

❖

Mari sat back and stared into Wyatt's beautiful eyes. Despite the doom and gloom surrounding her since she'd arrived, this woman next to her represented a giant ray of golden light. Her heart swelled, and her breath came soft and easy. "It did," she finally said. "It absolutely did."

Wyatt's smile was soft. Heartwarming. "So, about tonight."

Mari leaned in and kissed her. She didn't give herself time to think. Instead, she did something unusual for her. She went for it. Wyatt kissed her back, warmth flooding her. No more thoughts of going home.

"I take it that's a yes," Wyatt said against her lips. After a moment, Wyatt leaned back and looked into her eyes. "About that guest room…"

Mari laughed and stood. Without saying another word, she walked quickly down the hallway to Wyatt's room. She kicked off her shoes and pulled her sweatshirt over her head, dropping it onto the floor.

Wyatt leaned against the doorframe. "I like where this is headed."

Mari gave her a wink. "You started it."

"Well then, I suppose I need to finish it." Her eyes were narrowed, and a tiny smile turned up the corners of her mouth. Her shiny dark hair framed her face.

Mari turned, still wearing joggers and a bra, hands on her hips. "I suppose you better." Her heart pounded, and her breath wavered. Had anything ever felt this exciting before? Her nerves were on fire in a very good way. She reached out toward Wyatt. "Help a girl?"

She didn't have to ask twice. Wyatt reached her in a couple of steps, gently pulling Mari's sports bra up and over her head, their lips and tongues meeting as she tossed the bra to the floor to join her shirt and shoes. "You're so beautiful," she whispered into Mari's ear.

"I bet you say that to all the rangers." She laughed as she fell backward onto the bed and pulled off her joggers.

"Only the hot ones, and trust me, that doesn't apply to Ollie." Wyatt's clothes landed in an untidy pile on the floor in a matter of seconds.

Naked, they stared into each other's eyes for a few moments. "What?" She could see the question in Wyatt's eyes.

"Are you sure? I don't want to mistake this for something it's not." A flicker of darkness in her eyes.

Mari put a hand to her cheek. "I've never been so sure of anything. This feels, is, perfect." For a flash, she'd had the same thought. It fled as quickly as it had come.

"The timing sucks," Wyatt whispered against her ear.

"It does, and I don't care." She ran her hand over Wyatt's silky hair.

The smile returned to Wyatt's lips as she leaned back to look at Mari. "I could fall in love with you."

Now Mari laughed. "Love is great and all, but let's start here." She kissed her hard, sliding her hands down Wyatt's body. Firm, muscled, magical. Hot.

The real world faded away as they kissed, stroked, and tasted. A world of sensations that flowed like lava through her. Mari leaned her head back and cried out as release almost brought her up and off the bed. She returned the favor, smiling at Wyatt's not-so-quiet cries.

Warm and satisfied, she drifted off to sleep, Wyatt holding her close. The horror of the day disappeared in the warmth of her embrace.

The first time Mari woke up, inky darkness filled the room. Wyatt's even breathing let her know she slept well, her arm still circling Mari's waist. She couldn't remember the last time she'd felt this peaceful or slept this easy. She drifted back into blessedly dreamless slumber.

She woke up a second time with daylight beginning to creep into the room and Wyatt screaming.

❖

Royal sat in the kitchen sipping on a cup of coffee and making cryptic notes on a pad. The words made sense to him. To anyone else, they'd be gibberish. He'd developed his own brand of shorthand during law school and had been using it ever since. If his notes were discovered, they'd be impossible to decipher. He liked having that kind of advantage. Now, it was more an exercise to maintain focus. The hours were ticking away, and he had to keep everything together until the night of the moonrise.

He leaned back in his chair and smiled. It occurred to him how to turn this whole disaster to his advantage. He nodded to himself as he considered all the possibilities. It could work. He was tapping his pen against the pad when Claude walked in. As usual, he wore jeans, a tidy white shirt, and sneakers. How he didn't destroy the ubiquitous white shirts with his constant work in the gardens, he'd never know. Then again, if he thought about it, Claude could be that guy who simply threw them away when they got soiled and bought new ones.

At the counter, Claude groaned. "Man, you did it again."

"Did what?" His attention had returned to his notes.

"The coffee. You drank it all again. How long have you been up?" Claude took the carafe, rinsed it, and began to fill it with tap water. No need for fancy water purifiers here.

Royal glanced at his watch. "Couple of hours. Sorry. Should have made another pot but got sidetracked. Working on getting my ducks in a row." He didn't feel too bad about the empty pot. Claude could make his own coffee. Royal wasn't his housekeeper.

"I have faith in you, man. If anybody can turn this mess into gold, it's you. Always been surprised you're not sitting on the council. You're a natural for the more administrative side of things." He scooped coffee into the basket, and the scent of the fine grind wafted through the kitchen. Nothing like the smell of coffee to wake up the senses.

"Not in this lifetime. Not my kind of gig. I don't have a problem calling the council for help now and again, but sit on it? Not for me." Dealing with students had been plenty. Most of the time they were great. A few special. And a few giant pains in the ass. Keeping the secrets of the worldwide community of werewolves, just not his cup of tea. Or coffee.

"You call them yet?" Claude leaned on the counter as he waited for his morning cup of joe. The kitchen filled with the scent of the brewing coffee and the sounds of the drip, drip, drip into the waiting carafe.

"I did, right after I identified her body. They would have caught it on the news, and I sure didn't want to be on the receiving end of that call. Better to hear it from me." Those who sat on the council were not the kind to be screwed with. They were powerful in more ways than one.

"Wise decision, dude. What do we do next? We get any marching orders?" His coffee finished dripping, and Claude poured a mug.

"Harvest Moon." The next move was a given. Something he shouldn't need to tell Claude. For some reason, he seemed to be intentionally obtuse this morning. Again, it might be less on Claude's part and more on Royal's grumpy mood. Might want to pour himself another mug of the brew. Maybe it would help. Or not. Might simply be this pissy until after the Harvest Moon.

"Going to be tricky making it happen now." Mr. Optimistic this morning.

Bad mood or not, Royal maintained the belief they'd get through this and all would settle in as destiny decreed. "Not really. In fact, I'm confident I can make this work to my advantage. Soon enough, we will be a trio again, and maybe, once things settle down, you'll find yourself a mate. You and I both have been solo too long. Men are not meant to be alone." A mate might help Claude be less self-focused. Mellow him out. He could use it.

"Maybe. I kind of like to be the wild dog." Claude laughed. "A mate might drag me down, if you know what I mean."

He did. "Single and unencumbered does suit you." The playboy lifestyle had never appealed to Royal. He was more dialed into one woman at a time, not that he'd ever made a solid commitment to a woman in the past. No particular reason, only that he hadn't met anyone who looked like forever to him. At least not until he came home and got hit by lightning. Or that's what it felt like anyway.

Claude, well, he liked a good time and was open to all experiences. His good looks and charm brought men and women into his orbit, and he availed himself of the boundless opportunities dropped into his lap. Like Royal, he'd never known Claude to get serious about anyone. He played hard and loud. However, as he thought about it, it occurred to him how quiet Claude had become since moving here. He worked his gardens, complained about Inez, and hung out around the place. No wild nights or parades of women. That he knew of anyway. "Are you okay?"

Claude looked up, an expression of surprise crossing his face. His eyes narrowed. "I'm fine. Why do you ask?"

Royal shrugged one shoulder. "Before we came here, you were always up and out, and enjoying the finer things in life. I don't recall you ever missing a Saturday night in the city."

Claude shook his head. "Not true. I missed plenty of them while we were enjoying the far North. Running with the big dogs, you know?"

"Good point. You're right. Our time in the territories excepted, you didn't miss a chance to party in the city. Since the move, I haven't seen you head out for a single night on the town. You've kept yourself pretty isolated. What's up with that?" Compared to how things were in Vancouver, Claude had tapped into his inner Jekyll and Hyde.

His smile was soft. "I like it here. When we first moved down, I didn't realize how much I'd appreciate the quiet and the beauty. It settled on me real quick. It's refreshing not to have all the noise and the activity. A guy can think and tap into his inner psyche. Lots of room to run when the time is right."

"You going celibate?" A legit question, given Claude's SOP before.

He shrugged. "For the moment, maybe. This place gives me some peace, and for the moment, I'm okay with that. Plenty of time to tap back into my randy side."

"I'm glad you like it here. Problem is, we might have to make the move back. Inez kind of screwed us with her refusal to lay low. We've had more attention than I'm comfortable with, and we can't afford to have Lloyd looking at us too closely. We'll see in a few days if it's safe to stay or if we need to make a hasty exit from stage left."

Claude held up his mug and gave Royal a little salute. "After the Harvest Moon."

"Yup, after that." They were on the same page. Claude might be arrogant and full of himself, but he consistently displayed intelligence and good sense, something Inez had sorely lacked. Something that ultimately cost Inez her life.

Claude saluted him for a second time. "Copy that."

CHAPTER NINETEEN

No way did Wyatt see what she thought she saw. A man almost hidden by the shadow of a pine tree. Even in the darkness his nakedness was apparent. From behind another tree, she stared, confident he wasn't aware of her presence. His head tipped, his mouth opened in a scream. Ice slid down her back at the sound, but what she saw next turned the ice glacial. A naked man no longer stood in the circle of moonlight. A wolf, twice the size of any from the local pack, roared, his four massive paws pounding the ground. The screams turned into howls, and then the wolf fully stepped out from behind the tree. For a second, it paused, lifted its nose in the air, and then it ran straight in her direction.

She didn't hesitate. Wyatt took off running. The light of the full moon illuminated the forest, and familiar landmarks guided her in the direction of the parking area. Her legs pumped as she ran, her long strides taking her over fallen trees and across the fields thick with wild grasses. She had one goal: to get to her truck. Why didn't she have her bow? Her hand went to her waist. No knife either. How in the world did she end up out here in the middle of the night without a weapon?

The moon shone large and bright, shafts of light cutting through the trees. Wyatt ran as fast as her legs would go, her heart pounding hard enough she wondered if it would jump out of her chest. She glanced over her shoulder at the thunder behind her. The wolf was closing the distance between them. With its glowing *golden eyes, it stared at her. Not like any wolf she'd ever seen roaming the forest before. Huge, its paws hitting the ground like thunder as it relentlessly pursued her.*

She continued to run, her lungs starting to hurt, and the burning in her thighs yelling for her to stop. She couldn't. Her only hope for survival was to make it to the truck before the wolf caught her. Once more she glanced back. Too close. Far too close. The wolf leaped.

Wyatt woke up screaming. She slapped her hand over her mouth and blinked as visions of the forest disappeared, replaced by the warm morning light creeping in through the slats of the bedroom blinds. How in the world could a night that had been something from the very best of dreams end with a nightmare of the worst kind? The only good thing, Mari held her tight.

"You're okay. I'm here. You're safe," Mari whispered into her ear.

Her heartbeat steadied and her breathing slowed as the real world came into more focus. "I'm sorry."

"Sorry about what? No one has to be sorry about a nightmare." Mari brushed the damp hair off Wyatt's face, her touch gentle. "Pretty sure someone told me that about, what was it, twenty-four hours ago?"

"Appreciate it, but sorry to have dragged you out of sleep." She didn't want to say out loud how embarrassing it was to end their beautiful night like this. She'd be surprised if Mari didn't find a way to keep her distance from now on. Wyatt sure could mess up a good thing nice and quick.

Mari kissed her lightly, her lips warm and soft. "When I wake up next to a beautiful woman who needs my assistance, I feel powerful. Besides, you've done a ton for me and even came to me when I woke up screaming. Only fair to return the favor." Her smile was bright.

The fright of the nightmare faded in the face of Mari's sweet words. "You have a surprisingly good attitude for someone who's been through a whole lot of trauma lately."

"For some strange reason, I feel ready to take on the world. Amazing how a great night recharges a person." Her smile shifted to sly.

"Flattery will get you everywhere." If not for the nightmare, Wyatt would probably feel the same way.

"Oh, pooh." Mari frowned and reached over to pick up her ringing phone. "Hello?" Her expression darkened as she listened. "I'll be there in thirty." She got out of bed and started picking up her clothes from where she'd dropped them the night before. Between the two of them, it looked like a great wind had thrown all their things around the bedroom floor. Worth it.

"Ollie?" She had to think he'd be the only one calling her this time of the morning and requesting her presence.

She nodded. "I'm sorry to rescue and run." She jerked her shirt over her head, her hair wild.

Wyatt sat up, not bothering to pull the covers up over her bare body. "Go. I understand. Anything I can do to help?"

Mari smiled as she looked at Wyatt. "I can think of something, but alas, we don't have time."

Wyatt warmed all over. "Darn."

"Rain check. Ollie asked me to meet him at the sheriff's office to compile reports. Before I head in there, I have to buzz home and change into work clothes. I don't think they'd be too impressed with this." Mari waved toward her ultra-casual and very wrinkled clothes. She had a point.

"Come back later?"

Fully dressed and in the doorway, Mari turned and smiled. "Sounds great, but I don't know what will happen today. I don't want to promise something I may not be able to do. How about I call you later and let you know how things are shaking out?"

Disappointing not to get an immediate yes. She could also understand. Wyatt had to take a backseat to the current investigation. "Sounds like a good plan."

Mari took a few steps down the hallway and backed up. She looked around the doorframe at Wyatt. "What was the nightmare that made you scream?"

She shuddered as it all flashed through her mind like a movie on fast-forward. "A werewolf."

Mari's eyebrows drew together as she studied Wyatt. "Really? A werewolf?"

Wyatt nodded as the fear washed over her again. "A really big one, and he bit me."

❖

Mari stepped back into the bedroom and studied Wyatt briefly. Definitely serious, given the look on her face, which made her decide that Ollie and Lloyd could wait a few for her. Some things were more important. Some people were more important. "A werewolf bit you." Not a question.

"It was so freakishly real. I woke up screaming because of the pain." Wyatt's hand drifted to her left shoulder.

"Nightmares are like that." Wyatt's werewolf nightmare interested her. More than that, it echoed her own from the night before. She wanted to hear more about it.

Still massaging her shoulder, Wyatt said, "Do you know what folklore says about the bite of a werewolf?"

She might not be versed in many folk legends, but didn't everyone know about that one? "It turns you into a werewolf." That's what she recalled anyway, not that she considered herself well-schooled on the topic. Ask her about a gray wolf, and she could rattle off all sorts of details. Mythical creatures not so much.

"Gave me the creeps, and I'm telling you, the bite hurt so bad, I can still feel it. The weirdest part about it all is that something about that wolf felt familiar. Like I somehow knew it, or the man it was before it changed." A shadow passed over Wyatt's face, and now she grabbed the blanket and pulled it up as if she'd grown cold.

Mari would like nothing more than to plop back down next to her. She didn't dare. "I'd love to stay and talk this through with you. See if we can come up with why the wolf felt familiar. But I have to get into the office, and I'll already be later than I told Ollie.

I don't want to set more of a bad example my first week, or give Lloyd a reason to rethink his clearing me for Sherrill's murder."

"I get the feeling Lloyd isn't interested in you."

Mari nodded. "He's not. If I start flaking on my job, he might change his mind. I want to stay on Lloyd's good side." It was true. She'd left yesterday feeling that Lloyd had no reservations about her. She suspected he'd been around his fair share of killers throughout his career and knew bad when he encountered it. If he hadn't, he wouldn't have allowed her out there yesterday to assist.

Wyatt nodded and wrapped the blanket tighter. "I get it."

"Did I tell you the sheriff went to that same bar we did? Once I informed Ollie about what we'd discovered, anyway. He passed it along to Lloyd, and after I left last night, he'd said he planned to interview the manager. I think part of the plan this morning is to go talk to your friend."

"Royal?" Wyatt was pulling on a pair of sweats. "I wouldn't classify him as my friend, exactly. More of an acquaintance from our school days. One who wants to be more despite my consistent shut-down on his attempts."

"That's the guy." Mari hoped Lloyd would have more luck than they'd had when they tried to have a chat with his cousin. She took a step toward the hallway. Time to get in gear before it got any later.

"You think Royal is regretting his decision to move back here? Like with you, things haven't exactly been smooth. Not to mention..."

"Not to mention what?" Something about the way Wyatt said those three words made her hesitate, despite the fact she really did need to get her butt moving.

Wyatt pulled a sweatshirt over her head and then shook out her hair. "It's dumb really."

"Dumb sounds good right about now. Spill it."

"Like I said earlier, he appears to be fixated on me." Wyatt made a sour face. Old friend or not, she clearly didn't appreciate the unwanted attention.

"On you? Does he not see the obvious?" She chuckled. Some guys just couldn't handle the truth even when it stared them straight in the face.

Wyatt blew out a long breath. "Trust me, I've tried to be as diplomatic as possible and let him know he's knocking on the wrong door. For a really smart guy, he's not getting it. I don't know if he's one of those who thinks if I just give him a chance, I'll change my mind. Or maybe he's just oblivious. Either way, you'd think a law professor would be more savvy."

"Haven't we all run into those people?" She thought of a neighbor years ago who had to have asked her out half a dozen times. All her efforts to politely decline fell on deaf ears. Blunt and rude finally did the trick, though from that day forward, he gave her dark looks whenever their paths crossed.

"Way too often." Wyatt smiled slyly. "Maybe you can help me with Royal, and then he'll finally give up on his mission to be my boyfriend."

Mari laughed and saluted her. "I'll be more than happy to lend a hand or a kiss or…"

Wyatt's smile glowed. "Call me later."

"Done." She left Wyatt in the bedroom and hurried out to her car. It was possible she might have exceeded the speed limit as she raced toward her own house. It was also possible she didn't care.

After a three-minute shower, she dressed, grabbed a bottle of orange juice out of the refrigerator—one of just the very few groceries she'd had time to pick up—and managed to make it to the office forty minutes after her call from Ollie. She figured that ten minutes late didn't really count. No one seemed to notice her tardy arrival. All good.

"Come on in." Ollie waved her to his office, or was it her office? Too confusing. She'd stick with his office for the time being.

She sat in one of the visitor chairs. Ollie stood at the window, and the sheriff sat in the other one. Lloyd's knee moved up and down, and his fingers tapped the arms of the chair.

Lloyd turned to her. "Your tip about the bar paid off. I talked to Tyler last night, and he sent us a copy of the surveillance video. Now,

I want to go talk with Royal about his dead cousin. If she hadn't been killed out there, the woman would have some explaining to do. I'm hoping he can at least fill in a few of the blanks."

"You want me to come along?" This sure seemed like an interview that the sheriff's department, not a forest ranger, should handle. She wanted to go anyway.

"I do." Lloyd stopped bouncing his leg as she turned to look at him. The dark circles under his eyes aged him from the man she'd first met. No big mystery there. How often did he have to deal with what looked like the work of a serial killer? From all appearances, he didn't come across as the kind of guy who refused to ask for help. Though the help he asked for now gave her pause.

"Why?" Maybe she should just go and not ask a lot of questions. Pushing for more might not be appreciated from the new ranger in town. He didn't know it wouldn't be like her to just go along. Kind of like it wasn't like her to get over it, as her former boss had tried to suggest when they denied her the promotion. She'd set that POS straight.

Lloyd explained. "I have a hunch he'll be more willing to talk to you than me."

If she thought he'd made that statement because of her skills as a ranger, she'd be okay with it. But that's not how she saw it, and that's why she found it a touch insulting. "Kind of sexist, don't you think?" And off-base in her mind. Most men seemed to prefer to talk with other men, particularly when it came to the law. And she'd held out hope Lloyd would be more inclusive in his thoughts and actions. Maybe she'd read him wrong.

He laughed, and for a moment the weariness disappeared from his face. "Not where I was going, though, I admit, it could sound that way. I'm asking for your help because a lot of times we run into resistance in getting folks to talk to us because we're cops. The way I see it, a forest ranger is more neutral, which could be enough to get him to talk freely if you're the one asking the question. You, and Ollie, are less of a threat than the big, bad sheriff."

Part of it made sense. Still a critical piece missing. "Why not have Ollie talk with him then? Mano a mano."

He made a face. "Honestly, Royal doesn't know Ollie that well. Not much in terms of interaction between them before Royal left for college and stayed away for years. You're more of a contemporary, which we can use to our advantage."

Could be he was right. People did have a tendency to freeze up around cops. Throw in the little fact that Royal was a lawyer, and it doubled the likelihood he'd resist talking with Lloyd.

Despite the gun Ollie required her to carry on the job, when it was all said and done, she was a forest ranger, not a cop. Her job, first and foremost, would always be to preserve the parks, not solve murder cases. She glanced over at Ollie, who stood with his back to the window, his arms crossed over his chest. His expression remained calm, and he gave her a tiny nod. "Okay. Let's go talk to the lawyer."

The sound of car tires crunching down the gravel driveway interrupted Royal. After closing his laptop, he got up and walked out to the porch. Nothing shocking about the identity of the visitor. He'd expected Lloyd to show up sooner or later, and sooner seemed the most likely scenario. What he hadn't expected was to see Ollie and Mari come with him. New twist on a law-enforcement interview technique. Or at least what he was accustomed to.

"Hey, Lloyd. What's up?" He walked toward the marked car.

"Need to talk to you about your cousin. Got a few?" Mari and Ollie climbed out of the car as well.

"Can't tell you much." *Offer nothing.*

"We'll take whatever you can share." Mari stepped up next to Lloyd. Her brown hair had been tucked up under a forest-service cap, and her uniform looked clean and pressed. Made it clear that they'd come straight from the office. No messing around this morning. No forays back to the crime scene yet.

He studied Mari for a moment, working through scenarios for her presence here with Lloyd. He'd liked her well enough when they first met. She'd come across as smart, capable, and rational.

After he witnessed the interactions between her and his beloved, he liked her a lot less. That she showed up here with Lloyd just flat out pissed him off. Why he'd bring her along, he didn't have a clue. She had no business in this. *Go back to your forest and be a good little ranger.* In short, get out of his life and, more pressing, get out of Wyatt's life. Everything was progressing fine until Mari showed up.

Keeping his best courtroom neutral expression, he waved the visitors inside. "Sure. Come in. I'll make some coffee." Gave him a few minutes to gather his thoughts.

In the kitchen, he looked at what remained of the coffee Claude had made earlier and decided it would be enough. Probably not very tasty. It had been sitting on the warmer for a while. Didn't much care. Fresh coffee only encouraged visitors to linger. He took down four mugs. Outside in the garden farthest from the house, Claude worked, apparently unaware of their guests. Good. Lloyd questioning one of them was plenty, and even though Claude had been a top student, better to have the licensed attorney do the unwanted interview.

The trio had followed him into the kitchen, and they made small talk as he poured the coffee, brought out a small container of creamer, and handed each a mug. They took the offered mugs and sat around the table. "Okay. What are your questions about Inez? I've already confirmed one of the bodies found was hers, so what else do you need from me?" Take the offensive, basic strategy.

"Right, right, right," Lloyd said and reached for the creamer. He poured a little in, stirred it with the spoon Royal handed him, and then took a sip of the hot coffee. "Good stuff." He held up the mug.

He didn't buy the compliment. The brew had been sitting in the carafe long enough to be miles away from good. "Thanks. I try." He wanted to scream: *get on with it.* Instead, he waited. He narrowed his eyes as he noticed Lloyd give Mari a tiny nod that looked an awful lot like a "go-ahead" motion.

It was, because she lobbed the first question. "First, and most important, what was Inez doing with Sherrill at the bar the other night?" Mari hadn't touched her coffee. She stared at his face, her eyes intense and unreadable.

He shrugged, keeping a neutral tone. "Can't help you much with that one. I didn't even know she'd gone to the bar, let alone talked to your ex. She liked to go out at night every now and then, so it doesn't surprise me much she was there."

"Missed the action of the big city?" Mari still stared at him as though trying to see into his soul. The lady was super intense. Could be she'd missed her true calling by not becoming a cop like Lloyd.

"I suppose." If she thought she could rattle him, she'd be wrong. He'd been up against far more fierce adversaries. He continued calmly. "She seemed to be okay with the move here, but lately, she had mentioned being a little homesick. The night before you found her, Claude had driven her to the airport in Missoula. She was catching a flight back to Vancouver."

"Why?" Now at least she had wrapped her hands around the mug. The hardness in her voice hadn't softened.

"She said she wanted to go back, that she missed friends." The lies rolled off his tongue far more easily than he would have expected. Sounded pretty believable if he did say so.

"When were you aware that she didn't arrive?" The intelligent gaze never left his face. She would be one to watch...or, to take a page from Inez's playbook, to remove from the situation. Target practice. Couldn't believe he was actually leaning into something Inez would do. He considered himself above the base reaction. He'd have to work on that.

"Not until I got the call to identify her body. Only then did I talk with the friend who was supposed to pick her up from the airport and found out she never arrived. Or, to be more precise, never got on the plane in the first place, as we found out later." He was elaborating a little too much. If he were advising a client, he'd tell them to shorten their answers. A lot.

"She didn't say anything about meeting Sherrill?"

"No." Only a partial lie. After the fact didn't count.

"Even after you heard about Sherrill's murder? Surely, she'd mention that she'd talked to her the night before."

He shook his head. "You don't know Inez. Unless the meeting had led to something very exciting, it would mean nothing to her. She'd forget a person in the blink of an eye. I don't want to say my cousin is—was—self-centered, but the truth is the truth. It was about her. Always." Over the years, keeping himself safe had developed a razor-edged sharpness to his lies. Probably could have made millions as a defense attorney, if he'd had been so inclined. After this experience, he might seriously consider it.

Lloyd finally spoke up. "Okay if we take a look at her room?"

He'd anticipated that request and liked the appearance of cooperation he portrayed by leading them down the hallway. "Sure. Follow me." He swung the door open, knowing what the sheriff would see because he'd already gone through it after he'd loaded her into the car with Claude. Most of her things remained, as she'd taken only one suitcase when she left. He'd been concerned about where the suitcase was now and what she'd put in it. Frustrating that he could do nothing about it.

He stood in the doorway as Lloyd searched the room. Ollie and Mari stayed in the doorway with him. She might have done the majority of the talking in the kitchen, but looking for clues and evidence was clearly Lloyd's skill set. He checked the bed, the closet, the bureau. Almost the identical pattern he'd used when he checked through the room right after Inez left.

After ten minutes, Lloyd turned to them and shook his head. "I don't see anything."

"Honestly, Lloyd. I don't think she knew anything." He doubled down on his lies. Get him out of the house and out of his life.

"Had to follow the lead." Lloyd shoved his hands into his pockets.

Royal gave him a knowing nod. Just a couple of guys who understood the process. "I get it."

"I'm sure you do. Thanks for the help." Lloyd held out his hand. Royal shook it, Lloyd's grip bordering on a squeeze. He let go of Royal's hand before it tipped over into aggression.

"Anything I can do to help. I want to know who did all this as much as you. A serial killer in the Hamilton area is wrong in so many ways." Keeping up the helpful-guy persona.

"They seem to be everywhere these days. It's a goddamn plague." Lloyd took off his cap and ran a hand over his still-thick, though graying hair. He put the cap back on.

Ollie spoke up. "This is unthinkable, and it pisses me off that someone is spilling blood out there. Not the way I wanted to end my tenure."

"Sorry, Ollie." Royal patted him on the back. "I'm sure this is horrible for you. At least you've got some great help." He nodded toward Mari.

"She's getting more than she bargained for." Ollie looked over at Mari and frowned.

"Not your fault, Ollie. We'll get through this, and you can head to sunshine and warm weather." Mari gave him the ghost of a smile.

Royal took the opportunity to herd the unwanted guests down the hallway and toward the front door. "Well, if I come across anything, I'll let you know." Opening the door, he waited until all three walked out and then followed them to the car.

Before getting into the backseat, Mari held out her hand. "Thanks."

He shook her hand. No crushing grip from her. "I'm here to help, if I can." Probably wouldn't be the kind of help she wanted.

He crossed his arms over his chest and watched them drive in the direction of the highway. Mari, sitting in the back, turned to glance back at him. Sharp lady who might not be buying what he'd been selling. Her, he'd deal with later. He stood there until they were out of sight, and only then did her he return to his computer. Time to figure out who had invaded their territory and why. Once he did, he would kill them.

Chapter Twenty

R ather than sit around waiting to hear from Mari, Wyatt went to her workshop. Work always helped, and she'd been putting finishing touches on her latest custom bow order when an idea came to her. She set the bow aside, thankful she was ahead of schedule on this commission. Gave her the leeway to complete a new and special project.

First, she spent an hour on the computer researching. These days, not difficult to find anything, and today didn't disappoint. Taking what she learned on the internet, along with knowledge she already possessed, she made some three pages of notes before she started on a very particular creation.

Some hours later, Wyatt sat back and studied her handiwork. Six sterling silver broadheads ready and waiting to be installed. For longer than she should have, she debated with herself about which arrows to use them on. Finally, a decision made, she got to work again. Shortly after that, six arrows were ready and waiting in her quiver. Never thought she'd be loading her quiver with silver-tipped arrows, yet here she was.

Nobody else might believe her, and perhaps she doubted herself a little, but still didn't mean she shouldn't be prepared with the right tools for the job. The hardest part had been rounding up enough silver to make the broadheads. She'd hit the jackpot with a heavy necklace that had belonged to her grandmother. If the necklace hadn't been majorly ugly, she'd have felt guilty about melting it down. She told herself that Grams would find its new incarnation interesting and wouldn't be hurt by the repurposing of the silver.

Wyatt had made one trip away from the farm after the thought of silver occurred to her. While she could forge all sorts of things and routinely made her own broadheads, bows were her area of expertise. When she did custom bows, she crafted custom everything. Just her style and what brought customers to her from all over the country. But she didn't do bullets, given she rarely used a gun and didn't take orders for anything gun-related. Her business remained dedicated to bows and survival education, and she was smart enough to stick to what she knew best.

It occurred to her that if she equipped herself for the worst-case scenario, what about Mari? That's what prompted her to make a quick trip over to the house of her friend Bob. The guy knew his guns better than anyone she'd ever known, and that was saying something, given where she'd been born and raised. He also had all the equipment to make ammunition. She took him some of the silver, and he promised to deliver them before sundown. It was good to have friends, especially ones who had awesome skills and didn't question odd requests. In fact, he'd seemed downright pleased by her special order.

Weapons ready, now she needed to make sure her headlamps all worked. Normally, she handled this chore right before a class started, because at least one day of the program included night training. Nothing worse than getting out there in the pitch dark and discovering that a headlamp's batteries were dead. At least one student in each class failed to check theirs, even though every single student packet included the reminder. In bold letters. All caps. A good lesson for her students. A tactical error for the instructor. She didn't make tactical errors.

Keeping busy all day helped her to not focus on the fact that her phone never rang. No call came in from Mari. Made sense, considering everything happening. If Lloyd wanted Mari and Ollie to assist, he'd keep them running all day and maybe all night. She hoped he would limit it to the daytime. She also hoped Mari would stay with her again. The house felt empty now that she was here alone. She missed Tuesday, Addie, and Tripper. And she really missed Mari. In such a short time, Mari had managed to bring light into Wyatt's life. Light she didn't even realize she'd been missing.

Outside, she fed the animals, then checked to make sure all the water troughs were filled. They all acted happy to be back out in the pastures, and she hoped she wouldn't need to lock them inside the barn again tonight.

She pulled some weeds and took a couple of racks to the garden shed. Busy work, and it ran out pretty quickly. She did maintain a rather tight ship, disorder just not her thing. Tools were put away, supplies were in their proper places, and fences checked to be sure they remained in good condition. No new Daisy-created escape routes. Check, check, and check.

Out of farm maintenance to keep her busy, she headed back into the house. Dumb to just stand around. She hesitated, her gaze straying to the driveway. She hoped to see Mari's car drive down it. With a sigh, she turned and went into the house. For the next hour, she worked on the outline for the upcoming class. More like she tapped a pencil on her desk for an hour while staring at a blank notebook. Pushing the notebook aside, she turned to her computer. Not much actual work got done there either. With effort, she forced herself to focus and then sat up to lean closer to the monitor. A familiar and surprising name on the participant list. Royal's cousin, Inez, had signed up for the class. What in the world? Why hadn't he mentioned she'd planned to attend? What little she'd heard about Inez sure didn't suggest someone who would be interested in a women's survival course.

Leaning back in her chair, she closed her eyes and rubbed her temples with her fingertips. Her thoughts turned to her long-ago classmate. What was it about Royal that bothered her? He'd changed a lot since their school days, not that she ran in the same circle back then, and, well, none of them were those kids who had walked across the auditorium stage to collect their diplomas. What she did remember about him was quite different from the guy in the process of setting up a law practice downtown. Back then, he had seemed smart though extremely quiet. The kind of guy who blended into the background without any real effort. The Royal who returned to Hamilton definitely did not blend into the background. Still smart, though, and that gave her some pause. How smart, she wondered.

It was possible her reservations about him stemmed from his relentless attention toward her. Wyatt hadn't given him a single reason to believe she could or would ever be interested in him. Didn't seem to matter. He refused to give up. Like someone with obsessive-compulsive disorder, he didn't stop no matter how many times he ran face-first into rejection. With the murder of his cousin, perhaps he'd finally focus someplace else, and she could get on with her life without finding flowers on her doorstep or surprise visits with cups of Tracy's coffee on sunny mornings when she'd rather be doing something other than getting him to leave.

When her phone rang, she jumped and knocked a notepad onto the floor. Glancing at her phone, she smiled at the name on the display, and all grim thoughts of Royal evaporated. She leaned down and picked up the pad as she answered. "Hey," she said. "How's it going?"

"It's been a day." Mari sounded tired.

"That bad?" Wouldn't surprise her to find out that Lloyd ran her ragged. Not fair since the murder investigation was police business more than forest service. If she could, she'd tell Lloyd to run his own people ragged and give Mari, and Ollie, some breathing room.

"Not bad, exactly. No more new body discoveries so there's that to be grateful for." As she talked, the weariness started to fade from her voice. Wyatt liked to believe talking to her had a part in that.

"If it's any consolation, nobody expected what we found out there." She thought about her friends who came for a relaxing visit and instead got sucked into several days of intense searching. Tripper didn't seem to mind. That boy was ready to work 24/7. Tuesday and Addie most likely would have appreciated an uneventful visit, though the very nature of what they did meant a search could happen any time, any place. The karma they built up doing such selfless work would surely take them to a bright place someday.

Once this whole thing settled down, it might be her turn to travel their way and ensure the visit was quiet. Or not, given what both women did for a living. A human-remains team and a PI were way more glamorous than her simple lifestyle. Yeah, she'd definitely have to make a trip to the Midwest. Maybe she could talk Mari into going with her.

She stood and stared out the window, smiling. Wyatt wasn't a total off-the-grid type. She had modern conveniences like water, heat, electricity, and wi-fi. She believed in being self-sufficient, but she also believed in living in the real world. Things went forward, and those who didn't keep up were left behind. Blending the old with the new had merit, and she told her students as much, even as she taught them how to build a fire without matches or create a shelter from natural materials or make tea with the appropriate plants.

All these thoughts raced through her mind as she tried to think of a good reason for Mari to come back here tonight. It wasn't like the power might go off in this weather or the grocery stores would run out of food. No major storm on the way. No wildfires threatening the town. The only thing she could think of was companionship. Close companionship. Could be enough.

Weariness came back into Mari's voice. "No, I suppose not. Evil like this isn't something people invite in."

"It definitely isn't. This is generally a lovely place to live, and when everything settles down, you'll see it."

"I hope you're right because right now, this whole relocating to Montana has been an adventure I didn't see coming."

"Or me?" Dumb, dumb, dumb. Why did she say that? Why did she put Mari on the spot like that? Again. If only she'd stuck to the conversation at hand. She held her breath.

There was a lightness in Mari's voice now, the tiredness seemingly gone. "Definitely not you, but thank the gods you were here, or I think I'd have lost my mind through all of this."

Relief had her sitting back down in her chair. "That's a really nice thing to say."

"I mean it. You have made everything better. A bit of light in an otherwise dark time."

Her heartbeat sped up. "Do you want to come over?" Not impressed with how breathless she sounded. Seventeen-year-old Wyatt making an unexpected return visit.

"Yes."

❖

Mari should have exercised more restraint. Everything was moving at an uncomfortable speed right now, and a woman with any brains would take her time and slow down her roll. She'd never get away from the reality that she'd made a huge error with Sherrill, and she didn't want to put herself in the position of making another one. To mistake passion that arose from a heightened emotional situation for something deeper wouldn't end well.

All the stern self-talk didn't make a damn bit of difference. Mistake or not, she needed to see Wyatt. Wanted to as much as needed to. She changed her clothes, took along a clean uniform, just in case, and started driving a route that was quickly becoming familiar. Despite the hunt for a serial killer, this thing between her and Wyatt felt right. Sometimes bad timing turned out to be the right timing. Or that's what she told herself anyway.

The thought of Wyatt made her smile. Such an interesting woman in a dozen different ways. And, so far, not a wisp of mental instability. One and done in that arena. It had taken a while for her to look at her relationship with Sherrill in a clear and truthful way. Only then did she realize how many red flags she'd missed, or ignored, if she was being honest. Sure, she'd seemed attentive and stable at first, but the signs had been there. The flickers of madness beneath the high intelligence and beauty.

Eyes wide open now, she was pleased that none of those frightening flags showed in Wyatt. Quite the opposite. Bright and capable, with a subtle sense of humor and a mighty calm in the face of a storm. Sherrill never would have handled the sight of a body like Wyatt had. She'd been organized and thoughtful as she'd called in the authorities. Admirable, and it had drawn Mari even more to her. She didn't pitch a fit when Mari got called in on the investigation of the other victims while she'd been sent home. Sherrill would have had a meltdown of epic proportions to have been sent away like that. Wyatt had shown nothing but grace, topped off by a kiss that made her tremble just thinking about it.

She didn't even want to get started on making love to her. Almost wanted to send herself to the corner for jumping in so quickly, and if it hadn't felt so right, she might have made herself stand down. No corners for her tonight. No standing down. She anticipated a warm dinner, soft words, and a bit of romance.

The porch light glowed bright when she pulled in, and as she neared the front door, moths flitted toward the buttery glow. The moon rose high and golden, the air clear and fresh. If not for death beyond the trees, it would be perfection. She brought her hand up to knock on the door. Before she could, it swung open. Wyatt stood in the open doorway, her eyes bright and beautiful.

"Hey." Wyatt reached out to pull her into a hug, her arms around her, warm and comforting. Mari melted into her, grateful. All the stress and drama of the day faded away. How she could get used to this.

Mari kissed her on the cheek. "Thanks. You have no idea how much I needed that." She didn't want to move out of the embrace. Hungry as she might be, she could stand here like this all night.

"Come on." Wyatt took her hand and led her into the living room. "Have a seat and put your feet up. I'll get us something to drink."

Before Mari could say anything, Wyatt left her alone. Normally, given she was in someone else's home, she would sit with her feet on the ground. But Wyatt's home made her feel comfortable. This wasn't a house for show; it was a house meant to be lived in. Warm, inviting, friendly. She kicked off her shoes and put her feet up. Her head leaning back, she sighed. Tension flowed out of her. She changed her opinion. It was a house made to be lived in and loved in.

"Try this." Wyatt came back into the room, making barely a sound because, like Mari, she wore only her socks. "I think you'll like it."

Mari took the offered glass and put it up to her nose. It had a deep fruity aroma. "You make this one too?" The dandelion wine she'd served them before had been floral and refreshing. The blackberry wine, light and fruity. This one was deep red.

Wyatt smiled and nodded. "Of course. I may have to open my own winery one of these days. Raspberry this time."

"Seriously?" She caught the scent of raspberries and wasn't sure what else. She took another sniff. Then a sip. "Okay. That's good. More full-bodied than the other two."

Wyatt beamed. "Thanks. That's what I was going for with this one. I like to play with creating the wines from the things I grow. Takes a ton of time and effort, but it's fun, and they usually end up tasting good, although I had to tinker with the raspberry version a few times before I finally got it right. I put this particular vintage up three years ago."

"I would never even think to make wine out of things like dandelions or blackberries or raspberries." Mari sipped again, amazed how good it was.

Wyatt flashed a smile. "My grandmother is the one to thank for the creative vintages. She liked her toddies, and I guess I take after her. On the non-alcoholic side, I make a killer dandelion tea too. I've been experimenting for years with different fruits and flowers for both wines and teas. A little side gig with one customer. Me."

Mari's admiration grew, if that were possible. Wyatt would survive an apocalypse pretty darned well. She would be the person to follow if the world went to hell, and the way things had been going since she got here, that was a definite possibility. Mari planned to be one step behind her or, better yet, hand-in-hand.

Wyatt sat next to her on the sofa, putting her feet up on the ottoman beside Mari's. Talk about instant relaxation. Despite the unthinkable going on outside the house, inside it was like the world didn't exist. She wished she could stay here forever, sitting beside Wyatt and sampling her wonderful wines. Here was nothing but warmth and companionship.

"How is this all happening? How can I feel this wonderful and like we've known each other forever?" She turned to Wyatt and stared into her eyes. "So right. So fast."

Wyatt took a sip of her wine and smiled. "So perfect, if it's what I think you're referring to."

"Is it real?" She let the question in her mind pass her lips. Would it offend Wyatt? She had to know if it was all in her head or if it could possibly be genuine. The urge to cross her fingers came rolling in strong.

Wyatt put a hand on her cheek. "It feels real to me, and that's the truth."

Her heart did a little flip. For a few seconds, her mind raced to see if she'd missed any red flags. Nothing came to her, and once more her heart did that little flip. "It feels real to me too." She leaned and kissed her, the flick of her tongue pushing between Wyatt's lips.

The doorbell rang.

Royal's hand shook as he pushed the doorbell. More like he laid on the doorbell. He wanted to go inside right damn now. *Hurry up and open the door.* He glanced back over his shoulder at the car parked beside his, Oregon plates. That new forest ranger was like a bad rash he couldn't get rid of. While he didn't mind serving as her legal counsel, it pissed him off to no end that she kept clinging to Wyatt like a love-sick teenager. She wasn't even close to good enough for her. She appeared to be bright and not unattractive, but an alpha? The only one suitable to spend a lifetime with Wyatt was him. Period. End of story. He would fight to the death for her. Would the ranger? He doubted it.

Wyatt's expression was neutral as she opened the door, though he detected a bit of color in her cheeks. He didn't like the look of that. "Hey, Royal, what's up?" She glanced around him as if looking to see who might be with him. Why she thought he'd bring someone else along, he didn't know. This was always about the two of them.

"Royal?" She asked again when he didn't respond right away.

He flinched at the sharp tone of voice, though tonight, he would give her a pass. The last few days had been hard for everyone. Her, him, everyone, whether she realized it or not. He could grant her that grace as he understood that, in time, the irritation would fade away, as would the memory of the other woman who undoubtedly sat inside. All she'd need would be him. He gave her a small smile. "I'm checking on you. It's the neighborly thing to do."

"Why?" Still an edge to her voice.

He shrugged and smiled, hoping that his anger at her clear attempt to stall didn't show in his face. Let him in already. Was that so hard? "That's what friends and neighbors do, and since we're both, here I am making sure all is good with you."

"I'm fine." No need to be snippy.

He could take the high road when he needed to. She'd appreciate it in time. "All right then. I'll let you get back to your guest, but if you need anything, please don't hesitate to call. I can be here in a jiffy." She had no idea how fast he could cover ground if he let himself change. His fingers curled into fists as he peeked over her shoulder. Mari stood down the hallway, watching. He could solve that problem right now if he allowed himself to call on the power of the moon.

"Will do. Have a good night." She shut the door. In his face, no less. Not quite a slam. Not quite a friendly close. Her—it was that ranger gumming everything up. Definitely needed to do something about Mari, and the clock was ticking.

Back at his house, he paced. For an intelligent guy, he felt decidedly stupid at the moment. He had spent a massive amount of time and energy creating his perfect world. He was so damn close he could taste it, and then Mari walks in and fucks it all up. Not just Mari, but damned Inez too. Why couldn't she have just gone back to Canada like a good girl? Why couldn't she have stayed out of trouble here? Why? Why? Why? A million questions and not a single answer.

He went to the fridge and pulled out a beer. Not much of a drinker even before the change. He'd witnessed how it affected his father and never wanted to go that route. Still, every once in a while, a bit of alcohol helped smooth the rough edges. Tonight was one of those nights. A beer or two and maybe he'd come up with a brilliant solution. If not, he could always toss off his clothes and go for a run, murder investigation be damned. They'd never be able to catch up with him anyway.

The back door slammed, and a few seconds later, Claude sauntered in, pulling a dirty T-shirt over his head. The pristine white had turned splotchy brown. Some serious digging had gone on out there today. Claude tossed it toward the laundry room, though it fell short. Royal closed his eyes for a second. The irritation passed quickly. Claude tended to be cavalier about things, including keeping the house tidy. He would eventually pick up the shirt and actually put it in the laundry basket. Until the urge struck him, he would walk over it, and if someone else picked it up, all the better

"What's bugging you?" Claude reached into the refrigerator and grabbed a beer for himself. Royal had more concern about Claude drinking tonight. Not because he couldn't control himself. On the contrary, he'd shown himself to be trustworthy. More about recent events that had Royal thinking the party boy might want to stay sober. He opened his mouth to say something about the beer and then shut it. He sat here with one in his hand. Pot. Kettle. He decided to answer the question lobbed at him instead. "Why do you think something's bothering me?"

"Dude, you only go for the beer when you're pissed off. Social drinker, you're not. That's me and Inez's territory." Claude laughed and took a long swig, his head tilted back and his six-pack on full display. Royal sort of hated him for that. No matter how hard he worked out, his abs never looked like that.

"You know me well." Again, the comment showed Claude's quiet intelligence. He studied and took in information, storing it away for when it might be needed. One of those people who listened more than they talked. A prized asset in their profession.

"You sound surprised, dude. I listened to your lectures for almost three years, and we've been family for how long now? Yeah, I know you well. Better than you know me." He laughed and tossed the empty beer bottle into the trash. He turned and looked at Royal, a somber expression on his face despite just downing an entire bottle of beer. "It's that woman, isn't it? I told you, she's more trouble than she's worth. One of these days you have to start listening to me. I'm not all good looks and sparkling personality."

He set the bottle on the table, hard. "She's my chosen mate." He shouldn't have to say that.

Claude leaned against the wall. "You could choose another mate, one without all the complications."

Not true at all. Once chosen, that was it. Had he taught Claude nothing? Then there was the other undeniable piece. "I want her." That first day he'd come back and run into her in Tracy's café, his world came full circle. Everything made sense, and he knew why he'd felt compelled to return. Certainly the danger they'd face in the territories had a great deal to do with the decision. But something else had drawn him back, and until he'd seen Wyatt, he hadn't understood. At this point, there was no do-over. Destiny would not be denied.

"Okay, okay. I can tell I'm never going to be able to talk sense into you about her, so what's the issue? Moon's almost here, and honestly, I think it will be easy to lure her out. Five minutes, and boom. She's one of us. Can't see the problem."

"That other woman is the problem. The one whose ex-wife Inez killed. She's stuck to Wyatt like glue. In less than twenty-four hours the Harvest Moon rises, and I have to get to Wyatt then or the mating ceremony won't happen. Every time I see her, she's with that woman. I have to figure out a way to separate them."

Claude made a face. "Makes her a real pain in the ass."

He leaned his head down and ran a hand over his hair. Claude had hit it right on. Everything had been going great until that woman showed up. He'd been making ground with Wyatt, at least enough that tomorrow night would have gone smooth and easy. Mari should have stayed down in Oregon where she belonged. He was born and raised in Montana. She wasn't. He belonged here. She didn't. If she had stayed in Oregon, Inez wouldn't have killed her ex, and he wouldn't have a problem with her now.

He blew out a long breath. "She's a massive pain in the ass."

"Look, bud. I can help." Claude pushed away from the wall and walked closer.

He brought his gaze up and stared at him. "What do you mean?" He had no idea where Claude was going with this. The problem was his, and he'd figure it out before tomorrow night.

Claude shrugged and smiled. "I've given it a little thought, and it's easy."

"Easy?" Still couldn't fathom what grand plan was playing through Claude's mind.

"Yes, easy. All I have to do is waylay her, and you get it on with Wyatt. Problem solved. By the time she can get to her, it will all be done, and there's no turning back at that point. Am I right or am I right?" He took a bow. Sometimes Royal thought that Claude should have gone into acting.

Royal considered what Claude had suggested. In some way, yes, he could see it working. The man had a way with women. He could charm a snake. The problem, as he saw it, Mari wasn't a woman who would go for it. Point in fact, she had an ex-wife. "She's not into guys." A distinction he had a hunch Claude had missed somewhere along the line.

"Oh, come on. You've seen me in action. No one can resist me when I turn it on. Even if she doesn't want to jump in bed with me, I'll bet you a hundred bucks I get her to go for a drink. I mean, how long to you need? An hour. Two, tops?"

He was beginning to like the way Claude thought. It's possible the resident pretty boy might just pull it off. "Okay."

Claude's smile grew. "Okay?"

Royal shook his head. "Yeah. You keep the ranger busy when the Harvest Moon rises, and I'll deal with Wyatt. We'll be back on track for the perfect pack in no time at all."

Claude clapped him on the back before he grabbed a second beer from the refrigerator. He took a long draw and belched. "Your wish is my command."

Chapter Twenty-one

Wyatt came awake with a start. A dream she couldn't' remember but that left her unsettled lingered. She turned on her side and smiled. Mari sleeping beside her banished the uneasy feeling. Her dark hair curled around her face, her breathing soft and easy. She sure could get used to waking up like this every single morning. She didn't care that it all came about because of tragedy in their community or that it happened in what amounted to the speed of light. While she wished that no one had lost their life out in the wilderness that she loved so much, this woman was the silver lining to the dark clouds.

She put a hand on Mari's hair, silky and tangled, beautiful. How bizarre to have this happen now. "Good morning." She kissed her head and breathed in the scent of her.

"Good morning." She blinked and smiled at Wyatt. Light shone in her eyes. "I slept great. Thank you very much."

"I did too." A little white lie, given that the whisper touch of the dream kept tapping at her. "I wish we could stay here and pretend the world wasn't outside." She laid her head on Mari's shoulder and silently wished death hadn't tainted everything.

Mari leaned into her. "That sounds magical, but the sooner we get out there and solve the crimes, the sooner we can explore this thing between us." Mari sat up and swung her legs over the side of the bed. "Unfortunately, I have to shower before I head to work."

Wyatt smiled as she scooted over to her. "Strangely enough, so do I."

"Well, then, it seems like the only prudent thing to do is conserve water and shower together." Mari now stood naked in the open doorway to the bathroom.

Wyatt didn't linger. Her feet hit the floor, and she raced Mari to the shower. Best one she'd had in, well, ever. Longest one she'd had in, well, also, ever. Both of them were smiling now that they were dressed and sipping fresh coffee out in the kitchen. Same as she always made, yet somehow this morning it tasted like the best coffee in the world. "Call me when you can."

Mari set her empty mug in the sink. "I will, but I don't know when that will be. If today is anything like yesterday, it will probably be past dinner time."

"I understand. But it would mean a lot to me if you still call me when you can." She wanted to go with her, to have her back whatever went down out there. "Wait just a minute." She jumped up from the table and ran to her workshop. She came back a few minutes later, grateful that Mari had waited. "I have something you need to take with you."

After Royal left last night, they'd let the rest of the world go and enjoyed their time together. It had been beautiful and passionate and all-consuming. She'd forgotten the day's projects and the beautiful silver bullets Bob had brought half an hour before Mari arrived. "Here." She slid them into Mari's palm. The morning light glittered on the polished silver. Bob had done a most excellent job of making them.

For a few seconds, Mari stared at her palm. "Are these what I think they are?" She rolled them in her hand, sparkling and clinking.

"Yes, indeed." Couldn't tell at this point how Mari was taking the gift and what it actually meant.

Mari looked up and stared into Wyatt's eyes. A little smile pulled up the corners of her mouth. "Silver bullets. You made me silver bullets."

The tension in her shoulders released. Hadn't even realized until this second that she worried about what Mari would think when she gave them to her. "Safety first."

"Not to seem ungrateful, but isn't this taking the whole werewolf thing a little too far? I'm pretty sure there's a logical, very human-based, explanation for those deaths."

Wyatt couldn't let go of the Fenrir thing, no matter how hard she tried to lean into a run-of-the-mill serial killer, if one could classify a killer like that in those terms. "And you may be right. Doesn't change the fact that there are still a lot of things in the world that can't be explained. My philosophy: it doesn't hurt to be prepared for all scenarios."

Mari glanced down at her hand. "In case I run into a werewolf."

Wyatt shrugged. After all, what more could she say? The bullets were, in fact, in case she ran into a werewolf, as were the arrows she had placed in her own quiver. Better safe than sorry was an undying expression for a reason. "In case you run into a werewolf."

Mari shook her head, but she was smiling. "You are sexy and interesting and weird as hell."

The tension rolled back in. Damn. "There could be some truth in that comment. Does it scare you?" Lord, she hoped she hadn't just run off the most exciting woman she'd ever met. It had been a calculated move, and regardless of what Mari might say next, it was worth the risk if it kept her safe.

"Not in the least." Mari took out her gun, unloaded the traditional bullets, and reloaded it with her new silver ones. "There, locked and loaded and ready for any preternatural creatures that cross my path."

"One more thing." She hesitated to even bring it up. Could be a deal breaker. Could also be important. "How about we share location?" She didn't suggest the tracking app lightly. Especially when it came to Mari. The last thing in the world she wanted was for her to believe Wyatt was leaning into stalker behavior. That had nothing to do with why she made the suggestion.

Mari's eyes narrowed, and Wyatt could almost see the wheels turning in her mind. She was convinced she had, in reality, taken it one step too far. Surprised her when Mari nodded. "Okay. Normally, I'd say no way in hell. I don't need someone following me every step of the way. You know, been there, done that. But these aren't normal times, and that's why I'm on board. Let's do it."

"Thank you." She almost cried. The thought of losing her when they were only beginning to know each other was too unbearable to consider.

They loaded the apps on their respective phones, and after syncing them up, Wyatt kissed her hard. "Be safe and call me."

"I will when I can." Mari stood tall and straightened her shirt. She held her cap in her hand.

"I understand. Come back when you're done, and I'll make you dinner." She smiled and touched Mari's cheek. She really wanted to pull her into a tight hug.

Mari nodded, a light in her eyes. "Looking forward to what home vintage you have for me tonight. Something wild like pickled-beet wine?" She chuckled and made a face.

Wyatt winked at her. "Get back here when you can and find out. I promise, no pickled beets." She smiled before she lost her nerve, leaned in to kiss her one more time.

From the front doorway, she watched Mari drive away, dread settling in the pit of her stomach. If she were brave enough, she'd jump in her truck and follow. She stayed in the doorway watching. Only when Mari's car disappeared from sight did Wyatt close the door and think about how to keep herself busy all day. It stretched before her like a big, empty tunnel. Cold and alone.

Wyatt spent the rest of the day ignoring the bad sensation that made her feel as though she could throw up at any moment. Gave up on completing the bow she'd been working on, her concentration too horrible to do the work. She puttered in the yard for a while, weeded the gardens, and walked the pastures to check the fences. The animals were uneasy, as if they picked up on her mood. Not unsettled enough to forgo their feeding, and once she had them taken care of, she wandered back to the house. Every few minutes she'd pull out her phone and stare at it as if willing it to ring, which it didn't. She prepped dinner, opened a bottle of the good stuff she'd gotten from an award-winning winery, and set the table. No home vintage tonight.

Outside, the day gave way to darkness. Still no call and no Mari. She walked out to the front porch and sat in one of the chairs, resisting the urge to open the locator app. The cup of tea she'd made sat on the small table beside her growing cold. The bad feeling bore down heavier and more ominous as she got up and stood on the porch. The moon, huge and full, rose in the sky. The sound on the wind seemed to whisper to her: beware.

❖

The day stretched on with endless questions, telephone calls coming one after another, and different officials arriving in town. Serial killers were a big deal, and it was an all-hands-on-deck situation. Recaps of the last few days were on repeat with the arrival of each new agency. The day flew by, with lots of people and little progress. Mari found it discouraging. They should be able to come up with more. The best and the brightest had been sent in, yet nothing.

About two, Ollie told her to head out to the Bob Marshall Wilderness Area and look around. Fresh eyes could maybe spot something. Happy to do it and get out of the endless meetings and discussions. Sitting around a table with a bunch of cops wasn't her idea of a good use of her time. All they seemed to want to talk about were profiles and investigative plans. Nobody was actually doing anything.

Mari jumped at the chance to get outside. "I'm on it," she said as she put her cap on and grabbed keys to one of the official trucks.

Ollie put a hand on her arm, stopping her race to the door. "Be back by six at the latest. We lose the light earlier this time of year, and I don't want anyone out there after dark, civilian or official. We're closing it tight at sunset. Got it?"

"I do. I'll hike around a bit and see if there's any additional disturbance. Talk to anyone who's decided to come out, because we know there will be those out there looking for whatever, and I promise to be back before dark." She left Ollie with the sheriff and a couple of deputy US marshals, sliding out without anyone noticing her departure. Mari figured that by the time she came back, the FBI would be there too. It would likely be her only chance to survey the area without an entourage.

After hours of trekking around, she returned to her truck and started back toward the office. It had been a bust, and darkness was starting to fall, so she didn't see the point in staying out here any longer. Nothing out of the ordinary. Thankfully, no more bodies.

In the truck, she pulled out her phone. "Hey," she said when Wyatt picked up.

"Are you okay?" Tension. Worry. Relief.

"I got cut loose from the endless meetings a couple hours ago and have been out looking around for anything out of the ordinary. I'd have checked in with you earlier but kept thinking I'd have something concrete to tell you."

"And?"

"Not a single thing. I'm heading back now."

"Then you'll come here?" Hope now.

Mari smiled. "Yes."

"Can't wait. See you soon."

Mari put the phone back in her pocket and started the truck. As she drove, she thought about the upcoming dinner with Wyatt. Something positive and lovely to look forward to. Her attention was drawn away from her pleasant thoughts and to the side of the highway, where a disabled vehicle had pulled onto the shoulder. When a handsome man, wearing blue jeans and a white shirt, stepped back from the open hood, scratching his head, she figured she'd better stop. Something about him struck her as familiar, although she wasn't sure she'd actually met him. Likely someone she'd seen in passing since coming to Hamilton. With the state of things being what they were, people and faces were a blur.

"Hi. Do you need some help?" She got out of her truck and walked to where he stood at the front of his car. This was a guy who would have every woman for twenty miles stopping to help. Super-hot with an aura charged with masculine energy. Not her type. Didn't have to be her type to get her help.

He ran a hand through hair she suspected was intentionally messy. A practiced move designed to be alluring. She found it amusing. "Damn thing just quit on me, and I have no clue why. I'm no mechanic." He laughed and held out his arms, displaying a pristine white shirt. Definitely not the kind of guy who worked on a car.

She leaned in to look, not that she was a mechanic either. When it came to vehicles, her skills likely exceeded his, which wasn't really saying much. A quick scan under the hood showed her nothing. It was clean and, at first glance, as it should be. She turned to tell him as much when she felt the prick in her neck. She jumped and put her hand on the spot. "Ouch." Her vision grew blurry in seconds, his face fading from clarity but not before she saw his smile. Her knees weakened, and she dropped to the ground, gravel cutting into her elbows and cheek, warm blood trickling toward her mouth. The last thing she saw was his shoes. Gucci loafers.

Full darkness had fallen by the time Mari's eyes fluttered open. Her stomach rolled like she had a bad case of the flu, and she went to put a hand to her eyes but couldn't lift her arms. "What the hell?" Her voice sounded breathy, a sour taste rising into her mouth. "What did you do to me?"

Hot truck guy stood leaning against a tree, moonlight providing enough light for her to see his face. The soft look he'd had on the side of the highway was gone. Still handsome, only now it showed a hardness he wasn't bothering to hide. "Oh, a little cocktail I learned about from dear old Dad. A doctor with sketchy morals, you see. I learned a lot from the old man that has come in handy here and there. There for you." He laughed as he tapped the side of his neck.

"Why?" Her thoughts were muddled as she tried to make sense of what had happened, where she was, and why this man had gone after her. A little voice in the back of her mind kept whispering, serial killer. Was this who they'd been looking for the last few days? Was he the one dropping the bodies of women throughout the wilderness?

His smile grew, as did the hardness in his face. "Fun, mostly. You might not get it, but trust me. It's a hoot."

"Fun? Drugging strangers on the side of the road? What is wrong with you?" Her mind was clearing slowly. Enough to get somewhat of her bearings back.

Now he laughed large. It changed him from handsome to deranged. "Depends on who you talk to. Borderline personality disorder. Bipolar, among others. Narcissist from most everyone. Personally, I don't think there's anything wrong with me. I just like what I like."

"Drugging a law-enforcement officer is a federal crime." He had no idea of the hell coming his way. Given the darkness, she had to believe Ollie was already, or would be soon, out looking for her. She didn't return, she didn't radio in, and he wouldn't be able to get her by phone. All three would equate to a silent 9-1-1.

"Oh, sweetie, that's the least of my so-called crimes." Now he looked at his fingers as though she were boring him. "I'm a regular scofflaw."

"What do you mean?" His words gave her a bad feeling about where this was heading. As the drugs lost their potency, things were coming into focus. He was becoming clearer, and she didn't like what she was seeing.

He pushed away from the tree and began to pace as he looked out into the dark forest beyond. "The bodies you found out here, that was all me."

"Why? Why kill them?" She struggled against the effects of whatever drugs he'd injected, hoping to command her body to move. Her fingers flexed. It was something.

He stopped pacing and looked at her like she was a child incapable of understanding a simple situation. "I like to have fun, and trust me, it's fun. Been doing it for a long time, but after the change, it's become even more exciting."

"What change?" She stilled as she studied his face. She'd sort of been following him until now. He'd taken an unexpected turn, and she had no idea where he was going. His eyes glowed a strange shade of gold in the moonlight.

"Come on. You're a smart broad and have to know what me and Royal are by now. Inez too, before her sad, sad death. A shame. We were one big happy family. *Were* being the operative word." His laughter was ugly on the night air. Chills raced up her arms, and she struggled once more to move. The drugs were still holding her limbs hostage, though her fingers had begun to tingle.

"You and Royal?" Things were starting to click into place. An unbelievable space that made sense of the silver bullets in her gun.

"Yes, silly. We're a pack. Royal is our alpha, and he brought me and Inez into the family. That's how it works. Bitey bite and voilà, you'll love the moon too." His laughter started to take on an unhinged quality.

"She killed my ex-wife." The thought came to her as he talked, and, in her mind, she could see the two women struggling. It made sense. They'd left the bar and come out here, Sherrill probably thinking she'd have a quick lay and then brag about it to Mari. Make her jealous, an old song and dance that once upon a time might have worked. It wouldn't even have occurred to Sherrill that someone would do anything to her except hook up.

He made a tsk-tsk sound with his tongue. "Now there's the fun part. She didn't actually kill your pretty little ex. Oh, she killed the goat for sure, during one of her unauthorized joy runs. Your ex, she only toyed with her. Inez brought a handgun with her after Royal ordered her not to hunt, and she shot it at her. Dumb bitch left her thinking she'd killed her, but all she'd really done was scare the shit out of her. Your ex fainted." He laughed so hard, he doubled over. After he recovered himself, he continued. "If she'd waited around like a normal person, or, rather, a normal werewolf, Inez would have known that she was a shit shot and your ex was still alive. Neither one of them caught a clue that I'd followed them. I was happy to take up the slack and put a bullet in her forehead. Not my preferred method of escorting women out of this world, but fun just the same. It's the end result that really matters."

"Why me?" The sensation in her fingers morphed from a tingle to warm pain. Her body waking up. Never thought she'd be ecstatic about pins and needles in her toes and fingers.

"Let's just say it's a combination of fun and necessity. Fun for me. Necessity for Royal. You were in his way, like all the time. What you have no capacity to understand is that Wyatt belongs to him, and you need to be gone. Here I am to oblige my alpha." He held his arms wide. "A werewolf wingman, if you will." He laughed again.

"You won't get away with this."

"Sweetheart, I've been getting away with this since I was a teenager. My father knew and covered for me time and time again. Too bad you can't look up my work in Canada. You'd understand how good I am. Daddy dearest was quite pleased when I came to Montana. That's the thing about a professional like him. He understands I won't stop. At least now I'm not playing in his backyard anymore. I'm a thoughtful son, you know, giving him a little break and all."

Her stomach rolled again, and she willed herself not to throw up. Show no weakness was the thought racing through her mind as she watched and listened. "You killed all those women." The sickness she felt now didn't come from the drugs he'd injected her with.

"Part of my well-thought-out game. They run. I change. They run more. I hunt them down and kill them. Predator and prey, a really old story, and a fucking awesome story. I am king of the forest." He raised a fist to the moon.

"You're going to kill me." She wiggled her toes.

"Of course, I am. It's the best way to get you out of Royal's hair and free up Wyatt to become the chosen mate for my alpha. He's been planning to bring her into the pack since we relocated here. It's written in stone. Problem is you're in the way, so it's bye-bye for you. It has to happen this way. Sorry. Not sorry."

"What about Inez? Who killed her?" She didn't doubt he'd killed all the others. If they were all part of a pack, it didn't make sense that he'd kill her.

His smile was ugly. "She took one for the team, you might say. Made it look like she'd been a very bad girl and wanted it to stay that way. To do that, she had to go, so she did." He shrugged. "Like what's going to happen to you."

Her body tingled all over now, movement sliding back in. Her mind whirled with thoughts on how to get away, and she swept her gaze over the immediate area. Damn. Her gun and the special bullets were tucked into the waistband of his pants, her phone in his hand. She'd run out of luck. He began to undress, folding his clothes neatly and setting them beneath the tree, her gun and phone laid right on top. Could be her luck had just changed.

❖

Royal kept busy all day despite the intense buzzing in his body. Earlier, he'd gone into the office and packed up boxes he'd previously unpacked. Over the last few hours, he'd reached a decision. It seemed prudent to prepare to return to Canada once he had secured his mate, which would happen within hours. Things had become too messy here, and he'd be better served to find a way to protect his pack from the dangers that had sent him south.

Claude would be the right-hand man he needed to make sure it all went to plan. Inez had messed up everything else, and he'd wanted to be angry with her, but the price she paid was high for her transgressions. He believed in discipline and order. Death was a last resort. His plan to send her to face the council would have been sufficient punishment. Sometimes best-laid plans did go awry.

Tonight wouldn't be one of those nights when things went sideways. His confidence high, he was smiling when he walked into Tracy's café. Surprised him that she still stood behind the counter, given she'd opened at six a.m. and it was long past sunset now. "Long day?" He stepped up to the counter.

"Busy day with all the visitors in town. Everyone came in for coffees, sandwiches, and cookies. Couldn't lay the whole burden on my staff. If you're looking for food, I'm sold out of most everything. One of the reasons I'm still here. A bit of baking to do, or we'll have an empty case in the morning."

He shook his head. "Late-day coffee is on my agenda." A jolt of caffeine sounded good. Already buzzed, he'd let the kick take him to the next level. "Hear anything good?" A dose of local gossip couldn't hurt either while he waited for the moon to rise high in the sky. The air in the café smelled sweet, attesting to her baking in progress. A decided lack of coffee scent, which also told him he was the only one wanting it this time of night.

At the espresso machine, Tracy worked the buttons that turned coffee beans into magic. "Oh, man, I'm telling you, it's been something else. Every deputy is front and center, the feds have come like locusts, and have you heard the latest?" She looked up from her work, the hiss of the frother loud.

"Latest?" That sounded ominous. Did Inez leave more bodies out there? He hoped not.

"Yeah. Mari, the new forest ranger, is missing. She didn't show back up when she was supposed to, and when they sent someone to look, they found her truck abandoned along the highway. No sign of her anywhere. Her radio was still in the truck."

"Truck along the highway?" Claude's work. Had to have been. Made him wonder what he'd done to get her out of her vehicle. Not that it mattered. The nuisance was out of his way, thanks to his wingman, and operation-forever-mate could kick into full swing. He took the coffee she handed him, keeping his expression appropriately somber. What he'd really like to do was pump his fist in the air. "Thanks, Tracy." He put his money on the counter and turned.

"Be safe," she said as he moved toward the door.

"Same to you, and don't hang around here too late." He tried to maintain a casual pace, though it was hard to not leave at a dead run. Her latest news scoop filled him with excitement. So close now. So very close.

"I'm almost out of here. One more tray of rolls and I'm locking 'er up. See you tomorrow, Royal."

He gave her a back-handed wave and left. It hadn't occurred to him after his conversation with Claude last night how his snatch of Mari would give him the perfect opening to get Wyatt out where he needed her to be tonight.

He smiled as he drove away from town and down the now very familiar stretch of highway. The coffee went down hot and tasty.

All was right with his world at the moment, and soon it would be even better. Every nerve in his body hummed, a combination of the coffee and the upcoming rise of the Harvest Moon to the center of the sky, where its power would reach its zenith. The moon seemed to be singing to him already. As he turned down Wyatt's driveway, he shifted his expression from one of happiness to one of concern. Maybe he was the one who should have considered a career in acting.

Wyatt was coming out the front door when he pulled to a stop and lowered the driver's side window. She had both a bow and a quiver draped over one shoulder. Dressed in hiking pants, a fleece pullover, and sturdy boots, she was the picture of a confident, beautiful woman. His woman. "I heard about Mari and came as quick as I could," he said as he got out of the car. Oh, how concerned he sounded.

"Ollie called me when she didn't show back up at the office. I'm on my way out to look for her." Wyatt's voice trembled, and concern was etched into her face. She was into Mari deep. No time to waste in bringing her into his pack. Soon enough, she'd be forever linked to him and would never think of Mari again. Couldn't happen quick enough. He glanced up at the sky, calculating the time left before the moon hit mid-sky.

"Jump in. I'll drive and help you look." He leaned across and opened the passenger's door.

She glanced at her truck and back at his car with the open door. "I can drive myself."

"Come on," he said. "Of course you can drive yourself. I'm offering my assistance. Two is better than one. Twice the ground covered in half the time. You know I can help."

Her hesitation was brief. "You're right. Okay, yeah, I appreciate the help." He wasn't sure if she was trying to convince herself or if she really meant it. Didn't matter as long as she got in his car and they made it to the woods together.

"You need that?" He pointed to the bow and quiver. Pretty serious equipment, and though he couldn't see them well, it almost appeared like she had silver-tipped arrows. That could be a problem he hadn't anticipated. Why would she have those at all?

She nodded. "With everything going on out there..." she looked toward the mountains... "I'm not going anywhere unarmed. I'm better with a bow than anything else."

"Fair enough. If I remember correctly, you won an award or twelve for your shooting. Toss 'em into the backseat. Where do you want to start?" He didn't really care where they went, as long as they were in the wilderness. With the moon beginning to rise, the golden hour was almost upon them. Hard not to be giddy.

Wyatt was looking down at her phone, the glow of the screen lighting up the inside of the car. "I know exactly where she is."

"Oh" is what he said. *Shit* is what he was thinking. The last thing he needed was for Wyatt to find Claude and Mari. Had to keep them apart long enough to make her his.

She held her phone up. "I've got a tracking app. Follow my directions, and I'll tell you where to turn. We should be able to get to her relatively quickly."

He almost panicked. But after he gave himself a few seconds to think, he decided it wasn't so bad. Claude knew what would happen tonight, and he could make sure Mari didn't interfere. Once he turned Wyatt, and she became his mate, none of it would matter anyway. Crisis averted.

"Navigate away." He backed out of her driveway and pulled out onto the highway.

Chapter Twenty-two

Wyatt sensed something was off with Royal, although at the moment she didn't give a good goddamn what his problem might be. For once, his presence didn't irritate the hell out of her. With Mari missing, she appreciated the extra set of eyes. Anything to make sure Mari was safe, and right now that equated to taking any and all help—annoying pest, Royal, included.

No one had ever lit up her world like this beautiful forest ranger, and she wasn't about to lose her now. For a long time, she'd thought she'd be alone, one of those ladies who had a job and a bunch of cats. She had plenty of people in her life that kept her engaged and interested. Friends, some distant cousins, women who came into her orbit as students and stayed as friends, like Tuesday. Until Mari walked into her world, she would never have categorized herself as a lonely woman. Since Mari, she saw things in a different light. The filter had come off, and she could clearly see that she'd allowed herself to become isolated emotionally. Easy to do when no one was around to hold her accountable. Her parents would have called her on it. Definitely her grandmother. With all of them gone, she'd slid into her solitary existence with ease. It had become easy and comfortable.

In this moment, she hated it. She wanted Mari beside her. Right this second. Forever. Not too much to ask for, right? She kept her eyes on her phone and the little line with the moving arrow leading to the yellow flag on her screen. "Turn here," she told Royal. "Left," she added.

"Where from here?" The road had no lights, and darkness dropped over them even deeper the farther away they got from the highway, broken only by the rays of the rising moon.

"Maybe half a mile. There should be a turnout up here. You'll see some trailheads. Not the major ones but still maintained."

The parking area, like the road in, had no lights, and the darkness grew deeper the farther in they drove. The headlights of Royal's car swept across a car parked on the far edge. Shadows made it hard to see. Hard to identify.

"That's not good." He pulled to a stop at the opposite side of the gravel area with his headlights still pointed toward the other vehicle. "You recognize it?"

Yes and no. Pretty sure she'd seen it in town. Didn't help her at the moment. She hadn't paid any attention to the driver, and now she wished she had. Brought home the reality that a killer had been in her town all along, and she'd paid no attention to him. Her downfall when it came to things in town. She saw and heard everything in nature and the mountainous areas she loved to her core. In town, quite a different story. People were fine, just not as interesting as the natural world. Now, that inattention could cost Mari her life.

"No." She took a picture and sent it to Lloyd.

Royal had reached out and put a hand on hers, and it seemed like he had been trying to get her to not send the picture. It was already on its way to Lloyd when he asked, "You sure that's a good idea?"

She looked at him, and the uneasy feeling fluttered through her again. "Why wouldn't it be? Lloyd needs to know. He will more than likely recognize it." Unlike Wyatt, Lloyd kept a keen eye on everything about his town. Oh, he'd know the car all right.

"True. I'm just thinking we're wasting time. Let's get out there, and then we can let Lloyd know what we find. He'll have all the necessary info and be in a position to show up prepared for the threat."

His logic sounded skewed. She wanted Lloyd to be in the loop one hundred percent, start to finish. Animals she could deal with. Bears. Moose. Cougars. Those she understood. Serial killers were outside her skill set. "He needs to know whatever we know as soon as we know it. I'm not waiting to send him anything." She was beginning to think that bringing Royal along had been a poor decision. She could get to Mari a lot faster without him questioning every little step.

"You're right, of course. Don't know what I'm thinking. Come on." He opened the door and got out. "Let's get out there and find your friend."

"Oh, I can find her all right." Harder in the dark but not impossible. She still had the tracking app up, and she set a mark for the car on her GPS. Once that was done, she turned tracking on and put the GPS unit into her pocket. She hadn't bothered to grab a pack or chest harness when she left the house, only took a compass and the GPS unit. Both were in her pocket. "Let's go." Reservations about Royal aside, the faster she got out there, the faster she'd locate Mari. She grabbed her bow and quiver from the back seat and slung them over her shoulder.

"I'll follow you." Was that excitement she heard in his voice? Was he breathing harder? What in the actual hell? He'd always been different. He was downright weird now, and it left her uneasy.

Out of necessity, she brushed the feeling aside and looked at the locater app. Finding Mari was more important than worrying about an oddball companion. Only took her a few seconds to calculate the distance and location. "This way." She took off at a run and didn't worry about whether he could keep up. She wasn't about to slow down to accommodate an out-of-shape lawyer. If he got lost, the local search-and-rescue crew could come find him. She was focused on Mari. End of story.

Behind her, the clomp, clomp, clomp of his feet let her know he followed. Good. In truth, confronting a killer alone wasn't high on her list. She glanced every few seconds at the app line between her location and the flag for Mari, grateful it was growing smaller. Getting closer. The moonlight helped. Bright and buttery, it shone through the trees like a giant spotlight.

Up ahead, she finally saw them. Two figures. One human. One wolf. She stopped, readied her bow with the silver broadhead.

The wolf, big and menacing, was poised to leap at Mari. Without hesitation, Wyatt pulled back and took the shot. Only as she watched the arrow fly through the night did she realize the sound behind her had changed. Instead of the clop, clop, clop of Royal's shoes against the hard ground, now came the sound of four paws softly hitting the forest floor. She turned in time to see a massive wolf lunge at her, and pain roared through her as his teeth sank into the soft flesh of her shoulder.

❖

Defiant about running from the handsome serial killer after he'd transformed from man to wolf, a sight she'd never be able to erase from her memory, Mari had believed this was the end. If he'd wanted to take her life, he could jolly well do it right here and right now. But she wouldn't give him the satisfaction of becoming his prey. They'd squared off, the wolf with the glowing gold eyes and the all-too-human rebellious woman. The drugs fading from her system, she'd risen to her feet and faced him, feet hip-width apart and arms held wide in a come-and-get-me stance. Her knees still wobbled a little yet Mari dared him without words, and he took the challenge, four legs spread apart, giant white teeth bared. A low growl came from his throat.

When, out of the corner of her eye, she caught sight of Wyatt, she'd managed to keep still and continue to hold her ground. The wolf had been so intent on her, he hadn't even turned his head at Wyatt's approach. No one had ever looked as good as Wyatt emerging from the darkness, her bow over her shoulder. In the moonlight, Wyatt had stopped, brought her bow forward, and readied the silver-tipped arrow. The whoosh of the arrow as she let it fly at the same moment the wolf leapt sounded like a sonic boom. It struck him in the heart and dropped him inches from his prey: her. A hundred yards away, as the arrow left Wyatt's bow, a second wolf attacked, hitting her hard and sending her to the ground. Mari screamed and dropped to her knees, pain shooting through her legs at the impact. Though the moonlight pushed away some of the darkness, it was difficult to see all that was happening from where she knelt on the hard ground. It looked like the wolf had latched onto Wyatt's shoulder. She hoped it was her shoulder and not her throat.

Inches from her, the wolf remained motionless, a dark lump of hair and teeth. For a few seconds that felt like an hour, Mari didn't move either. Was he dead or simply playing dead? Fear immobilized her. Her heart beat so hard and fast she feared that a heart attack was imminent and she'd end up dying anyway.

The moonlight created a surreal vision here in the middle of the woods. Two women. Two werewolves. One dead. One killing the woman who made her heart pound in a good way. Not in the need-CPR kind of way. That thought pushed her to her feet, and she took a step toward Wyatt, not knowing what she could or would do, only knowing she had to do something. She couldn't let Wyatt die. Not now and not after she'd come to save her. Pretty boy didn't twitch. Dead.

The second wolf lifted his head and stood over Wyatt as if she belonged to him, blood dripping from his teeth. Clarity came to her in that moment. Royal, claiming his mate just as handsome had described. His deep growl, low in his throat, sounded like thunder in the quiet of the moonlit night. Definitely resource guarding.

He hadn't killed the other women. That wolf lay behind her, or so he'd professed to her earlier. She'd believed him when he told her and still did. He hadn't faked the pride in his words. She shuddered. A serial-killer werewolf. In what universe did something like that even happen? She glanced back, shocked to see the wolf slowly disappearing as his human shape began to reappear.

The growl came again and brought her back to the here and now. No more time to stand around and think. Time to act! Wyatt had come for her, had saved her life. Then she remembered. The silver tip of Wyatt's arrow had taken down handsome, as the folk legends promised. The silver had stopped him. She gazed at the pile of clothes beneath the tree to her left. Could she?

Better to not stop and calculate odds. As her dad used to say, no guts, not glory. She jumped up and ran. Either she surprised the wolf or he continued to resource guard, afraid to lose his potential mate if he went after Mari. In seconds, she made it to the tree where the pile of clothes still lay folded and tidy. On top lay her gun. She dove, grabbed the gun, and rolled behind the tree.

The wolf sprang into action. Could he have seen the gun, or did he react to her movement once he realized she'd moved away from his pack mate? Royal, she thought again as she stared at him from behind the cover of the large pine tree, the guy who wouldn't leave Wyatt alone no matter how many times she rebuffed him. The same guy who lived with both Inez and handsome. A guy who had transformed into a wolf, and she didn't have to be a ranger to understand that wolves moved in packs. She sure as hell hoped there weren't more of them.

On her knees, she brought the gun up and held it with both hands. Sighting in on his face, she steadied her hands, her arms outstretched. The reality of the situation didn't escape her. She'd have one shot, and one shot only. She took it and went flying backward. At first, she thought it was recoil. A second later, she realized the wolf had slammed into her. Her gun went tumbling into the darkness, landing somewhere off to the right with a thump. She waited for the pain of the wolf's bite. It didn't come. All she felt was pressure as she lay on her back, pine needles poking through her shirt, the dead weight of the wolf on her chest.

"What in the actual hell is going on out here?" Bright lights lit up the forest, bouncing like a disco ball. The calvary had arrived. Too late. Wyatt might very well be dead, and the damn wolf might have broken Mari's back.

She struggled out from beneath the wolf's body, hot and unmoving. Rolling it to the side, she stood. No broken back. Good. Now, she had to get to Wyatt. Tears streamed down her face as she dropped next to her and pulled her into her arms. "Please, please, please don't leave me." Wyatt didn't move, blood staining her shirt and soaking into Mari's pants, warm and frightening.

"I ask again. What the hell?" Lloyd's mag light shone down on them. "Did I just see you shoot a wolf?"

Werewolf, she thought. She'd shot a werewolf. With a silver bullet. "Yes," she said. She continued to cradle Wyatt in her arms.

She had to be okay. If not for her and her believing enough to make the silver arrows and bullets, they'd both be dead.

"Then why am I seeing two naked guys on the ground, one with an arrow in his body and one with a bullet hole in his chest?" Lloyd took off his cap and scratched his head. "And why did I see two huge-ass wolves two minutes ago? Where in the hell did they go?"

"Werewolves." She hugged Wyatt tighter. "Lloyd, they were werewolves, but that doesn't matter right now. We have to get Wyatt to a hospital."

"Nope. Just nope. Naked men who are freaks, that's all." Lloyd clicked his radio. "Get the EMT in here now."

"Come on," she said in Wyatt's ear. "Open your eyes, beautiful. I need to see your eyes."

Lloyd knelt next to her. "What happened?"

Mari glanced over to where the wolf had charged Wyatt. Royal's naked body now lay in the spot. "He bit her."

He shone his light on Wyatt's shoulder. "Sonofabitch, those are some big-ass bites, and no way anyone will buy that one of these guys did that with their little human teeth. Problem is, we're gonna have to come up with a better story than werewolf. Nobody in their right mind will believe that."

She looked at him. "I don't care if they believe it or not. It's what happened. I was here, and you saw it. You're going to tell me you don't believe in werewolves?"

"Ranger, I don't know what I believe at this point, but if we tell them…" he pointed to the lights headed their way… "that a couple of werewolves tried to kill you two ladies, we'll all end up in the hospital. You and I will be on a lock-down floor."

Despite the truth of what she'd experienced and witnessed, Lloyd was right. They'd both get an unscheduled vacation in a psych ward. "Two whacked-out serial killers?" she said. "I mean, they are naked, which plays pretty well toward the whacked-out part."

"Yeah." He stood and waved the EMT over. "Let's go with that."

EPILOGUE

Three months later

Wyatt walked out of the doctor's office smiling. Mari waited in the car. "All clear," she declared when she slid into the passenger's seat. "Wounds are healed, bloodwork is clear, and I'm more than ready to get back to work. No rabies. No infections. No nothing. I'm golden."

Mari took her hand and brought it to her lips. "Fantastic."

"You're missing the best part." Wyatt laughed.

"No. No, I'm not. We also know that the folk legends are absolutely true. If you get bit by a werewolf, which does exist, and it dies before you change, you're all good. No transforming into a wolf when a moon rises."

Wyatt laughed and was happy that she could laugh about it now. "You're right on that one. Who knew? I tell you what. I'll be thinking about those old stories a whole lot differently from now on."

"Kind of makes my work a bit different now too. I look at the animals out in the woods, and I wonder, is it really an animal, or is it a were-something-or-other?"

Wyatt squeezed her hand. "No worries, beautiful. I'll be there to protect you. I still have the rest of those silver broadheads."

"I send up thanks every day that you thought to make those and my silver bullets. If you hadn't..." Mari shuddered.

Now Wyatt leaned near and gave her a hug. "Don't dwell on it. I did, and you used the best tool at hand. That's all that matters."

"Not to mention, law enforcement got their serial killer. Or, rather, serial killers. Do you think Royal knew what Claude had been up to?" Mari tapped the console.

Wyatt had given that one a lot of thought. She shook her head. "I don't. I believe he was fixated on me for his mate and didn't spend much energy policing either Inez or Claude. From what you've told me about Claude's confession, he used Royal's focus on me to his advantage. He could do what he wanted without any scrutiny."

"He was a piece of work and way too smart for his own good. Couple that with wealth, and who knows how long he could have gotten away with killing."

"Royal wanted to start over back in his hometown, but you know what? For a smart guy, he made some bad choices. Fatal choices." Over the last three months as her body healed and Wyatt had time to make sense of what had happened, she'd been able to put some of the pieces together. His intense focus, his refusal to give up on his pursuit of her, his plan to get Mari out of the way.

"Good thing Lloyd has an open mind. Don't know how this would have gone down very well if he hadn't been there to do damage control."

Wyatt chuckled. "I told you from the get-go, he's a good guy, although I will say that even I was surprised by the spin he did on this." From what Mari told her, he'd been initially dumbfounded by what he'd seen and then regrouped. By the time the rest of the crew arrived, he was business as usual. As if a couple of werewolf killers were anywhere near usual.

"I'm just glad we're getting back to normal." Mari turned and smiled at her.

"Speaking of normal, have you given it any more thought?" Wyatt held her breath.

Mari turned the key in the ignition, and the car roared to life, though she kept it in Park. "Funny you should ask. I got a call from Tuesday while you were in the doctor's office."

Wyatt turned in her seat and stared at Mari. "Tuesday called you?"

"Sure. We've chatted quite a bit over the last few months."

"You didn't mention it." Not a single word. What were they up to?

"Something we've been working on."

"Really? And that is?" This was an interesting twist.

"Well, it seems that Tuesday isn't really a Midwest kind of woman after all and thought that moving back West would be a good idea."

Wyatt's heartbeat quickened. "Addie was born and raised there. I have a hard time seeing her move away."

"True enough, but you know sometimes a change can be good. Look at me, for example. I was born and raised in Oregon, yet here I am and settling in quite nicely."

Mari was playing with her now. "Are you going to make me drag it out of you?"

Mari laughed, the sound light and beautiful. "So, it's like this. Tuesday and Addie thought that Hamilton would be a good place to start a new life, and that means they need someplace to live. Someplace like my house."

"I thought Addie didn't like all the mountains and trees. She said they made her feel claustrophobic. She wants to buy your house?" Wyatt was trying to connect all the dots, and there were big holes.

Mari nodded. "She does. She's willing to work on her claustrophobia. A new challenge, if you will."

"Hmm, okay…and you'll live there with them?" Still not filling in the blanks.

She tilted her head and smiled. "No. I don't think so. You remember Sarah, my realtor?"

Wyatt nodded. Everyone in the area knew Sarah. She kicked butt when it came to selling real estate. "I do."

"Well, she's already drawn up the paperwork for Addie and Tuesday to buy my place. I think Tripper is going to like it a lot, and you know Lloyd would love to have them on hand for searches."

Anticipation built in Wyatt's heart. "You're going to buy another place?"

Mari shook her head. "I'm hoping not, because I have a better idea."

"Hit me with this better idea." Did she dare hope?

"I really like the bed at your place." Mari's smile was bright, her eyes twinkling. Yes, twinkling, and here she thought that was just a word writers used.

Wyatt threw her arms around Mari and pulled her close. For weeks now, a deep truth had lived in her heart, though she hadn't found the courage to let it pass her lips. She did now. "I love you."

"I know." Her words were happy and playful. "I mean how can you not?"

"You're a brat."

Mari stared deep into her eyes. They were filled with joy. Mari's palms were warm as they cupped her face. "I love you too."

About the Author

Sheri Lewis Wohl grew up in northeast Washington State, and though she always thought she'd move away, never has. Despite traveling throughout the United States, Sheri always finds her way back home. And so she lives, plays, and writes amidst mountains, evergreens, and abundant wildlife.

Sheri likes to write stories that typically include mystery, murder, and mayhem along with a bit of the strange and unusual. Always with a touch of romance. With multiple novels Golden Crown Literary Awards finalists, her novel *Twisted Whispers* was a 2016 Golden Crown Literary Award winner for Paranormal/Horror, and *The Talebearer* was a 2019 Lambda Literary Award finalist.

A former nationally certified human remains detection K9 handler, Sheri and her German Shepherd partner, Zoey, deployed throughout the Northwest. She continues to train with her youngest dog, Deuce, is working on running half marathons in all fifty states, and puts her acting chops to use every chance she gets. You can catch her in television shows such as *Z Nation*, *Grimm*, and *Going Home*.

Learn more about Sheri at her website www.sherilewiswohl .com, her blog sherilewiswohl.wordpress.com, and Facebook: @SheriLewisWohl.

Books Available from Bold Strokes Books

Anywhere with You by Margo Glynn. On a road trip through the Great American Southwest, two friends discover nature, hope, and each other. (978-1-63679-907-0)

Burning Bridges by Lesley Davis. Can Clancy and Jude crack the case of nine missing women—and the secrets of their own hearts? (978-1-63679-872-1)

Dreams Entangled by Sophia Kell Hagin. Amid self-doubt, secrets, a pandemic, fear of attack and attempted murder, Pirin and Gracie's attraction turns to love and their lives will never be the same. (978-1-63679-892-9)

Echoes of Love by Catherine Lane. As Hazel's and Jo's paths intertwine, they're swept up in a whirlwind of long-buried secrets, sizzling chemistry, and memories that won't be denied. (978-1-63679-835-6)

Moonlight Obsession by Sheri Lewis Wohl. All it takes to stop a clever killer is moonlight, love, and a silver bullet. (978-1-63679-831-8)

My Boyfriend's Wife by Joy Argento. Amid betrayal and heartbreak, can two women discover a love that could heal their pasts and rewrite their futures? (978-1-63679-866-0)

Tapout by Nicole Disney. A struggling MMA fighter finds her edge in an underground ring, but as she falls for the magnetic and ambitious promoter behind the matches, their dangerous world threatens to destroy everything they've fought to rebuild. (978-1-63679-924-7)

The Fame Game by Ronica Black. Wild child Hollywood actress Luna Kirkman begins dating Hollywood's leading man, only to fall for his straitlaced sister instead. (978-1-63679-858-5)

An Extraordinary Passion by Kit Meredith. An autistic podcaster must decide whether to take a chance on her polyamorous guest and indulge their shared passion, despite her history. (978-1-63679-679-6)

That's Amore! by Georgia Beers. The romantic city of Rome should inspire Lily's passion for writing, if she can look away from Marina Troiani, her witty, smart, and unassumingly beautiful Italian tour guide. (978-1-63679-841-7)

The Unexpected Heiress by Cassidy Crane. When a cynical opportunist meets a shy but spirited heiress, the last thing she plans is for her heart to get involved. (978-1-63679-833-2)

Through Sky and Stars by Tessa Croft. Can Val and Nicole's love cross space and time to change the fate of humanity? (978-1-63679-862-2)

Uncomplicate It by Kel McCord. When an office attraction threatens her career, Hollis Reed's carefully laid plans demand revision. (978-1-63679-864-6)

Vanguard by Gun Brooke. Beth Wild, Subterranean freedom fighter, is in the crosshairs when she fights for her people and risks her heart for loving the exacting Celestial dissident leader, LaSierra Delmonte. (978-1-63679-818-9)

Wild Night Rising by Barbara Ann Wright. Riding Harleys instead of horses, the Wild Hunt of myth is once again unleashed upon the world. Their ousted leader and a fey cop must join forces to rein in the ride of terror. (978-1-63679-749-6)

Heart's Appraisal by Jo Hemmingwood. Andy and Hazel can't deny their attraction, but they'll never agree on the place they call home. (978-1-63679-856-1)

Behold My Heart by Ronica Black. Alora Anders is a highly successful artist who's losing her vision. Devastated, she hires Bodie Banks, a young struggling sculptor as a live-in assistant. Can Alora open her mind and her heart to accept Bodie into her life? (978-1-63679-810-3)

Fearless Hearts by Radclyffe. One wounded woman, one determined to protect her—and a summertime of risk, danger, and desire. (978-1-63679-837-0)

Forever Family by L.M. Rose. Two friends come together after tragedy to raise a baby, finding love along the way. (978-1-63679-868-4)

Stranger in the Sand by Renee Roman. Grace Langley is haunted by guilt. Fagan Shaw wishes she could remember her past. Will finding each other bring the closure they're looking for in order to have a brighter future? (978-1-63679-802-8)

The Nursing Home Hoax by Shelley Thrasher and Ann Faulkner. In this fresh take for grown-ups on the classic Nancy Drew series, crime-solving duo Taylor and Marilee investigate suspicious activity at a small East Texas nursing home. (978-1-63679-806-6)

The Rise and Fall of Conner Cody by Chelsey Lynford. A successful yet lonely Hollywood starlet must decide if she can let go of old wounds and accept a chance at family, friendship, and the love of a lifetime. (978-1-63679-739-7)

A Conflict of Interest by Morgan Adams. Tensions rise when a one-night stand becomes a major conflict of interest between an up-and-coming senior associate and a dedicated cardiac surgeon. (978-1-63679-870-7)

A Magnificent Disturbance by Lee Lynch. These everyday dykes and their friends will stop at nothing to see the women's clinic thrive and, in the process, their ideals, their wounds, and a steadfast allegiance to one another make them heroes. (978-1-63679-031-2)

A Marvelous Murder by David S. Pederson. When a hated director is found dead in his locked study, movie star Victor Marvel, his boyfriend Griff, and friend Eve seek to uncover what really happened to Orland Orcott. (978-1-63679-798-4)

Big Corpse on Campus by Karis Walsh. When University Police Officer Cappy Flannery investigates what looks like a clear-cut suicide, she discovers that the case—and her feelings for librarian Jazz—are more complicated than she expected. (978-1-63679-852-3)

Charity Case by Jean Copeland. Bad girl Lindsay Chase came home to Connecticut for a fresh start, but an old, risky habit provides the chance to save the day for her new love, Ellie. (978-1-63679-593-5)

Moments to Treasure by Ali Vali. Levi Montbard and Yasmine Hassani have found a vast Templar treasure, but there is much more to the story—and what is left to be found. (978-1-63679-473-0)

The Stolen Girl by Cari Hunter. Detective Inspector Jo Shaw is determined to prove she's fit for work after an injury that almost killed her, but a new case brings her up against people who will do anything to preserve their own interests, putting Jo—and those closest to her—directly in the line of fire. (978-1-63679-822-6)